The Real McCoy

Also by David Evans Katz

SIN OF OMISSION

add MARINES ON PG. 171.

The Real McCoy
by
David Evans Katz

Library of Congress Control Number: 2013930464

ISBN: 978-0-9800098-7-3

Koenisha Publications
3196 – 53rd Street
Hamilton, MI 49419
telephone or fax: 269-751-4100

Dedicated in loving memory to my father, a World War II combat veteran of the battles for New Guinea and the Philippines, and to my mother, who waited for him to come home.

Acknowledgments

I want to thank David Dunham for his beautiful dust jacket photograph of the 1929 Ford tri-motor airplane, and my editor and publisher, Sharolett Koenig, for her patience and dedication.

Show me a hero and I will write you a tragedy.
— F. Scott Fitzgerald

My father was a stranger to me. I still can't remember much about him that I learned firsthand. In fact, most of my knowledge of him came from what I read, or from what other people told me. Even though I hardly knew him, he was a larger-than-life hero to me when I was a little boy. I suppose all kids see their fathers as heroes—that's the way it ought to be.

I'm an old man now—eighty-eight or eighty-nine. I have to do the math, and the counting always tires me out. I usually start by remembering that I was twelve years old in 1932 when my mother left my father and took me to live in Boston with my grandparents. I can count up from there, and it helps if I can picture my teachers from every grade, or something that happened to me or in the world. But then I get distracted and my thoughts digress, and it takes so long to reach the end. Sometimes I have to start over, and that just makes me angry, so I let it go and I think eighty-eight or eighty-nine is close enough. It's not important that I know it exactly.

I have a hard time remembering events from last week or last month, and last year seems to run into the year before or the year before that. But forty, fifty, or sixty years ago is no problem. My long-term memory is just fine. Sometimes, I'll look out the window and see things that aren't there anymore, like cornrows in a field from another time and another place, or a face belonging to someone long dead. It's just a trick of the mind. If I wake up sweating, I'm back in the jungles of the Pacific, feeling the crush of humidity choking my lungs, but then I remember it was fifty years of smoking that did that. Some things I wish I could forget.

My head is filled with small, inconsequential facts that, when aggregated, mean nothing. They just stay in my mind and won't go away. That's why I don't have room for yesterday or last week. I remember trivialities I learned as a child, like the fact that Wild Bill Hickok was holding aces and eights when Jack McCall shot him in the back in the Number 10 Saloon in Deadwood in 1876. That one clear memory consists of five things about a man who died almost half a century before I was born.

My three grandsons are in their late twenties. They had million-dollar educations, but they probably have no idea who Wild Bill Hickok was, let alone what cards he was holding when a deranged drifter murdered him in a saloon. That's fine. They don't need to know that. They're not related to Wild Bill Hickok. When I was their age, I barely knew five things about my own father, and I still have a hard time sorting out what was real from what wasn't.

I get confused about what he was and what I wanted him to be, and then I have to go back and remember again from a particular point in time, just like when I want to count my age.

CHAPTER 1

I always start remembering in Boston, on a narrow cul-de-sac running diagonally from St. Louis Street toward Huntington Avenue. Ours was a brick and granite house, a unique building separated by a cobblestone alley from six adjoining bow-front brownstones. On the face of the house, a wild rose bush climbed the wall and a brass lantern hung above a red front door.

Van Houghton Row was set apart from Huntington Avenue by a small delta that was, before the war, a private park enclosed by a black wrought-iron fence. The homeowners of Van Houghton Row owned and maintained the park, and access was limited to residents only. When I returned from the war, it was gone. Sometime while I was overseas, the park had been razed and turned into a Cities Service gas station. Van Houghton Row was no longer a pretty little private courtyard with brick sidewalks and flower boxes. Most of our neighbors had moved away, and the brownstones were divided into low-rent apartments catering to married college students. My mother must have hated that.

Like Van Houghton Row, I, too, had changed. Physically, I was taller, leaner and more muscular than the twenty-one-year-old boy who'd gone off to war more than four years before. It was a beautiful late March day in 1946 when I came home, but the aroma of car exhaust stifled the incipient smell of spring blossoms. I hauled my duffel bag over my shoulder and stepped off the trolley at the Museum of Fine Arts, only a block from Van Houghton Row. As I rounded the corner, I saw a little girl skipping rope on the sidewalk, singing a lilting jingle to the rhythm of her steps. *Cinderella, dressed in yella, went to the ball to meet a fella.* I was glad that little girls still jumped rope and sang silly songs.

I had just spent a miserable four days creeping across the country by train, first on the Sunrise Special from L.A. to Chicago, and then on the Wolverine from Chicago to Boston by way of Detroit. Both trains were crowded with GIs on their way to or from discharge centers, and a party atmosphere prevailed all the way from Los Angeles. I wasn't in a celebratory mood, so I tried to ignore the raucousness. I could tell by looking at them that most of the almost-veterans hadn't seen a lick of combat. Had I given it any thought, I might have been resentful, but my mind was stuck halfway between Manila and Boston. Though I outranked most of them, discipline had evaporated and I couldn't have done anything to keep order if I wanted to.

On the morning after I changed trains in Chicago, I escaped to the rear observation car hoping for some quiet time. Fortunately, the car was nearly empty—two elderly couples played bridge in a booth at the front, and a dark-haired rugged-looking sergeant sat alone in the back staring out the window. I almost took a seat in the middle—away from the others—when I noticed the sergeant's shoulder patch. Like me, he wore a Ranger insignia. I walked close enough to see the campaign ribbons on his chest, and I saw some of the same ones I wore: Solomon Islands, New Guinea and the Philippines. He had six bronze battle stars—one more than me.

I walked over and asked, "You one of General Krueger's boys?"

He glanced up, spotted my captain's bars and started to rise.

"At ease, Sergeant. We're almost civilians, now." I held out my hand and said, "Jamie McCoy, Thirty-Second Infantry."

"Al Merloni, Thirty-Fourth." He shook eagerly and smiled, revealing a chipped front tooth. "Jeez, Captain, I was starting to think I was the only one on the whole train." He jerked a thumb forward, indicating the rowdy garrison troops in the other cars.

"'They also serve who only stand and wait,'" I said.

"Yeah, but do they hafta stand and wait so loud?"

We both laughed. I sat down in a well-padded chair and leaned back, taking in the view. We both knew the score—it was manifest in the premature age-lines on our foreheads and the campaign ribbons on our chests.

"Where's home?"

"Coney Island," he said.

"I hate to tell you this, Sarge, but this train's headed for Boston."

The smile erupted again. "I know. That's where my fiancée lives. I'm gettin' married in seven days."

"No kidding? Congratulations." A newspaper article I'd read in L.A. said that marriage license applications were up more than a thousand percent since V.J. Day. "Childhood sweetheart?"

"No, nothin' like that. I met her before I went overseas when I did my amphibious training at Camp Edwards. We've been writing ever since." He reached into his breast pocket, removed a well-worn photograph and passed it over to me. "I carried Beth next to my heart for four straight years."

Beth was stunning. I looked at the photo with unabashed envy, lingering over it longer than decency permitted.

Sergeant Merloni held out his hand and said, "All due respect, Captain, but get your own girl. This one's spoken for."

I handed it back, trying to cover my embarrassment with a grin. He was gracious, though, and accepted my bad manners with good humor. He eased into an expansive monologue, telling me all about Beth, and about his people in New York, and the more he spoke, the more I wished that I, too, had family anticipating my return.

Eventually, the subject turned to our war experiences. In civilian life, two words wouldn't have passed between us. We were from different worlds—Al was an Italian kid from New York and I was a Yankee WASP—but we were kindred spirits in this one thing, and there were damned few people on the home front who could or would understand.

As his battle stars suggested, Al had hit the beaches six times—once in the Solomon Islands, three times in New Guinea and twice in the Philippines. All but the last—Lingayen Gulf—had been brutal. At Lingayen, the Japs left our landings unopposed and waited inland. After the deceptive calm, Al fought for thirty-one straight days on the road to Manila, only to find a city reduced to rubble and ashes, and a civilian death toll beyond counting—all killed by retreating Japanese troops. Japanese Marines took four thousand civilian hostages and holed up in the ancient fortress of Intramuros. For four days, the Americans laid siege, and the Japanese Marines responded by slaughtering a thousand women and children. Al couldn't help feeling that the Americans might have prevented it, but he couldn't articulate how. The horror of seeing all the bodies haunted him, and he knew he couldn't discuss it with Beth or anyone else who'd spent the war out of harm's way.

We watched the outside world whisk by in silence for a while. I didn't volunteer any of my own horror stories, though I had more than enough of them. Al was spent, and I didn't want to diminish his catharsis.

At last I said, "You're one of the good guys, Al. You did your job the best you could and you're not responsible for enemy atrocities. You're only responsible for your own behavior in battle. That much I know."

I also knew that my own behavior hadn't always been above reproach.

He nodded, accepting my dispensation. At the far end of the car, we heard one of the bridge players shriek, "Grand slam!"

Al laughed and said, "Beth tells me her mother and three aunts are fanatical bridge players. I can't wait to see them in action."

He was already getting back to normal.

I didn't talk with anyone else for the rest of the trip to Boston. Mostly, I sat in the club car staring out the window at the rolling panorama of America. The last time I'd been cross-country, it was in the other direction in a blacked out troop train heading for my point of embarkation in San Francisco.

At night, when there was nothing much to see out the windows, I read a dime novel and did about thirty crossword puzzles—it was better than thinking about returning to an empty house. Although I'd lived there during my teen years, I didn't think of Boston as home, and with my mother gone, it never would be.

I would have loved the joyous homecoming Al Merloni was expecting. Instead, I had to face my mother's lawyer, Arthur Wiseman, and settle her estate. I thought about how terrible it must have been for my mother to die without seeing me one last time. My grandparents, too, died while I was overseas, within six months of each other, and my mother faced that twin ordeal alone.

I didn't even have a key to the house—I'd have to break in unless the handyman and housekeeper were still there. I didn't know if Mr. and Mrs. Glendenning had stayed on after my mother's funeral; they were old, and they'd been living at my grandparents' house for a long time before my mother brought me there. I tried to telephone from Back Bay Station, but the number had changed sometime during the war, and the operator couldn't find the new listing. HUNtington-7334 had been as familiar to me as my Army serial number. Now both numbers were useless.

A halting sadness gripped me as I knocked at the red door. The little girl stopped skipping rope and watched me. Her attention would make breaking in awkward. After a moment spent pondering the problem, I prepared to knock again. Before I could, the door opened to reveal Mrs. Glendenning—in a worn blue housedress and a frayed cardigan sweater—looking at me without recognition. Her posture was bent and her head tilted forward on her long wrinkled neck, like an ancient crane.

"Yes, sir? May I help you?" She spoke in the flat Irish accent that grated on the ears of proper Bostonians.

"Mrs. Glendenning, it's Jamie."

She began to close the door. "Jamie's not here. He's overseas in the Army."

"No, Mrs. Glendenning. *I'm* Jamie. I'm home."

Mrs. Glendenning furrowed her brows and looked me up and down. She removed a case from a pocket in her sweater and unfolded her eyeglasses, reluctantly putting them on as if doing so would reveal her age more than the wrinkles on her face or the liver spots on her hands. She looked at me again, more carefully, but didn't smile in recognition. She just opened the door wider and motioned me into the house.

"You didn't send word you were coming, Mr. McCoy."

I'd sent a telegram to the lawyer, of course, as soon as I disembarked from my troopship in Los Angeles. And perhaps Arthur Wiseman had told the Glendennings, but it wasn't out of the question that Mrs. Glendenning's senility played a part in the miscommunication.

"I'm sorry," I said. "I wasn't sure if you and Mr. Glendenning would still be here."

She glared at me. "And where else would we be? Ain't this been our home for twenty-seven years?"

I lifted my duffel bag from the landing and brought it into the foyer where I dropped it, much to Mrs. Glendenning's dismay. Although they'd been my grandparents' employees and worked for my mother after my grandparents died, the Glendennings had always been too possessive of number 7 Van Houghton Row.

I removed my cap and loosened my tie as I looked around the foyer and up at the portraits of my Winant family ancestors lining the walls of the stairway. In a world where everything had changed, nothing was different inside this house. When Mrs. Glendenning closed the front door, its stark thud preceded the once familiar sound of the parlor clock ticking rhythmically in the other room. My grandfather's ebony walking stick still reposed in the brass stand in the corner, my grandmother's umbrella beside it. I crossed the parlor threshold and gazed at furnishings that recalled another era. They seemed out of place without the presence of my mother and grandparents. It was like seeing a stage set without the actors.

I scanned the room, mentally cataloguing the items scattered about the tables—copies of *National Geographic*, a crystal vase, matching china figurines, a marble bust of Plato. I imagined my grandfather reading in his chair by the fireplace while my grandmother and mother sipped sherry on the chesterfield by the window. God—how I missed them.

Mr. Glendenning came into the room, wiping his hands on a towel. He recognized me immediately and smiled. "Welcome home, Captain McCoy. Mr. Wiseman told us you'd be coming home soon. It's good to see you back safe and sound. Can I fix you something to eat?"

I looked at Mrs. Glendenning for a reaction to her husband's announcement that I'd been expected after all but, if she noticed the discrepancy in her own recollection, she didn't reveal it. I turned back to Mr. Glendenning and said, "Thank you. I'd love a sandwich and a glass of milk if it's not too much trouble." I really wanted a Scotch and soda, but it was too early in the day.

"No trouble at all. I'll fix you up quick." He retreated down the hall toward the kitchen.

I opened the double pocket doors to my grandfather's study and walked over to the telephone table in the corner. Mrs. Glendenning followed me, hovering at my side as if to prevent me from stealing anything. Assuming an air of authority, I said, "Please bring me a telephone directory. I wish to call Mr. Wiseman right away."

Mrs. Glendenning complied with my request and left me alone to place my call. When I finished, I retrieved my duffle bag from the foyer and climbed the stairs, grasping the polished oak banister, allowing my hand to caress its smooth grain as I ascended to the second floor landing. I stopped there briefly, looking through the archway at the closed door of my grandparents' bedroom at the front of the house. Also on the second floor were my mother's bedroom and a large, comfortable guest room.

I continued up to the third floor, where the Glendennings maintained a suite and where my bedroom was located—directly above that of my grandparents. I opened the door to my room and let the duffle bag fall to the floor again. After everything I'd been through in the Pacific, having slept in the mud and sand and grit of New Guinea and the Philippines, I had expected to relish the thought of falling down on my own bed and sleeping for hours, but nothing in the room seemed right to me. My mother had turned it into a shrine, cluttered with my baseball trophies, sports paraphernalia, academic awards and a decade's worth of Jamie memorabilia.

It wasn't really my room, after all. I'd spent every summer at my grandparents' cottage in Maine. I'd gone off to Groton when I was fourteen and to Harvard four years later. Six months after graduation, America was in the war and I was in the service. My old room at Kirkland House in Harvard Square was more familiar to me than this boy's bedroom where I'd slept only during holidays and school vacations.

I opened my closet and saw my old boarding-school uniforms and several suits hanging on the rail. I assumed none of my civilian clothing would fit, so I resigned myself to wearing my Army uniform until I could manage a trip across the river to J. Press.

At the foot of the bed was an old steamer trunk in which I'd stored my personal belongings before I left for Fort Devens. I knelt down, lifted the lid and reached through the folded shirts and sweaters until my hand touched a large manila envelope. It was still there.

* * * *

Arthur Wiseman arrived at three-thirty. Mrs. Glendenning prepared tea and set the tray on Grandfather Winant's mahogany desk. Without waiting to be dismissed, she closed the pocket doors and left me alone with the lawyer.

Wiseman was middle aged and paunchy. He was a fast talker who articulated his words with darting hand gestures. On someone else, the waving might have been distracting, even amusing, but it enhanced Wiseman's otherwise stodgy personality. This was a man who could punctuate a closing argument with a grand sweep of his right arm and an outstretched finger as though he were performing Shakespeare for the King. He wore thick wire-rim glasses perched over a bulbous nose that betrayed his ethnicity. His suit had seen better days, despite the fact that he was a senior partner in a prosperous firm. He dressed more like an avuncular college professor than the brilliant lawyer he was. I'd known him since I was a boy, and I liked him a lot.

During the thirties, Wiseman achieved notoriety as lead counsel for the Boston chapter of the American Civil Liberties Union. He met my mother, Helen McCoy, at an ACLU fundraising dinner. Eventually, she became his client and, to my grandparents' chagrin, his dear friend. Grandmother and Grandfather Winant were cordial to him, but not friendly. His Jewish heritage was inconsistent with their Episcopal beliefs, and they were unsubtle about letting my mother know he was simply NOKD—"Not Our Kind, Dear."

He was a widower, and even I could see he loved my mother, but she kept things on a purely platonic and professional basis. After his wife died in 1932, he buried himself in work, but my mother's simple acts of kindness, a casual touch, an unexpected laugh at one of his silly gestures, softened him. I think he would have died for her.

Wiseman opened his briefcase, fussing with its contents as he spread a stack of papers across the desk while I poured the tea. He sat down in my grandfather's chair and sipped, bidding me to sit as well. He stared at me over the rim of his china teacup, assessing me like a rare painting, watching my every move.

"You look like your father," he said. "Well, at least you look like the newspaper photographs. I never actually met him in person."

Wiseman offered me his condolences, both for my mother and my grandparents, though my grandparents had died three years before. I saw that he, too, was still grieving for my mother. It was an awkward moment for both of us, but it passed quickly and we got down to business. He stood up and paced the oriental carpet as he spoke, informing me of the basics: Helen Winant McCoy had been executor of her parents' estate in 1943; upon her death, he, Arthur Wiseman, had been named executor. I, Jameson Hale McCoy III, was sole heir to the estate of my mother and that of my maternal grandparents. Not including the house and its furnishings and the property in Maine, I would inherit from my grandparents, after estate taxes, a little more than eight hundred thousand dollars in cash and approximately two million in securities.

Wiseman watched as I let out a low whistle and leaned back in my chair. The Winants were old Boston money, so the amount didn't surprise me. They had, after all, supported my mother and me for years, even paying my prep school and college tuition.

The lawyer continued, "There's more. As you know, your parents never divorced after they separated in 1932. Before your father disappeared in 1934, he established trust funds for you and your mother in the amount of a million dollars each. Your mother never touched her money and, as a result of sound investment policy, it has more than doubled in value."

At hearing this, I stood and walked to the window, stammering my response. "M-my god! And I was worried about what I'd do for work. I'll never have to work again." I immediately recognized the stupidity of my remark.

Apart from my combat service, I'd never worked a day in my life.

Wiseman continued, "Your father's attorneys in Hartford turned most of his affairs over to your mother shortly after he went missing. She had some matters to deal with in Connecticut, which I've listed in these papers, including having your father declared legally dead in 1941. I handled it all for her, and it made me quite unpopular with the locals in your hometown."

I was puzzled by his last remark, but I let it pass.

"Your father was once a very rich man, Jamie, worth close to seventy-five million dollars I'd say. Unfortunately, only a fraction of his net worth remained intact after I wound up his interests. Still, it's a little more than a million in cash, after taxes, and about five million in various stocks and bonds—that's in addition to real estate holdings and the money in the trust funds. Also, your paternal grandparents' house in Granbury has been maintained. This was one of your father's express wishes. He wanted you to have the house and property."

Wiseman showed me the details in the papers, and had me sign several others. He offered his services to help with anything I needed, including a few issues still outstanding in Connecticut, but I was distracted—overwhelmed by the news that I was now a multi-millionaire. He gathered his remaining papers and stuffed them into his briefcase.

I thought about how my father had provided for me financially, and how he failed to provide for me in any other way. "You know, Arthur, my father never once contacted me after my mother and I came to Boston."

Wiseman sighed. "I know, Jamie. I don't understand why, but I know it was your mother's wish that he stay away. As I said, I never met your father. I only know what I read in the newspapers and saw in the newsreels."

"It's funny, but that's how I knew him, too. I remember growing up in Granbury, but not much about my father. I was twelve when we left, and I can only picture him in his flying gear, stepping into the cockpit of his plane. Once we moved to Boston, my mother never mentioned his name again, even after he disappeared."

Wiseman said, "Jamie, your mother was a very private person. She didn't share anything with me about her relationship with your father. But she did talk about you—endlessly. She was proud of you, especially when you won the Distinguished Service Cross for what you did in the Philippines. I'm sure your father would have been proud, too."

"Thank you for saying that, Arthur. I appreciate it, but I wasn't a flyer like my father, and I wasn't quite the war hero he was, either. He won the Medal of Honor, after all."

"Don't measure yourself against him, Jamie. It was a different time and a different place and different circumstances. What you did saved hundreds of men from certain death."

I walked over to the sideboard and poured myself a whiskey from my grandfather's crystal decanter. I offered one to Wiseman, but he declined. I sat down again, and the two of us stared at each other in silence for a few minutes.

It was after five when Arthur Wiseman left. The traffic noise was growing out on Huntington Avenue as downtown workers headed home to Jamaica Plain, West Roxbury, Brookline, Newton and points beyond.

I walked upstairs to my bedroom, whiskey in hand, briefly glancing out the window at where the little park used to be, seeing instead the green tiled roof of the Cities Service station. I knelt down at the steamer trunk again, and this time I removed the envelope from the bottom. Sitting down on the bed, I spread out its contents. The newspaper clippings were dated the first week of April 1934. The *Boston Herald* had the biggest headline:

FAMOUS AVIATOR LOST OVER THE ATLANTIC

The *Boston Globe*'s was smaller and less dramatic:

HARRY MCCOY MISSING—PRESUMED LOST AT SEA

The Traveler trumped them both with its double headline:

MCCOY DOWN AT SEA
WAR HERO DIES IN ATTEMPT TO SET AVIATION
RECORD

I propped my head on the pillow and re-read the stories. I'd kept them hidden from my mother, because she would have been upset if she knew I had them. I still held bitter memories of wanting to take the train from Groton down to Granbury to see my father take off on his flight to Capetown, and my mother refusing permission. Instead, I'd remained cooped up in my dormitory room and missed the last opportunity I would ever have to see my father. My mother and I never spoke about it, and now that she was dead, my grudge would remain forever unresolved.

As I spread the yellowing newsprint on my lap, I heard Mrs. Glendenning rattling pots and pans downstairs. The unsubtle smell of something burning in the kitchen penetrated all the way to the third floor, and I considered offending the old bat by going out to dinner. I had much to think about, but I'd already decided I wanted no part of Boston. I'd keep the house open—I could afford it—and I'd let the Glendennings live there as long as they wanted to stay, but I needed to get the hell out.

CHAPTER 2

I spent the next two weeks settling my mother and father's estates. With Arthur Wiseman's assistance, I signed and filed the appropriate papers with the probate court and set up the bank and brokerage accounts I needed to provide me with a handsome income. I visited J. Press, the Cambridge haberdashery I'd used as an undergraduate, and purchased a new wardrobe along with a leather Gladstone bag and two large suitcases. As far as I was concerned, the sooner I got out of uniform, the better. I never again wanted to think about the Army or the war; I just wanted to start a new life.

Arthur Wiseman arranged for my late father's Hartford lawyer to open the house in Granbury. I received a telegram from E. Biddle Franklin, Esq. of Selwyn & Macy informing me the house would be ready by the first of May, and inviting me to telephone for instructions. The caretaker, Henry Dietz, would meet me at the Granbury train station whenever I chose to arrive.

Throughout all my preparations to leave Boston, Mr. Glendenning was helpful, but Mrs. Glendenning continued treating me like an unwelcome visitor. One evening, as I sat in my grandfather's study reading the newspaper and smoking a cigarette, Mrs. Glendenning barged in and announced, "Mrs. Winant never allowed smoking in her house."

I fought to control my temper. I took a deep drag on my Lucky and exhaled a cloud of smoke. I looked directly at her and said, "My grandmother died three years ago. This house belongs to me now, and I'll do whatever I please in it."

The woman turned scarlet and opened her mouth to reply, but no words came out.

I leaned forward in my grandfather's reading chair. "Your memory must be failing you, Mrs. Glendenning. There's a humidor on my grandfather's desk with a dozen stale Havanas inside. Perhaps you forgot he was accustomed to smoking cigars in this very room."

She turned and left without saying anything more, and I stubbed out my cigarette, resolved to hasten my departure.

After the cigarette incident, I took every opportunity to stay away from Number 7 Van Houghton Row, but there was little for me to do around town. I tried looking up old friends, but everyone I knew before the war had either moved away or was serving overseas on occupation duty. One of my old roommates, Geoff Rendell, had been killed in action in France, and the other one, Bert Goodenough, was still in Germany. There were no former girlfriends, either. Although I'd dated a few attractive girls in college, I had never formed a close relationship with any of them. I always thought there would be plenty of time for serious romance after college; I hadn't counted on the war.

On April 29, I made my final arrangements. I went to South Station and purchased a one-way ticket to Granbury for Wednesday morning, May 1, on the Albany and Hartford Railroad via Framingham, Worcester and Springfield. Before I left the station, I stopped at the Western Union desk and sent a telegram to the caretaker, Henry Dietz. A confirming wire arrived two hours later. That afternoon, I received a call from Arthur Wiseman asking me to stop by his office.

I arrived at 15 Court Square at 4:30 p.m. A secretary escorted me to a corner office that bespoke Arthur's senior status in the firm. He greeted me warmly, grasping my shoulder with his left hand and offering a firm handshake with his right.

"Thank you for coming, Jamie. Please sit down. Would you like a cup of coffee, or perhaps some tea?"

I settled into a side chair. "No, thank you, Arthur. What did you want to see me about?"

He returned to his desk and sat down. He offered me a cigarette, which I accepted, and we both lit up. "It's fine that you're returning to your hometown, Jamie. Granbury's a beautiful place—quintessential New England. But I wanted to warn you about a few things before you left."

"Warn me? About what?"

Wiseman sighed and took a deep puff on his cigarette, looking like a man struggling with a dilemma. As he spoke, ashes fell on his desk. "Your father was a hero in Granbury. The people there idolized him." He paused. "Unfortunately, they're not quite as charitable toward your mother. In fact, they despise her. And me, too."

"I don't understand. Why would they despise my mother? And what do you have to do with it?"

Wiseman removed a file folder from the middle drawer of his desk and opened it on his blotter. He silently reviewed its contents for a few moments, flipping pages and running his finger along the lines of writing. Leaving the file open, he spoke at length, telling me some things I already knew about my hometown, and quite a few things about my father and his family that I didn't. I knew my father was descended from a collateral branch of the same family that produced the Revolutionary War spy Nathan Hale, and I was vaguely aware that my family name was attached to a manufacturing company one of my ancestors founded, but I knew little else.

Granbury was on the Connecticut River north of Hartford. It had once been a prosperous farming community—mostly shade tobacco. A few farms remained in the area, but Granbury, like many other towns its size, became dependent on manufacturing during the late nineteenth century. My great-grandfather, Charles Jameson McCoy, built a machine tool factory in Granbury—the McCoy Machine Works—shortly after the Civil War, and it became the principal employer in the area. My paternal grandfather, Jameson Hale McCoy, Sr., inherited the company in 1905 and converted it from machine tools to engine parts. He ran it until his death in 1925, making it one of the top manufacturers of automotive and aircraft engine parts in the northeast. My father, Jameson Hale "Harry" McCoy, Jr., subsequently took control and managed the company for a few years, but he was more interested in flying than operating a factory, so he sold it to a couple of men from New York in 1928.

The new owners ran it into the ground, and the stock market crash made matters worse. By mid-1931, they declared bankruptcy. The bank foreclosed, took over the property and shut the place down, bringing the population of Granbury to near ruin in the process. In an extraordinary act of generosity, Harry McCoy re-purchased the factory from the bank and re-opened it in 1932. Despite a poor market, he poured millions of dollars into the company, running three shifts a day until he disappeared in 1934.

Wiseman finished his cigarette and continued, "After your father disappeared, your mother sent me to Granbury to evaluate the business and pick someone to run it. Most of the employees cooperated at first—after all, they wanted to protect their jobs. But I soon discovered something was wrong. There was no backlog. The company had only two customers, but all their orders had been completed. Even though the invoices were recorded as paid, there was no money in the company accounts.

"I brought in an outside auditor from Hartford, but he couldn't figure out what happened. Your mother feared embezzlement or worse—that your father was involved in tax fraud—so I hired a former Treasury agent to investigate."

I was alarmed. "What did the T-man find out?"

"He discovered the two customers were dummy corporations. We suspected your father funneled his personal fortune through these two companies to purchase engine parts just to keep the factory running. By the middle of 1934, the McCoy Machine Works was insolvent, and your father's personal assets were depleted to about a million in cash and a few million in stocks and bonds—still a considerable sum, but only a fraction of what he once had."

Wiseman paused to give me time to react, but I had nothing to say.

"We had no choice, Jamie. We had to close the factory again. As you can imagine, the people of Granbury weren't pleased. It was the middle of the Depression, and the shutdown took a terrible toll."

"So you and my mother were pariahs there."

The lawyer widened his eyes. "To say the least. The threats got so bad that I feared for my life."

I was shocked. "You mean they actually tried to kill you?"

"Someone set fire to my car, and I didn't stick around to find out if I was going to be next."

I let out a low whistle. I thought about Arthur's revelations and said, "There's something I don't understand. What happened to all the parts the factory sold to the dummy corporations?"

Wiseman closed the file folder and handed it to me. "All we have is in here. You're welcome to keep it. It's one of two copies. I have the other one."

"Who has the original?" I asked.

"Your mother; but I believe she destroyed it."

"Did the T-man keep a copy?"

"Your mother asked him not to, but I really couldn't say."

I took the folder, opened it and scanned its contents. It consisted of a typewritten report on the letterhead of Goddard MacFarlane, Private Investigator, Graybar Building, New York City.

Wiseman said, "Page 42 has the information on the dummy companies. As you can see, there isn't much."

I turned the pages and came to the appropriate references. The first one was the New York Engine Company, John Niemand, proprietor, 345 East 86th Street, New York. The second was listed as Yorkville

Exports Ltd., Henry Nirgenz, proprietor, also at 345 East 86th Street.

Arthur said, "The address belonged to a doctor named Griebel who knew nothing about the two companies. MacFarlane couldn't find corporate listings for either one, and there were no listings anywhere in New York or New Jersey for either Niemand or Nirgenz. I could have saved him the trouble had he given me the names before he checked. Although I don't speak German, Yiddish is close enough, and I know 'niemand' means 'nobody' and 'nirgenz' or 'nirgends' means 'nowhere.' The factory had shipped the parts to an address in Perth Amboy, New Jersey, but it turned out to be an abandoned warehouse."

I was puzzled. "Was my father breaking the law?"

"There's no crime in looting funds from yourself, and your father was sole owner of the McCoy Machine Works. Your mother was worried about tax fraud, but the auditor discovered that your father overpaid his taxes during the period in question."

"He left no other clue about what he was doing?"

"Nothing we found. It appears he was only providing employment for three hundred people who desperately needed work. Maybe he was hoping the economy would turn around and justify the expense, or maybe he was just a generous guy who felt obligated to help his neighbors."

I took the file with me, planning to read it on the train to Connecticut. It was unfortunate that my mother's name was tarnished in my hometown, but at least Wiseman prepared me for it. I resolved to ignore any negative comments I might hear about her in Granbury. After all, I wanted to rediscover my past and reconnect with the memory of my father, not alienate my future neighbors.

CHAPTER 3

The train ride to Connecticut was pleasant and uneventful. I sat in the parlor car drinking coffee and reading the MacFarlane file. My copy of the report was a Photostat—that is, white letters on a black background. The photostatic copying process was expensive, I knew, but it was preferable to handling messy carbon copies.

In some places, the report was articulate and specific, but in others, it was incomplete, with sentences cut off in the middle and thoughts left unfinished. The whole thing seemed a bit of a jumble with no conclusion—it read like a committee wrote it. This made it difficult to follow, and I wasn't impressed. Goddard MacFarlane hardly seemed worth whatever my mother paid him.

I was struck by MacFarlane's opinion of Granbury. He wrote that the people were surly, uncooperative, and suspicious of him as an outsider. He attributed this to Yankee aloofness, but he also felt that those in a position to know my father were hiding something. In the end, he decided my father's actions were unexplainable. He presented several possibilities, two of which Arthur already summarized for me in his office: either my father was the most generous man alive, or he was engaged in a scheme to hide money from the Internal Revenue Service. However, there was no evidence for the latter scenario, as attested to by the audited financial statements and tax returns, all of which appeared to be in order. MacFarlane also considered that my father could have been a terrible businessman who simply ruined his company, or that third parties—the owners of the dummy companies in New York—had been defrauding him.

Naturally, I wanted to think the best of my father, so I assumed his actions were in keeping with the family tradition of philanthropy. My greatest concern was how I would be received in Granbury. Would these flinty Yankees welcome me as a returning native, or treat me as an outsider, as they had Arthur Wiseman and Goddard MacFarlane?

The train rambled through the western Massachusetts farmlands and turned south along the Connecticut River toward Granbury, passing a dozen or more factory rail sidings. As my destination approached, I considered that one of them might have belonged to the old McCoy Machine Works.

I arrived in Granbury a few minutes before two o'clock on May 1, expecting Henry Dietz to meet my train. The station was a sturdy brick relic of the last century, built in the days when railroads ruled American commerce and passenger traffic. The conductor offered me a hand down onto the wooden platform and I looked around for Dietz, but the place was all but deserted. An elderly porter struggled at the far end of the train pulling my suitcases from the baggage car, and the stationmaster spoke with a janitor at the other end. I strolled toward the stationmaster who, upon seeing me, began walking in my direction.

When he was only a few feet away, he stopped abruptly, staring at me. "Good Lord! You look just like Colonel McCoy."

I smiled. "No, sir. I'm his son, Jamie."

The stationmaster smiled in return. "Jamie McCoy! You're the spit—"

"I know," I interrupted. "I'm the spitting image of my father. I've heard that all my life." I held out my hand to shake.

The stationmaster took it and pumped up and down. "It's great to have a McCoy back in town. I'm Hector Cummins, son; I knew your daddy well. Used to work for him, in fact." He waited for a sign of recognition from me, but when he saw there was none, he said, "Aw hell, you were too young to remember anyway."

"It's nice meeting you, Mr. Cummins."

"Just call me Heck. Everybody else does."

"Thanks, Heck. And please call me Jamie." I was glad to have things on a first name basis—it was a good sign I might not be treated as an outsider after all. I told Heck Cummins about the wire I'd sent Henry Dietz asking him to meet me at the station, and asked if Heck had seen the caretaker anywhere about.

Cummins laughed out loud. "You're lucky if Hank Dietz remembers what day it is. He told me you'd be coming, but he didn't say when."

I sighed. There was no way I'd be able to manage my Gladstone bag and suitcases without a car.

Heck patted me on the shoulder. "Why don't you check your bags with the porter and walk over to the Noll

Tavern down by the green. Hank'll show up there eventually. He usually does about this time of day."

"How will I know him?"

"Don't worry Mr. McCoy—I mean Jamie—he'll recognize you."

I made arrangements with the porter to check my bags and tipped him a dollar, a veritable fortune. I walked out of the station and crossed a gravel lot toward a sign directing me to the center of town. Beyond the sign was a cobblestone footpath that wound its way up a grassy slope. At the top of the footpath, I came to a white clapboard church with an imposing four-story spire. In front was a signboard identifying it as the First Congregational Church of Granbury—the Reverend Arnold Hopewell, Pastor. I vaguely remembered the building, but I couldn't recall ever having been inside. My mother raised me as an Episcopalian; I had no knowledge of my father's denomination. The church fronted on a main thoroughfare, the Old Hartford Turnpike, a two-lane road marked by a weathered signpost indicating Springfield, Massachusetts was twenty-two miles north, and Hartford, Connecticut was seventeen miles south.

The center of Granbury lay before me. Across the road from the church was the town green, a rectangular expanse of lawn stretching westward the length of three football fields. At the foot of the green was a nondescript two-story brick building I recognized as the school I attended as a child. To the right of the school was the courthouse—built of solid granite and as ornate as the school was plain—and next to that, a wooden firehouse.

I began recollecting images from my childhood. Arthur Wiseman had been right—Granbury was the quintessential New England town, straight off the cover of the *Saturday Evening Post*. On the north side of the green, close to the Old Hartford Turnpike, was a large Romanesque brownstone structure I recognized as the McCoy Memorial Library, a building my great-grandfather had donated to the town. I remembered being taught in school that it was one of the last public buildings designed by the great architect, H.H. Richardson.

Farther down the north side of the green, along Ferry Street, was a line of stately homes, some built of brick, others of white clapboard, mostly private residences. In the center of the green stood a covered octagonal band shell, and in front of that, Granbury's Civil War Memorial, a weathered granite statue of a Union infantryman clutching a rifle and gazing somberly down at an ancient cannon aimed, incongruously, at the schoolhouse. Oak, chestnut, elm and maple trees dotted the lawn, all of them just beginning to reach their fullness.

On the south side of the green, along Albany Road, were the municipal and commercial buildings—town hall, the police station, a bank, a dozen small storefronts, and the Noll Tavern. Pre-war cars drove slowly up and down the roads on both sides of the green, and pedestrians walked along the brick sidewalk on Albany Road in front of the storefronts. If the Depression and the McCoy factory shutdown had affected the town, it must have recovered since. Everything looked neat and prosperous to me.

I crossed the Old Hartford Turnpike and walked across the green toward the Noll Tavern. I smiled at the people I saw and they smiled back. It felt good to be home at last.

When I entered the tavern, it took a few moments for my eyes to adjust to the dim lighting. The room was cozy, with solid oak tables and chairs scattered in the front and a narrow brass-railed bar at the back. The décor was purely colonial American, with a framed color portrait of George Washington adorning the left wall. On the right wall hung crossed muskets, a saber and a powder horn. I couldn't tell if they were genuine or merely reproductions. A sign near the entrance read, "Tap Room." I inferred there was a dining room elsewhere on the premises.

Several men were at the tables, some of them eating light snacks, most of them just drinking draft beer and chatting quietly. I headed for the bar, intending to inquire about Henry Dietz, but I didn't get halfway across the room before the bartender came out from behind the bar and strode toward me, announcing to the room, "Listen up, everyone. This here's Colonel Harry McCoy's son."

I was taken aback. The dozen or so men at the tables put down their drinks and crowded around, patting me on the back and competing to shake my hand.

The bartender introduced himself as Ernie Thayer, proprietor of the Noll Tavern. "Heck Cummins telephoned from the station to say you were on your way here. Glad to have you, son."

That explained the welcome. "Thank you, Mr. Thayer. I'm glad to be here."

"Hell, son, it's just plain Ernie."

"And I'm just plain Jamie."

Ernie clapped me on the back and introduced me to the other men. I didn't remember a single name.

"Come on over to the bar and have a beer, Jamie. I've got a few things I want you to see."

I obliged. As Ernie poured a draft, I said, "I'm trying to find Henry Dietz, the caretaker of my father's house. He was supposed to meet me at the train station, but he never showed up. Heck Cummins said I might find him here."

Ernie laughed. "That's old Hank for ya. Never where he's supposed to be. That son of a bitch'll be late for his own funeral."

He handed me a beer, and I drank it in small sips.

"Don't worry, though, he'll be along soon," Ernie said. "He always shows up sooner or later."

"I guess I'll just have to wait for him here, then."

"And you're welcome to do so." Thayer wiped his hands with a towel and reached under the bar, bringing out a cracked and fading leather album. "I want you to see this, Jamie. It's a collection of photographs and newspaper clippings of your father. He was quite a guy, and a good friend."

Ernie opened the album on the bar and I looked at the first page. It was a newspaper article from the *Hartford Times* dated June 1, 1919. The headline read, "WAR HERO RETURNS." There was an accompanying photograph of my father in his American Flying Corps uniform. Below my father's picture was another photograph of a parade scene in what I supposed was downtown Hartford. The story described Harry McCoy's return from France with his new bride and the tumultuous welcome he received. I turned the page to find that the story continued with more photographs—of my father alone wearing his decorations, of my mother and father smiling at the camera, and of my father standing between my paternal grandparents who were beaming proudly.

The next page had a sidebar story summarizing the events leading to my father's Medal of Honor. I read it while Ernie looked on.

While returning alone from a reconnaissance flight over the Western Front, Lieutenant McCoy of the 27th American Air Service Squadron encountered five German planes strafing a company of U.S. Marines who were trapped and nearly surrounded by German infantry. According to Major Theodore Derwent, commanding officer of the Marine company, McCoy tore into the enemy planes and immediately shot down two of them. With the other three in close pursuit, he executed a death-spiral dive, spun out at the last minute, climbed above his pursuers and shot down another one.

For the next several minutes, as Marines and German soldiers watched in awe, the two remaining German flyers attacked Lieutenant McCoy's plane, each in turn taking their best shots at him while McCoy deftly evaded their assaults. Finally, the American airman downed his fourth plane, but the last German was about to close in for the kill. As enemy troops cheered from below, the German flyer aimed his machine guns at McCoy, only to have them jam. The German veered off and McCoy maneuvered underneath him ready to fire. The German was at his mercy.

Instead of firing, Lieutenant McCoy pulled up alongside his enemy and motioned him to land behind the American lines. Reluctantly, the German complied, whereupon the American Marines captured him and his aeroplane.

Furious, the German troops on the ground resumed their withering mortar and rifle fire at the Marines, while machine-gunners aimed their bullets at McCoy in the air. Undaunted, as bullets tore into his aeroplane, McCoy maneuvered into another steep dive, this time strafing the German troops mercilessly. After making several passes at the enemy, with devastating results, the German commander ran up the white flag and the Marines carried the day.

It was a lucky thing for McCoy that the Germans surrendered when they did, because he was out of ammunition, nearly out of gas and his plane was falling apart. As his engine sputtered, the daring young American airman landed in the meadow below next to the German plane he had spared from destruction just moments before. Jubilant Marines immediately surrounded Lieutenant McCoy and carried him away on their shoulders.

Next to the story was a grainy photograph of General Pershing placing the Medal of Honor around the neck of a newly promoted Captain Harry McCoy. I'd seen a copy of this picture before when I was a child; it was autographed by Pershing, and hung in my father's library.

I continued turning the pages while Ernie provided commentary to accompany each of the photographs and newspaper clippings.

Ernie pointed out another series of newspaper photos. "That was when your father broke the airspeed record to Miami. Damn, that was something. Your old man beat Wiley Post's record by nearly an hour, but the American Flying Club refused to give him the prize because he took off from Granbury rather than Roosevelt Field. Well, Colonel McCoy just gassed up his plane, turned around and flew right back. On the way, he flew low over Long Island, buzzed Roosevelt Field, and dropped a dye marker right in the middle of the runway. When he landed at Granbury, he had beaten his own record by thirty-eight minutes. The next day, Wiley Post himself drove up from New York and personally handed your father his own trophy."

I beamed. My father must have been quite a guy. I only wished I had known him better.

The next few pages recorded Harry McCoy's solo flight from New York to Rio. Ernie related some more amusing anecdotes and laughed at a picture of my father, sound asleep under the fuselage of his old Lockheed Vega. Ernie's laughter abruptly died as I turned the next few pages. The photographs and accompanying news stories were similar to the ones I'd kept hidden in my Boston bedroom for years.

"That's the last flight."

"I know," I said.

In the photographs, crowds of well-wishers surrounded a grinning Harry McCoy as he made his way to the special tri-motor plane he had designed and built just for this flight. This was the takeoff my mother had refused to let me attend when I was a freshman at Groton. He would have been the first man to fly solo across the Atlantic the long way—north to south from Granbury, Connecticut to Capetown, South Africa.

I stared at a photograph of a tall beautiful woman, also dressed in flying gear, kissing my father goodbye. I asked, "Who's the woman with my father?"

Ernie didn't have to look at it. "That's Greta Huffmann. She was a famous flyer, too—from Germany. She's the one who gave your father the idea to make the flight."

I gave him a questioning look, and Ernie related a story that, perhaps, explained why my mother refused to let me come to Granbury for the takeoff.

In July 1933, Greta Huffmann and her husband Rudy, while flying from Berlin to New York, became lost in the fog over Long Island Sound and crashed into a swamp near Bridgeport, Connecticut. Their plane was wrecked and they were badly bruised and shaken up, but otherwise unharmed. My father drove down to Bridgeport to offer his assistance, later accompanying the couple to New York City.

My father paid for their rooms at the Plaza Hotel, and he stayed there, too. He entertained the couple regally, introducing them to Wiley Post, Amelia Earhart and her husband George Putnam, and arranged a visit to Eleanor and Franklin Roosevelt at Hyde Park. Rudy Huffmann later returned to Germany, but his young wife stayed in America with my father for several months, causing quite a scandal.

The Huffmanns had been planning a New York to Capetown flight, but with their plane destroyed and Rudy back in Germany, Greta Huffmann soon convinced my father to make the attempt. He had recently completed work on a new tri-motor airplane—a fast, powerful aircraft built especially for long-distance flights—and it seemed like the perfect opportunity to prove his design. The plane was a veritable flying gas tank, carrying more than three thousand gallons of aviation fuel, and, with its three powerful Pratt & Whitney Wasp engines, it was capable of speeds approaching two hundred and fifty miles per hour.

Harry McCoy took off from the private airfield on his Granbury estate on the morning of April 2, 1934. The seven thousand mile, nonstop flight was expected to take thirty-six hours—a test of endurance that would have eclipsed Charles Lindbergh's 3,600-mile flight from New York to Paris seven years earlier. He was sighted forty-five minutes after takeoff by a Coast Guard cutter as he flew over Montauk Point, Long Island; he was never seen or heard from again.

Harry McCoy had pre-arranged a series of radio checks with private ham operators in Bermuda, the Caribbean, South America and West Africa, but no one ever heard him broadcast. Three U.S. Navy ships and several merchant vessels in the Atlantic attempted radio contact, also without success. There was no search at sea because no one knew where to look.

After my father disappeared over the Atlantic, Greta Huffmann returned to Germany, having reconciled with her husband. A year later, they flew from Berlin to Capetown, setting a new record for the trip. The Huffmanns divorced in 1936.

I listened to the story of my father's disappearance, relieved at hearing someone discuss it openly for the first time. The subject had been taboo at my maternal grandparents' house in Boston, and my only source of information until now had been newspapers and magazines. I was never allowed to grieve properly. At least now I thought I understood my mother's silence—shame over her husband's public affair with another woman. But I was still puzzled. My mother had left my father almost a year before the affair, taking me with her to Boston with no explanation.

Ernie continued turning the pages. "Here's something a bit more pleasant."

It was a black-and-white glossy of my father on the Granbury green, arm-in-arm with six other men, all clad in white shorts and undershirts, smiling foolishly at the camera. Names were written in the margin below each man in the picture, and it was dated May 30, 1928. The event was vaguely familiar.

"That was the eighth annual Granbury Road Race," Ernie said. "Your father started it in 1920, and it became a town tradition."

I smiled. "I think I remember. It started as a wedding anniversary celebration for my parents." My parents met in Paris shortly after the First World War, when grandfather Winant went to the Versailles peace talks as an advisor to President Wilson. He brought his daughter—my mother—along as his personal assistant, and she fell in love with the dashing war hero, Harry McCoy. They eloped in Paris, much to the chagrin of both families.

Every year thereafter, Harry invited his closest friends to Granbury for a two-day celebration that culminated in a five-mile footrace. After the first few years, others began competing, and it soon became a major event drawing runners from as far away as New Haven and Boston.

Ernie identified some of the men in the picture, pointing at each one. "That's Major Derwent, commander of the Marines your father saved during the war. This one here's John Barrow, your father's closest friend. They went to Choate and Yale together. He's a federal judge now, in New York. Used to be the Attorney General here in Connecticut."

I recognized him—Uncle John. He wasn't really my uncle, but I had called him that when I was a kid.

"We haven't had the race for the past four years—because of the war—but Mayor Gibbons is starting it up again. He invited your father's friends to come back for Decoration Day, and there's gonna be a ceremony in your father's honor right on the green before the race."

"That's great," I said. "I'd love to meet these guys."

"Well, I don't know if they're all coming, but you being here might convince 'em to show. After you get settled in, drop in and see the mayor. He'll put you in touch with your daddy's friends."

Just then, Hank Dietz walked in and came up to the bar. He was tall and lean, like me, but he was at least twenty years older. He had a three-day growth of beard, gray thinning hair that looked like it hadn't been washed in months, and he reeked of stale sweat and beer. He held an old baseball cap in both hands, and he looked down at his feet as he spoke. "Jeez, Mr. McCoy, I'm awful sorry about missin' you at the station. I finally remembered, and Heck Cummins told me you'd be waitin' here at the Noll."

"That's all right, Mr. Dietz. Why don't we just go pick up my bags at the station and head over to my father's house."

"No need to fetch the suitcases, Mr. McCoy. I already got 'em in the back of my truck. And you can call me 'Hank.' Everyone else does."

"Thank you, Hank." I didn't invite him to address me by my first name. He was my employee, after all, and I'd gotten the impression from both Heck Cummins and Ernie Thayer that Dietz wasn't particularly well respected.

I turned to Ernie and thanked him for the beer and the reminiscences of my father, promising to be a regular visitor at the Noll, and to call on Mayor Gibbons at the first opportunity. As I left with Hank Dietz, I waved goodbye to the other men at the tables.

Outside, Hank opened the passenger door of a rusting Ford pick-up truck that looked like it had been built sometime in the early thirties. Empty beer bottles littered the floor of the cab and the bench seat had a spring sticking out of the fabric.

Hank said, "Let me throw a hunk of wood over that spring. That oughtta keep it down." He reached behind the seat and brought out a foot-square scrap of wood that he placed atop the passenger seat.

Climbing into the truck, I stepped on the running board and it almost gave way. Hank shut the door behind me and walked around to the driver's side. He started the engine, which turned over with difficulty, and we lurched forward. At the corner, we turned right onto the Old Hartford Turnpike and drove south.

I said, "I'm going to need a car, Hank. Do you know where I can buy one?"

"You already got a car, Mr. McCoy. I been takin' care of your daddy's roadster for the past twelve years like she was my own. I got her all gassed up and ready for you at the house."

I winced. If Hank Dietz had been taking care of my father's car like it had been his own, then it was probably a rusted out hulk like the pick-up truck.

CHAPTER 4

As we drove south, the landscape began to change. Close to town, large Victorian homes with manicured lawns dotted the roadside; after a mile, colonials, Cape Cods and saltboxes prevailed; then came low farmhouses and empty rolling meadows. We came to a low stone wall on the right, behind which stretched acres of newly planted corn.

Hank said, "That's your daddy's land. Used to grow shade tobacco, but it's leased to local farmers now, and they just plant cow corn."

"Who decided to lease it out?"

"Your mama, I 'spect. Some lawyers in Hartford handle the details. They was the ones as called me and said you was comin' back. I had to hire a dozen hands to get the place in shape. Ain't no one lived here in years, and the house needed a lot of work. You know—cleanin' up, turning on the electricity and phone, flushin' the pipes and all. Had to replace some roof tiles, fix some shutters and a bunch of other stuff. Nothin' big, mind you, just a lotta little things."

"Thank you, Hank. I appreciate the effort."

"Well, there's still a lotta stuff as needs doin' ya know. There ain't no electric refrigerator in the kitchen, just an old icebox. I figure iffen ya want a Frigidaire, I can call down to G. Fox in Hartford and have 'em send one up."

"Thanks. That's a good idea."

"My oldest boy and me can handle the groundskeepin' and the maintenance chores, but I figured you'd need some household help besides that, so I hired on Mrs. Hanratty as housekeeper and cook. She lives nearby. I hope that's okay with you."

"I'm sure she'll do just fine." After four years overseas, I thought a housekeeper—any housekeeper—would be a luxury. I just hoped she was more personable than Mrs. Glendenning.

As we drove along and I listened to Hank speak, it occurred to me that he wasn't a native New Englander. His accent sounded almost southern, but not quite. "Where you from, Hank?" I asked.

He grinned and said, "Ya could tell, huh? Came from a small town in western Pennsylvania, but I moved up here after the Big War. Didn't feel like workin' the farm no more and there was a lotta factory jobs up north. Gotta job at yer granddaddy's factory, but I got my hand caught in a lathe and that was the end of my business career."

I looked at his left hand and noticed it was missing two fingers.

"Yer granddaddy was a good fella, though. He hired me to work around the house, and I been here ever since."

"Even after my father disappeared?"

"Yer daddy was even nicer than yer granddaddy. He had a provision in his will that kept me on the job as long as the house and property stayed in yer family."

We came to a set of granite gateposts, and Hank turned the truck past open wrought-iron gates onto a tree-lined gravel road. On the right-hand side was the red clapboard saltbox where my father was born. It was more than two hundred years old, and had been home to generations of Hales and then McCoys until my grandfather built the mansion.

We continued up the gravel drive past an open field with a weathered tobacco barn at one end.

Hank said, "That was your daddy's private airfield. He used the barn as his hangar."

He slowed down to give me a better look. There was still an old windsock hanging limply on a pole by the barn.

The driveway curved to the right and, around the bend and up a slight rise, I saw my family's mansion. I hadn't seen the place in fourteen years, but it was just as I remembered it—imposing and grand. My grandfather built it at the turn of the century, copying the same Romanesque style H.H. Richardson used on the Granbury library. When I was a little boy, I had called it The Castle. Its red sandstone walls towered above the landscape, blocking the vista beyond. It was too much for one person, but in the old days, there was a platoon of servants catering to my grandfather's every whim.

I never knew my paternal grandmother—she died before I was born—but I remembered my grandfather fondly. I was his only grandchild, and he doted on me. The old man died when I was five; afterwards, my parents and I moved from the red saltbox into The Castle.

As we approached the house, I noticed a faded gray discoloration on the wall that resembled a lightning bolt pointing down at the arch over the front door.

"What's that mark on the wall, Hank?"

"What do you mean?"

I pointed at the stain. It was unmistakable, and Hank couldn't have missed it. "Right there, over the door. It looks like someone painted a lightning bolt on the house."

"Oh that. That's uh—It's just a water stain. We had some trouble with the roof tiles awhile back."

I looked at him like he was crazy. "That's a pretty artistic water stain. Are you sure it wasn't painted on?"

"No, Sir. I mean yes, Sir. I'm sure. It's just a water stain."

I let it go.

Hank pulled the truck into the circular driveway under a *porte-cochère* and came to an abrupt stop directly behind my father's roadster. I opened my door and got out, walking over to the sleek sports car. It had deeply polished brown fenders and running boards, and a tan body. I ran my hand along the sides, admiring the car's crisp lines.

Hank walked over. "You like what I done with 'er? She's quite a beaut, ain't she?"

"Yeah, Hank, she sure is."

"It's a 1928 Mercedes Benz SSK."

I looked at the leather-covered steering wheel and the dials on the wooden dashboard. Bolted on the face of the glove box was a brass plate inscribed, *To Colonel Jameson Hale McCoy, Jr. in commemoration of the tenth anniversary of his gallant exploit—Karl Erich, Graf von Sielau, 1928.*

Hank watched me examine the inscription. "The car was a gift from the German pilot your daddy spared in the Great War. He came over here in '28 for the Road Race."

I was speechless.

I stepped up to the broad verandah as Hank removed the suitcases from the back of the truck and followed me to the front door. Mrs. Hanratty must have been waiting for us, because she opened the door immediately, surprising me.

"Hello, Captain McCoy," she said, smiling. "I'm Gladys Hanratty, your housekeeper. Welcome home."

I smiled back at her. "Thank you, Mrs. Hanratty. I'm glad to be here. It's been a very long time. Too long. And please, ma'am, I'm not a captain any more. My military career is over."

"Yes, Cap—Mr. McCoy." She stepped aside to let me enter.

Hank leaned over and whispered, "Lotta folks'll call you Cap'n no matter what you say 'cuz yer daddy liked to be called 'Colonel'—know what I mean?"

"I get it, Hank. Thank you."

The front hallway was enormous—a brass and crystal chandelier hung from the center of a two-story vaulted ceiling; a six-foot high stone fireplace dominated the far wall, above which hung an oil painting of my grandfather; a curved staircase swept up the wall on the left. To my right a set of double doors opened into the library and my father's study beyond, where my mother and I had spent evenings on the soft leather sofa reading to each other.

I had many fond memories of my mother in this house, but few of my father—he never read stories to me when I was a little boy. Harry McCoy was always off flying somewhere, setting new records, or at least competing for them. My grandfather and Uncle John Barrow were the male figures I remembered most from when I lived here before.

Hank brought the suitcases in and carried them upstairs to the master bedroom. He then went back to town for groceries, promising to return to give me a tour of the property. Mrs. Hanratty unpacked my suitcases and put my things away while I washed up in the master bathroom.

A half hour later, I had changed my clothes and returned downstairs to explore the house, ending up in the library trying to rekindle more memories. On the wall above a small writing desk was the photograph of General Pershing hanging the Medal of Honor around my father's neck. To its left was his citation, and next to it was a framed diptych. The left side of the diptych was a letter written in heavy German script surmounted with an elaborate family crest. On the right was—I presumed—the English translation:

> Dear Captain McCoy,
>
> I am writing to express my gratitude and that of my family for the extraordinary act of chivalry you displayed in aerial combat against my son.
>
> Savagery is commonplace when nations are engaged in war; gallantry is rare. That you refrained from killing my son when he was at your mercy is a kindness his mother and I will long remember. It is thus also that your generosity toward a helpless enemy has

earned you the accolades of your government and your comrades-in-arms.

My son and many of the soldiers captured as a result of your action have written home to tell of your exploits. His Imperial Majesty, the Kaiser, has been informed, and he has recorded your name in one of the weekly dispatches to the General Staff recognizing acts of individual heroism. It is the first and only time an enemy officer has been so honored.

It is my hope that, when the current hostilities have ceased, I may have the privilege of meeting you and thanking you in person.

[signed]
Karl Gustave
Graf von Sielau und Kurland
18 August 1918

I read the letter a second time. My father's wartime heroics had been well reported in the newspapers, but I never knew this detail. His actions had merited recognition even from the Kaiser. I wondered what my father must have thought of that. I understood well that battlefield courage is often a spur of the moment thing— a reaction born of good training. My own experience had been different; I had reacted to baser instincts.

At that moment, Hank Dietz returned, ready for my tour of the estate. We began with the main house, which took some time because I was intent on examining every room. When we finally left the house, I insisted on driving the Mercedes, preferring its comfort to the rigors of Hank's truck. Hank happily agreed, showing me how to work the choke and the starter.

"This car's a real kitten," Hank said. "She's old, and her suspension's a little tight, but she rides like a dream."

I acquired my driving skills on the streets of Boston, and they had atrophied somewhat during my tour of duty in the Pacific. After stalling twice trying to ease the clutch into first gear, I finally got the car moving forward. I turned out of the driveway and, following Hank's directions, turned right and drove along a narrow dirt road that meandered through the fields behind the main house.

"I remember riding in a much bigger car when I was a kid. Is it still here?"

"Nah. That would have been the Cadillac touring car, but it wasn't nearly as sweet as this baby. Yer daddy sold the Caddy. Heh heh."

Hank was laughing at his little rhyme, and he repeated it.

"Yer daddy sold the Caddy."

The road took us through a stand of trees and over a bridge that spanned a wide brook. Hank said it was a great fishing spot for trout, filled with native browns and a few rainbows, but I paid little attention. I'd never been much of a fisherman; I didn't have the patience for it. We came to a clearing, and Hank pointed to a break in the trees where a narrow path led down to a spring-fed lake.

"There's a ton of fish in the lake. Got a small dory skiff tied up at the dock. Hope you don't mind that me and my youngest boy like to come up here sometimes to fish."

"I don't mind at all," I said. "You and your son are welcome to fish here anytime."

Hank pointed out two small outbuildings along the edge of the cornfields to the south. "Them's the tool sheds. I packed most of the equipment in Cosmoline years ago, so they's probably in good shape iffen you decide to start farmin' again."

"How much land is there, Hank?"

"All in, I'd say over four hunnert acres, give or take. Acourse, the house and main grounds takes up about ten of that, the lake and woods about twenty-five, and the roads and buildings about ten, so's I figure you can cultivate over three hunnert and fifty acres easy. You'd hafta wait 'til next year, though. The land's all leased out for this season."

The thought of becoming a gentleman farmer had some appeal, but I wasn't quite ready to make that decision. I had something else in mind. "I'll have to think about it, Hank. I'll let you know what I decide."

"Best decide afore harvest," he said. "That's when the bids come in for next year."

We drove on past the tool sheds and came upon a row of four small whitewashed houses with rusty corrugated tin roofs, each with a sheet-metal stovepipe sticking out of the center. Hank indicated this was where the farm hands had lived. I had no memory of farm hands. I did remember lots of other people—visitors, house servants and workmen. Some of them must have been farm hands.

Next, Hank directed me to turn left toward an enormous red barn shaded by three tall oak trees about fifty yards away. It was built on a rise so that its stone foundation opened at ground level in the back, but the main doors were on the first floor in the front. It was a beautiful old structure that, unlike the other farm buildings I'd just seen, had been very well maintained.

"The tobacco barns are all farther south, down by the Old Hartford Turnpike. This here's the main barn. In your granddaddy's day, this is where they kept the workhorses and plows. We got a couple a diesel tractors now. Acourse, the ridin' horses was kept in the old stables out behind the big house."

I stopped the car in front of the barn, and we both got out and walked up to the big wooden doors. Hank pulled on one of them with both hands and it yawned open, revealing a cavernous main floor littered with ancient hay. The noise of the creaking door startled a big old tomcat that darted out from one of the stalls and bolted past me into the field.

"That's old Buster. He jus' showed up one day and never left. Plenty of field mice for him here, I expect."

The barn smelled musty. We walked inside and roamed around, poking into all the little recesses, examining the stalls and the hayloft. Hank lit a kerosene lantern and we descended the stairs into the lower level together. It was cooler down there, and damp, too. Hank went over to the outside doors and pushed them open, bringing in the afternoon sunlight and a rush of fresh air.

Hank turned around and pointed. "Them's the tractors. They's good ones. John Deere. Both work, too."

I examined them from a distance, feigning interest, but it was really the building itself that fascinated me, not the tractors. Adjusting to the light, I noticed the details of the structure. I walked across the stone floor and felt the cool stone walls.

"Any idea how old this place is?"

Hank shrugged. "Beats me. Been here afore I got here, anyway."

I noticed a large closet in the corner. Its door was secured with a rusty padlock that clearly hadn't been opened in years.

"What's in here, Hank?"

"I wouldn't know, Mr. McCoy. Your daddy's stuff, I guess."

"Do you have a key?"

"No Sir," he said.

Hank became ill at ease and stepped back, trying to steer me away from the closet. He wasn't very good at disguising his discomfort, and it only made me more curious about what was inside.

I tugged on the padlock, but it didn't yield. I said, "I'd like you to break it open. Are there any tools about?"

He hesitated. "I think there's a hammer and a bolt cutter upstairs in the toolbox."

Hank went back to the upper level, returning in a few minutes with the tools. He arranged the pincers of the bolt cutter around the steel loop and squeezed the handles until it snapped in two with a loud crack. He then took the hammer and smashed the lock apart, taking the hasp with it.

"That oughtta do it," he said. "Sorry about the hasp. I'll replace it."

I opened the closet door and Hank held the kerosene lamp up over his head for a better look. Inside, stacked in two neat rows standing on their butt ends, were twenty-four U.S. Army-issue Springfield rifles. Twelve .45 automatic pistols hung by their trigger guards on a pegged rack just above the rifles. All the guns were swathed in thick grease to preserve them from rust.

My eyes went wide. "Jesus Christ. It's a damned arsenal." I turned to Hank and said, "What the hell was my father doing with these?"

"Well, sir, that weren't none of my business." Hank just stared at me, blinking, hoping I'd let the matter drop.

"Come on, Hank. You seem to know everything else about this place. What about the guns?"

Hank's eyes darted from me to the guns and back again. "Your daddy had a private gun club. A bunch a guys used to come up on weekends and shoot skeet and other stuff."

"What other stuff?"

"Hell, Mr. McCoy, I don't know. Just stuff. They used to dress up in uniforms and play army. I always figgered they was here 'cause your folks were ascared of kidnappers—you know, like the Lindbergh baby."

The story sounded strange to me, but of course I remembered the Lindbergh baby kidnapping. It happened just before I turned twelve, and I remembered being afraid that kidnappers would come after me, too, because my father was a famous aviator like Lucky Lindy. A few weeks after they found the Lindbergh baby dead, my mother took me to Maine for the summer, and we never came back to Granbury after that.

Hank volunteered something else. "Those fellers used to come up when the niggers were here. You know—just to make sure they behaved theirselves."

"What?" I glared at him. Hank's casual use of the word "nigger" unsettled me. My mother's ancestors had been staunch abolitionists before and during the Civil

War. Although Grandmother and Grandfather Winant didn't believe in mixing the races socially, they believed in treating people with dignity, and I was taught the word "nigger" was vulgar.

"Well, ya see, the last couple a years afore your daddy died, he used to bring up a buncha nigger farm workers from the South to pick the tobacco crop." Hank pointed through the open barn doors across the field. "See them buildings down there? Them's the ole stalls the niggers used as dormitories. The gun-club men camped out here in the barn and kept watch on the field hands, just so's none of 'em would go roamin' around."

I was appalled. It was like something out of the Reconstruction South.

Hank must have sensed my anger, because he stopped talking and closed the closet door. Then he said, "I'll get a new hasp and padlock for this here, Mr. McCoy."

"That won't be necessary. I want you to load these weapons onto your truck and bring them to the police station tomorrow. I'll see the chief and ask him to dispose of them."

"Whatever you say, Mr. McCoy. But if you're gonna be givin' 'em away, I could sure use another huntin' rifle."

I shook my head. "I don't know what you hunt around here, Hank, but I don't think you want a Springfield. These guns are old Army-issue. They're designed to be man-killers, not hunting rifles."

Hank nodded. "I don't mean to be tellin' you your business, Mr. McCoy, but if I was you, I wouldn't volunteer to be spendin' any time with Chief Eberhardt."

As we walked back to the car, I pondered the implications of my father's arsenal and his private little "gun club."

CHAPTER 5

I made two telephone calls the following morning—
one to Mayor Joe Gibbons and one to Police Chief Victor
Eberhardt. Mayor Gibbons was happy to hear from me
and said he looked forward to seeing me at ten o'clock.
Eberhardt was less enthusiastic. He initially pleaded a
busy schedule, but relented and told me to stop by after
meeting with the Mayor.

I put on a light blue sport jacket and tie, and set off
in the roadster at quarter of ten. As I turned onto Albany
Road at the center of town, I noticed people stopping and
pointing at my car. I pulled into an empty parking space
in front of the Noll Tavern, stepped out onto the sidewalk
and was immediately surrounded by a small knot of
people eagerly introducing themselves. I shook hands all
around, telling everyone how glad I was to be back in
Granbury. I hoped this wouldn't happen every time I
came into town.

Mayor Gibbons was waiting for me inside the town
hall, and he was as happy to see me as the people
outside. We chatted amiably in his office, catching me up
on fourteen years of Granbury life. Gibbons talked a lot
about my father; as far as he was concerned, Harry
McCoy had been the greatest man who ever lived.

I learned that the McCoy factory remained idle for almost six years after my father disappeared. Pratt & Whitney purchased it from my father's estate and reopened it in 1940 when military orders for aircraft engine parts made the plant viable again. The demands of the wartime economy revitalized the town, but there was still significant residual bitterness against my mother for having closed the factory in 1934. The mayor handled the subject of my mother diplomatically, saying only that he thought she was a beautiful woman; then he offered his condolences about her recent passing. I could tell the words left a bad taste in his mouth.

The mayor prodded me about my experiences in the Pacific, and I gave him an abridged version. He then segued to a discussion about his plans for Decoration Day.

"Jamie, I'd like you to consider wearing your uniform and serving as grand marshal of the parade."

"I left my uniforms back in Boston. I'll have to send for one."

"Then you'll do it?"

"I'd be honored."

"Wonderful! It'll mean a lot to the people of Granbury. We thought the world of your father. We're dedicating a small memorial to him on the green after the parade."

The mayor unfurled a drawing of the monument; he beamed as I admired it. Then he gave me a handwritten agenda for the planned Decoration Day events.

"I invited a few of your father's old friends to come for the occasion," he said, "but I've only heard back from Ted Derwent and Roger Willoughby. They'll both be here."

"I know who Derwent is, but who's Willoughby?"

"He was one of your father's school chums. Lives right here in Connecticut—down in Wallingford."

"What about John Barrow?"

"Judge Barrow? No reply. He's a pretty busy fellow. Now that you're here, though, maybe he'll want to come, too."

"If you could ask your secretary to give me their addresses and telephone numbers, I'd like to get in touch with the judge and the others and invite them to stay at my house."

"That's a great idea," he said. "I'll see to it."

Gibbons called to his secretary and asked her to get the information I requested. While she was doing that, the mayor told me about the plans for the five-mile footrace, and invited me to participate in that as well. I said I'd think about it, but I wasn't much of a runner.

Before I left, I asked him who else could tell me about my father. I said I was particularly interested in learning more about the last flight.

"The best person to talk to is Dulcie Patch, the town librarian. You might also try Freddie Crowell. He publishes the local weekly, the *Granbury Mercury*. It's not much of a newspaper—mostly public service stuff now—but the paper had a lot of great stories and photos of your dad in the old days. His office is next door to the bank. If you'd like, I'll give him a call and let him know you're coming."

I thanked the mayor and promised to call when I heard back from John Barrow and the others.

Just before noon, I left town hall and walked next door to the police station. A sergeant sat behind a raised desk in the lobby, writing something with a pencil. As I drew closer, I saw he was working on a crossword puzzle. Behind him was an American flag; next to it was a framed portrait of Douglas MacArthur. I'd have expected a portrait of President Truman, but in Republican Granbury, they displayed General MacArthur.

"Hi," I said. "I'm Jamie McCoy. I have an appointment with Chief Eberhardt."

The sergeant nodded and jerked a thumb behind his desk, where I saw a heavy wooden door with the words "Chief of Police" stenciled in faded gold lettering on the upper cross-panel. I knocked on the door. A gruff voice responded, telling me to come in.

I turned the brass knob and opened the door. The office was small and cluttered, but brightly lit from a double-hung window that overlooked Albany Road. There was a gun rack on the left wall, and next to that a calendar advertising the Travelers Insurance Company.

Chief Eberhardt had his back to me. He sat reading the newspaper in a worn leather swivel chair facing an antique roll-top desk. There were two candlestick telephones on the desk, a stack of papers and a thick memo pad, but not much else. The chief was a big man. Because he was seated, I couldn't tell how tall he was, but his girth was abundant, and he had a back that could have carried a hod of bricks. He straightened up a little, but still didn't turn around. His bald spot at the back of his head shone in the reflected sunlight coming from the window.

I cleared my throat loudly. "Chief Eberhardt? I'm Jamie McCoy. I spoke to you this morning."

The chief slowly, dramatically, turned in his chair to face me. Two black eyes fixed on me with an intensity that made me wince; the pupils were like spots on a pair of dice. His face was sallow and drawn, washing out the features that give a man character. He looked like a ghost.

I walked over and offered my hand. "Jamie McCoy," I said again.

The chief stood up, towering over me, and accepted my handshake. "Victor Eberhardt." He said it quietly and without inflection, as though his very name should awe me into submission. "What can I do for you, Mr. McCoy?" He motioned me to have a seat in the wooden side chair by his desk and he sat down as well.

"Well, Sir, I've just moved back home to Granbury, and I wanted to get to know some of the folks in town. The last time I was here, I was only twelve and, quite Frankly, I don't remember many people."

"Welcome home, then," he said.

It was as cool a welcome as I'd ever heard. "I was wondering, Chief, if you knew my father."

"Yep, I knew him. Good fella. Too bad he died."

"Thank you. Did you know him very well?"

"Guess so. As well as a country cop can know a celebrity like your father, I suppose."

He wasn't going to make this easy. "The reason I'm asking is that I found a locker in my father's barn that contained two dozen Springfield rifles and a dozen pistols. I was hoping you might know something about it."

The chief just looked at me impassively. "That's quite an arsenal. What makes you think I'd know anything about it?"

"Well, you *are* the chief of police, and I understand you've had the job for fifteen years. I assumed you would have been aware of such a large cache of arms in town."

"Look, son, your father was a private man. He didn't tell me his business, and I had no reason to ask him."

That was a lot of bull. My father was a very public man. He was a war hero and a world-renowned aviator who couldn't go anywhere without a herd of newspapermen and photographers recording his every move and every public utterance.

I tried a different tack. "Hank Dietz told me my father had a sort of private gun club that met on the estate. Wouldn't my father have had to register all those firearms?"

"Maybe he did. I can't remember. That was a long time ago. I really don't know anything about it."

I sensed Eberhardt was lying, but I didn't understand why.

"Chief, I'm just trying to find out a little bit about my father—what kind of man he was. My mother took me away from here when I was just a kid, and I never got a chance to know him. Now I come back, and one of the first things I discover is a hoard of guns hidden in the barn. I'm just trying to find out why."

"I wish I could help you, but I can't." He leaned back in his chair and folded his arms on his chest. "What do you plan to do with the weapons?"

I gave him my best sardonic grin. "I was thinking of invading Massachusetts."

He didn't even change his expression.

"Perhaps you'd better just drop those weapons off here at the station. I'll get in touch with the National Guard armory down in Windsor Locks and see if they want them, or if they just want me to destroy them."

"I'm way ahead of you, Chief. I already asked Hank Dietz to do just that. He'll drop by later today."

"That's probably for the best," he said. He stood up, a little unsteadily, signaling me that our meeting was at an end.

I stood up, too. As I did, I noticed Eberhardt's left foot pointed outward, and his left shoe looked different than the right. It was unworn at the top. I'd seen something like that only once before—a corporal in my company lost a leg, and the doctors gave him a prosthesis that didn't flex his shoe, leaving it unworn. Foolishly, I stared at Eberhardt's foot.

He saw me staring, and bent down and rapped his knuckles on his shin. The result was a soft wooden tap. "Hunting accident." He straightened up and smiled insincerely. "You planning on staying in town long?"

I was embarrassed, but recovered quickly. "Actually, Chief, I'm planning on living here permanently. I hope you don't mind."

"Don't mind at all. It'll be good to have a McCoy back in Granbury—that is, if you really are a McCoy."

"What do you mean by that?"

He backed up a little, managing his artificial leg with ease, and hitched his thumbs into his belt. "Well, like you just said, your mama took you away from here when you were a little boy. She raised you; Colonel McCoy didn't. Maybe you favor your mother's side of the family more than your father's, though you look a lot like your old man, I'll give you that."

I was getting steamed. "What if I was raised by my mother? What business is it of yours?"

"Let's just say the folks around here never took kindly to the way your mother handled things after your father disappeared. She sent that Jew lawyer down here to shut the factory for no other reason than she hated your old man. She had no right to take it out on us. The town took a long time recovering from what she did."

Eberhardt was twice my age, but a hell of a lot bigger than me, and a good five inches taller. I didn't give a damn. I was an Army Ranger, and I was prepared to lay him out in his own office if I had to, wooden leg or not.

"Mr. Eberhardt, I was born in Granbury. My family goes back in this town more than two hundred years. You might say my roots are here, and this is where I plan to stay. So you and everyone else had better get one thing straight right now—my mother did what she had to do. The factory was insolvent. My father practically bankrupted himself keeping people on the payroll for two years. By the time he died, there was no money left to pay anyone. My mother never discussed it with me—I was just a kid at the time—but knowing her the way I did, I'm certain she tried everything to keep the business going."

Eberhardt frowned. Neither of us said a word for almost half a minute; then he nodded his head slowly.

"Okay, kid. Think whatever you want. Your mother was a saint. But in my book, she shoved a knife into this town's back. And as for all the money she lost, well, you look like you've still got plenty left."

I glared at him, but I had nothing else to say.

"Nice meeting you," he said. "Don't be a stranger."

I left the chief's office angry as hell and strode across to the Noll Tavern. The lunchtime crowd was just starting, and I could see Ernie Thayer was busy, so I just grabbed a table in the taproom and asked the waiter to bring me a beer and a chicken sandwich. Just as I finished eating, a tall, dark-haired man came over to my table and introduced himself.

"Mr. McCoy? I'm Fred Crowell from the *Granbury Mercury*—Ernie Thayer's brother-in-law. The mayor gave me a call this morning and said you wanted to chat. I came in for lunch a little while ago, and Ernie pointed you out to me."

He was older than me by a good ten years, but considerably younger than his brother-in-law, Ernie. I stood up and offered my hand. "Please, call me Jamie. Have a seat, Mr. Crowell."

"Thanks, Jamie," he said as he pulled up a seat. "And I'm Freddie to my friends."

"Would you like a beer, Freddie?" I asked.

"No thanks, I'm working, but I'll have a Coke."

I waved my hand at Ernie over by the bar and got his attention. He came over, smiling, and greeted us both. Freddie ordered a Coke, and I asked for a refill on my beer. Ernie went to the bar and returned after a minute with the drinks, including one for himself, and he sat down to join us, despite the lunchtime crowd.

Freddie lit a cigarette and took a sip of his Coke. "The mayor tells me you want to see some of the *Mercury*'s back issues."

"Yeah," I said. I'd been thinking about what I wanted to do to occupy my time, and just sitting here, comfortable among my father's acquaintances, I blurted out something I thought I hadn't yet decided. "I'm writing a biography of my father, and I want a look at some of the newspaper articles from the old days. You know— background material and photographs."

Ernie said, "That's a great idea. You can use my scrapbook."

"Thanks, Ernie." I turned to his brother-in-law. "I'm sure I'll find some of my father's private papers at the house, and I know there's plenty of articles from the national newspapers and magazines, but I was hoping you might have some old articles with the hometown angle."

Freddie nodded eagerly. "Sure, sure. There's lots of stuff. Of course, my uncle ran the paper in the old days, back when it was a real newspaper and not just a local tabloid; but I've read all the back issues. I keep the morgue over at the library. There are articles about all your father's flights, and a few about his technical innovations, too—at least the ones that weren't top secret. Did you know he once built an engine so powerful that the plane couldn't hold it? After Lockheed strengthened the airframe, it made three times the speed of any other single-engine plane. They tried to pitch it to the Army as a fighter, but Uncle Sam was cutting back in those days, so it sat on the shelf."

"I didn't know that," I said.

"Your father was more than a stunt flyer, Jamie. He was a genius."

Ernie said, "You know, Freddie here is a pretty good writer. He could help you out."

"Thanks for the suggestion, Ernie. I'm sure Freddie's a great writer, but I'm just beginning the research phase. Hell, I just made the decision to do it. I'm not ready to write anything yet."

Freddie said, "I'm here if you need me. Call on me anytime."

"Thank you, I will."

"Meanwhile, just head on across the street to the library and introduce yourself to Miss Dulcie Patch.

She's the head librarian. Tell her I sent you, and she'll give you access to the *Mercury's* archives."

Ernie laughed. "He won't need an introduction, Freddie. Dulcie'll fall all over herself when she sees him."

Freddie asked, "Does she know he's in town?"

I had no idea what they were talking about, and it must have shown.

Freddie said, "Frankly, Jamie, you look a lot like your father."

I was still puzzled. "So?"

"Dulcie had a thing for your father," Ernie said.

"Do you mean this librarian and my father had an affair?"

Both men laughed loudly and shook their heads. "No, no," Ernie said. "Nothin' like that. It's just that she—"

Freddie cut him off. "She has a bit of an obsession with your father's memory."

"Yeah," Ernie said. "Dulcie knew your father real well before he went off to war. She used to write him all the time while he was in France, and I guess she got it in her head that he was in love with her. But your father's friends knew better. He wasn't interested in Dulcie that way."

Freddie said, "When your father came back to Granbury married to your mother, folks say that Dulcie took it pretty hard. She never made a scene or anything like that, but people could tell she was disappointed." He paused and looked over at Ernie as though he were seeking permission to continue. Ernie nodded almost imperceptibly. "Of course, I'm just repeating gossip, because I was off at college at the time, but I think when your mother and father separated, Dulcie half expected your father would turn to her, but he didn't."

Ernie said, "Your father was always kind to her, but he just considered her a close friend, nothing more."

"I don't get it," I said. "Why does any of this matter now? My father's been dead for twelve years."

Ernie sighed. "You see, Dulcie never married. She's been carryin' a torch for your father all these years, and it's—well, it's become kind of a town joke. It was all pretty tame at first. After your dad disappeared, she went into mourning—wearing black all the time. A few months later, she started telling people your father was in love with her, and before long, the stories she told got even more involved. She claimed she was the reason your mother left him, and your father even asked her to marry him just before his last flight."

I was stunned. This woman sounded like she was mentally ill. "I don't understand why everyone lets her get away with this morbid fantasy."

"It's harmless, really," Freddie said. "No one takes her seriously."

"Well I don't think it's harmless. In fact, I think it's craven. My father isn't around to deny her stories. What kind of woman would do such a thing?"

Ernie drained his beer and looked at me solemnly. "A very lonely woman, Jamie, and in some ways, a very powerful one in this town."

"How is she powerful?"

"Let's just say she's got a lot of clout."

Freddie said, "Take a walk over there and talk to her. Humor her. Let her make a fuss over you. You gotta understand that the library is her little fiefdom, and if you want to see the newspaper archives, it'll be a lot easier if you don't antagonize her."

"Aren't the archives the property of your newspaper?"

"Yeah, but I don't have the facilities to store the archives, and the library does. And Dulcie controls the library."

"Granbury's a small town," Ernie said. "If you wanna get along here, it's best not to upset the status quo, if you know what I mean."

"And Dulcie Patch is the status quo?"

"She's part of it."

I nodded my understanding, but I wasn't happy about it.

Freddie drained the last of his Coke and stood up. "Jamie, it's been a real pleasure." He extended his hand, and I stood up and shook it. "I've got to get back to the paper now, but give me a call if you need any help with that book of yours."

"Thanks, I will."

"And don't you worry about Dulcie. Like I said, she's harmless."

Freddie Crowell waved his goodbyes to Ernie and some of the other men in the bar and walked out the front door. Ernie was still at the table, so I sat down again and nursed my beer.

"Listen, Ernie," I said. "There's something else I want to talk about."

He glanced at his watch and looked over at the bar to make sure there was no one waiting to be served. "Sure. What is it?"

"I just met Chief Eberhardt over at the police station and, well, it wasn't exactly pleasant."

"That don't surprise me. Vic Eberhardt ain't the sweetest guy in town. What did you see him about?"

"Yesterday afternoon, Hank Dietz showed me around the estate, and we came across a stash of Springfield rifles and automatic pistols in the barn. I asked Hank to pack them up and bring them over to the police station. I wanted Chief Eberhardt to dispose of them for me."

Ernie furrowed his brows. "I see. What did Vic say?"

"It's not so much what he said as what he didn't say. I wanted to find out if he knew why my father kept an arsenal on the property, but he claimed to know nothing about it."

"So?"

"So, I could tell he knew something but wouldn't tell me. Hank said my father used to run a gun club—sort of a private army—on the estate, and it seemed pretty strange to me that the chief of police wouldn't know anything about it."

"Not so unusual." Ernie rested his elbows on the table, placing his chin on his folded hands. "Your father didn't tell everyone his business, and the chief wasn't one of his close friends."

I looked directly in his eyes. "But you were his friend. You knew about it, didn't you?"

He shook his head. "Your daddy and I were good friends, sure—knew each other since we were little kids. But he was a rich man's son. Your grandfather practically owned this town once upon a time, and your father traveled in some pretty fast circles. Hell, he even knew President Roosevelt. He always came back to Granbury, though, and he remembered his old friends here, but he didn't share everything about his life with us."

"So you don't know anything about his little arsenal or about the gun club?"

"Well, I didn't exactly say I don't know anything. I just don't know much, and Frankly, there isn't much to tell. Your father was a sportsman. Used to have a bunch of his friends up on weekends target shooting is all. I was never invited. No big deal."

"Hank said these guys kept watch on the Negro field hands."

Ernie straightened up and rested his hands on his knees. "Don't know nothin' about that."

I looked at him hard. If he did, in fact, know anything, he wasn't about to tell me.

"Okay," I said, and left it at that.

Ernie started to turn away. "Well, I better get back to my customers. You go on over to the library and meet Dulcie. It'll be a real treat for her."

"Thanks, Ernie. You've been a big help." We both stood up. "There's just one more thing I wanted to ask. How did you feel about my mother?"

He smiled. "Jamie, your mother was a beautiful and refined lady. Some folks around here may hold it against her for having run out on your father, and others may blame her for what happened to the factory, but I know better. I don't know why she left your father. He never spoke about it, and it was none of my business anyway. As for the factory closing, well, that's all water under the bridge. Things turned out all right in the end."

I got the feeling Ernie wanted to say something more, that he was holding back. I debated whether or not to press him, but decided against it. My silence must have prompted him, though, and he leaned closer and lowered his voice.

"Look, kid, there's somethin' else I'll tell you about your mother, but you gotta promise to keep it just between us. It goes no further."

"All right."

There was a bar rag hanging on Ernie's belt. He began kneading it, like it was a string of rosary beads. "When the Depression hit, I was in quite a jam. I had a big mortgage on this place—my wife and I live right upstairs, so it's my home, too. Business fell off pretty bad. I was behind in my payments, and the bank wanted to foreclose on me. Your father bought the mortgage from the bank and let things ride until I could get back on my feet."

Ernie's eyes were getting moist.

"Anyway, after your father disappeared, your mother sent a lawyer down here to clean up his affairs."

"I know him—Arthur Wiseman."

"Yeah, that's him—a Jewish fella from Boston. Anyway, I figured he was gonna demand payment on the note your father held on this place, and I was pretty scared, 'cause I couldn't come up with the money. He calls me up and says for me to come out and see him at your father's house, so I went, all the time thinkin' of what I'm gonna tell him to give me some time to pay off the note. When I get there, he hands me the note, and written across the front is 'Paid in Full' and it's signed by another guy—Biddle something—as your father's 'attorney in fact' or something like that."

"That means he had my father's power of attorney; he could sign things for him."

"Yeah, that's what that fella Wiseman said when I asked him if it was legal. He said it was a gift from your mother."

I didn't know what to say.

"Now look," Ernie said. "I don't wanna see a word about this in that book you're writing about your father. I'm only tellin' you 'cause I never got a chance to thank your mother properly. I don't care what anybody else around here thinks about her. She was aces with me."

"Thanks, Ernie. I appreciate your saying that."

"No problem, kid. And remember—you never pay for anything in here. You got that?"

I smiled. "Got it."

He turned and walked back to the bar, all the time wiping his hands on that rag. Not wanting to embarrass him further, I left quietly, thinking about my mother's gift to him. It couldn't have been a large sum to her, but it must have meant the world to Ernie.

CHAPTER 6

I strode across the green just as the clock on the firehouse bell tower tolled one o'clock. I looked back toward the police station and saw Hank's truck parked in front. The truck-bed was empty, so I assumed he had already unloaded the weapons while I was inside the Noll Tavern having lunch. It was turning into a beautiful day, and I walked toward the Old Hartford Turnpike and the library, thinking about driving back to the Castle in my father's Mercedes convertible. I'd spent four years walking or riding in Jeeps and trucks. I was getting used to being rich. It felt good.

The library was an impressive sight. It stood at the crest of a rise at the top of the green, set back from the sidewalk and surrounded by neatly trimmed evergreen bushes and flowering plants that were just beginning to bloom. There was a broad portico in front and a smaller one on the south side. In between was a large Palladian window flanked by four smaller rectangular windows, all of them paned in lead. The moldings and pillars could have easily adorned a French cathedral. The building looked out of place in this small New England town, as though it had been stolen from a larger city and moved in one piece to Granbury. Above the arched entranceway, the name "Charles Jameson McCoy Memorial Library" was deeply etched in Roman letters. My great-grandfather either had an enormous ego or grand visions about what he expected Granbury to become.

I walked up the brick path, climbed the stairs to the portico and entered through massive twin oak doors into a narrow foyer with a low vaulted ceiling illuminated by a row of brass wall sconces. It felt like a church. On the left hung two gilt-framed portraits—one of George Washington and the other of Abraham Lincoln. In an oval niche on the right-hand wall was a massive painting of my great-grandfather, dwarfing The Father of Our Country and The Great Emancipator. The people of Granbury apparently knew on which side to butter their bread.

Beyond the foyer was the main reading room, in the center of which was an oak counter that formed a circle directly under a pearl white two-story high rotunda supported by six oak columns. In fact, the interior was a forest of oak—the wall panels, the bookshelves, the tables and chairs—and it was enormous. Along each wall were recessed private reading areas; to the left was an open entranceway leading to the Reference Room, and to the right was a similar room set off as the Children's Library. In the rear was another entranceway that led to the main stacks.

I walked up to the counter where I expected to find Miss Dulcie Patch, but the woman on duty was clearly much too young—younger than me, in fact—and probably not long out of high school. She wore a bright green dress more suited to a county fair than a working day at the public library. The nameplate at the desk read

"Miss Marker," and I immediately thought of the Damon Runyon tale by the same name.

In my best library whisper, I said, "Hello. I'm looking for Miss Patch. Is she available?"

Miss Marker smiled and said, also in a library whisper, "Yes, Sir. She's in her office at the rear of the Children's Library. Is she expecting you?"

"No actually, she's not, but Mr. Crowell from the *Mercury* sent me over to see her, and I was hoping she could spare a moment."

"If you'd like, I'll call her on the intercom and tell her you're here." She picked up the receiver of what looked like a toy telephone. "What name shall I give?"

"Jamie McCoy."

She started to dial, but stopped and looked at me. "Did you say 'McCoy,' sir? As in the McCoy family?"

I smiled at her. "Yes, that McCoy. My great-grandfather's name is on the door."

She blushed, and so did I.

"Oh, I'm sure she'll see you, sir. Just a moment." She dialed two numbers on the toy telephone and cupped the mouthpiece with her hand. Despite that, I heard her whisper, "Miss Patch? There's a gentleman out here to see you. Mr. Crowell sent him over. He says his name is Jamie McCoy."

There was a pause, after which the librarian hung up the intercom phone. Then she looked at me again and smiled sweetly. "Please go right in, Mr. McCoy." She pointed toward the entrance to the Children's Library and said, "It's right through there, all the way in the back. Her name is on the door."

I thanked her and walked through the entranceway she indicated. The Children's Library was a miniature version of the main reading room. There were more oak tables and chairs, but they were smaller in proportion. It was empty except for a woman and a little girl, whom I presumed was her daughter, sitting at a table in the far right corner. The woman's back was to me. She hunched over in a child's chair reading to the little girl who was beaming with joy at something her mother had just read. I heard her giggle, and the mother laughed quietly, too.

There were two doors in the back corners of the room, one of which was labeled "Restrooms" and the other "Dulcinea Patch—Head Librarian." I briefly thought about using the lavatory first, but I changed my mind when the office door opened and Dulcie Patch came out to greet me.

I was surprised at what I saw. From the way Ernie Thayer and Freddie Crowell described her, I expected to meet a pinch-faced old spinster. Instead, Dulcie Patch was a beautiful woman. I knew her to be my father's age—he would have been fifty-three—but this woman looked to be no older than forty. She had long, dark wavy hair and deep blue eyes, and a dazzling smile. I wondered how such an attractive woman could have remained unmarried.

Before I could say anything, she came over, took both my hands in hers and kissed me on the cheek. "Jamie McCoy. My goodness, you look so much like your father. How wonderful to see you again."

"It's very nice to meet you, Miss Patch."

I must have had a puzzled look on my face. She tilted her head and wrinkled her eyebrows. "Of course you don't remember me. You were just a little boy the last time I saw you. But look at you now—you're all grown up, and a war hero, too, I understand."

Miss Patch ushered me toward her office. As I stepped aside for her to go first, I noticed the young mother in the corner had turned around to look at me. I smiled at her, and then entered the office and shut the door behind me.

"Please, have a seat, Jamie." She motioned for me to sit on a small settee by the wall.

I did so, and she sat next to me—just a little too close. Unlike the rest of the library, Miss Patch's office was bereft of oak. Her desk was blond maple, as were the side chairs, and the wainscoting was painted white. The office itself was small, but nicely decorated with check curtains on the two windows and four Wallace Nutting prints on the walls. On the wall between the two windows was a framed diploma from Connecticut College for Women, proclaiming "to all persons whom these presents may come" that Dulcinea Frances Patch had been conferred the degree *Ars Baccalaureatis, magna cum laude* on June 5, 1915.

She noticed me looking at her diploma and said, "I was in the very first graduating class, you know. My parents wanted me to go to Smith, but I insisted on going to Connecticut College. The school was brand new—it was started when Wesleyan stopped admitting women—and my parents were skeptical." She patted my leg and said, *sotto voce,* "I really went there so I could be close to your father. He was at Yale at the time."

I changed the subject. "Thank you for seeing me, Miss Patch. I really should have called ahead."

"Nonsense," she said. "I'll always make time for Harry McCoy's son. Now tell me about yourself."

I told her I had just returned from overseas seven weeks ago, and I'd decided to return to Granbury to settle permanently. I mentioned that my mother had passed away while I was still in the Pacific, but she offered no condolences, an omission I would have considered unusual but for what Ernie and Freddie had told me about her fixation on my father.

"How did you know about my war record, Miss Patch?"

"Why, Jamie, didn't you know? It was in all the papers. Come, I'll show you."

She got up from the settee and opened the door. She signaled for me to follow, and I did so, noticing the young mother and her daughter were still in the corner. The mother was kneeling next to her daughter now, and I saw her face. She was blonde, very pretty, and in her early twenties. As I followed Miss Patch, I stared at them, fascinated by the scene. Suddenly, the mother looked up and stared right back at me, smiling. I turned my head quickly, embarrassed at having been caught, and followed Dulcie Patch.

We walked through the Children's Library, across the main reading room and into the Reference Room. There, on the right hand wall, was a glass cabinet bedecked in red, white and blue ribbons and filled with photographs and press clippings of my father. To my astonishment, there was a section on the left with framed newspaper and magazine articles about my exploits in the Philippines. There was even a photograph of my fellow officers and me in full camouflage holding our Tommy guns. General Krueger's Sixth Army public relations team must have been responsible for this.

Miss Patch pointed to a second cabinet farther down along the wall. "There's a case down there where we have a memorial to the town's other heroes of both world wars. In Granbury, we know how to honor our own."

"I don't know what to say, Miss Patch, except that I'm a little embarrassed. There were a hundred and twenty-six men in my company and a dozen Philippine guerillas who deserve as much honor as I do."

"But you were awarded the Distinguished Service Cross, and *they* weren't from Granbury." She opened the case, removed one of the framed articles and handed it to me.

I read it—it was from *Look Magazine*. It mentioned my name prominently, and noted that we carried out our mission with only one American casualty. There was no mention that four Philippine guerillas lost their lives in the assault.

In February 1945, I commanded a company of Rangers on a mission behind enemy lines to liberate three hundred prisoners of war from a POW camp just outside the Philippine town of San Rafael. A squad of tough Philippine guerillas—men who'd lived and fought behind enemy lines for three years—led the way. Other units, too, had performed similar missions. A week before, a company of Rangers liberated five hundred starving and sick prisoners—survivors of the Bataan Death March—from a camp in Cabanatuan; a month later, commandos from Combined Operations rescued a thousand civilian internees from their prison at Santo Thomas University in Manila.

It had been more than a year, and the thought of that mission still tore me up. Liberating American POWs was a good thing, but I was sick at heart over the pleasure I took in killing the enemy. I felt raw hatred for the Japs then and—God help me—I hated them still.

I hadn't started out feeling prejudice against Japanese people the way so many GIs had. I'd met a couple of them at Harvard, and they were polite and cultured, but the American propaganda machine worked overtime manufacturing race hatred. I heard tales of Japanese atrocities in China, Manchuria and the other territories they occupied, and for a long time I treated all such stories with skepticism. It wasn't until my unit reached the Philippines that I began to hate.

My company advanced on the town of Abacajai where the local resistance group warned our battalion C.O. that the Japanese were preparing to evacuate a satellite prison camp located about fifty miles inland, and they were planning to kill the prisoners rather than take them on the retreat. We arrived at the camp after an all-night forced march through the jungle, only to find that the Japs had already left. There were a hundred dead GIs and only three survivors. The guards had herded the Americans into a brick shed filled with gasoline cans and tossed in hand grenades, incinerating the prisoners. Three survived the inferno only because they slipped away and hid in a latrine. Fourteen men had been in the camp hospital; the Japanese guards lopped off their heads.

When my company discovered what the Japs had done, we became incensed. The only thing we thought about for weeks was revenge, and when it came time to liberate San Rafael, we vowed to butcher every Jap bastard we saw. Our assault initially caught the enemy unaware, but they pinned us down in an open field. We would have been slaughtered, but I managed to lead a flanking maneuver that carried the day. From bitter experience, we knew Japanese troops rarely surrendered, but after having killed three quarters of them outright and securing the camp, almost thirty of them survived. We corralled the prisoners into a hog pen and I ordered every last one of them shot; none of my men hesitated. We were behind enemy lines and couldn't afford to drag thirty prisoners along with three hundred freed Americans through the swamps.

The experience didn't quell my rage or my hatred. I took no satisfaction from my revenge, or from receiving the DSC. All I had was a nagging sense of disgust that I'd sunk to the level of the enemy.

Of course, I shared none of this with Miss Patch. I hadn't shared it with anyone. Here I was, fourteen months and half a world away from the horrors of war, and I still struggled to maintain that distance— emotionally and physically.

I handed the article back to Miss Patch and said, "I hadn't seen these stories. It's nice that you kept them here."

She smiled sweetly and patted her hand on my forearm. "I'm happy to do anything for you, Jamie— anything at all." There was almost something sexual in the way she said it.

I mentioned my plans to write about my father and my wish to examine the back issues of the *Mercury*.

"The *Mercury*? Oh, well, of course. You're welcome anytime, but the *Mercury* archives are such a mess. I do wish you'd give me a day to straighten them out."

"I understand," I said. "Are you sure a day will be sufficient?"

"Yes, I think so."

I thanked her and promised to return the next day to begin my research.

Just then, Miss Marker came into the Reference Room and walked right up to us. "Miss Patch? I'm sorry to interrupt you and Mr. McCoy, but there's a telephone call for you at the circulation desk."

Dulcie offered her hand to me and promised to see me again.

I accepted her hand and said, "Until tomorrow then."

She left with Miss Marker. As I watched them walk toward the circulation desk, I couldn't help staring at Dulcie's attractive behind, wondering if my father did have an affair with her. I'm not sure I would have blamed him if he had.

CHAPTER 7

It was after two when I left the library. As I walked out to the sunlit portico, I spotted the pretty young mother and her daughter on the lawn. I smiled at them, expecting nothing in return, but they came over to me, the little girl skipping all the way.

"Hello," I said.

The little girl wore a pale pink sundress; her blond hair was cut in a pageboy with a pink bow in the back to match her dress. She looked to be about four years old. The mother wore a short-sleeved pale blue dress— considerably shorter in the hemline than pre-war fashions—that accentuated her shapely figure and beautiful legs.

The little girl curtsied and said, "My Mummy says you're a war hero like my daddy. Did you fight the Nasties like my daddy did?"

I knelt down beside her and said, "I don't think I know your mother, sweetheart. My name is Jamie McCoy. Why don't you introduce me to her?"

The mother laughed and took over the introductions. "Susan, this handsome man is Mr. Jameson McCoy. He is, in fact, an old friend of your mother's, only he doesn't remember me."

I truly had no idea who the mother was, and my confusion was surely written all over my face. Close up, she was even prettier than I'd thought in the library, not exactly a striking beauty like Dulcie Patch, but pretty in a wholesome way. She had high pink cheekbones and deep, jade green eyes. GIs used to talk about Hollywood glamour queens like Betty Grable and Veronica Lake, but they were the stuff of fantasy; here was the kind of girl we all really dreamed about—fair-haired, fresh faced, slender, leggy and athletic looking. If she hadn't already been married, and a mother to boot, I would have fallen in love on the spot.

"You have me at a disadvantage," I said with a chuckle. "You obviously know me, but I'm afraid I don't remember you."

"If I have you at a disadvantage, Jamie, it's a first. I think I'll let it stay that way for awhile."

"Aw, c'mon. Don't keep me in suspense."

She pursed her lips together and shook her head no. "You've got to try at least."

The little girl, Susan, giggled while I struggled to remember. But it was no use. I shrugged my shoulders in resignation and held up my arms in surrender.

The mother bent down and whispered something in her daughter's ear.

Susan looked up at me and said, "Mummy says that since you didn't guess her name, you have to buy us both an ice cream at Berry's Drugstore." Then she turned to her mother and asked, "Mummy, is this like playing Rumplestiltskin?"

"Yes, dear, I suppose it is."

"Okay," I said. "My treat for ice cream."

Susan stood between us and took her mother's hand and then mine, and led us across the green to Berry's Drugstore on the corner of Albany Road and the Old Hartford Turnpike.

When we reached the sidewalk, I asked, "Did we go to school together?"

"Now you're getting warmer."

"Alison Camden?"

"Not even close," she said. "Alison's family moved away in '42. Besides, Alison was chunky. Do I look chunky?"

I appraised her lovely figure and shook my head no. "I give up. Tell me and I'll spring for sodas, too."

"You really don't know?"

"I really don't know. I'm sorry, but I've been away a long time."

"All right, then. Allow me to reintroduce myself." She extended her right hand, which I took in mine, and she said, "Kathryn Well—"

I knew it before she finished. "Kate Wellnett—of course. Jeez, I'm sorry, Kate. I should have recognized you."

I held the door of the drugstore open and Susan skipped in ahead of her mother. When we were all inside, Susan tugged on her mother's sleeve and said, "Mummy, our last name isn't Wellnett."

"I know, dear, but that used to be Mummy's name before she married your daddy, and Mr. McCoy would remember that name, since he probably doesn't know that your daddy and I got married."

"Now *that* I can guess," I said. "I'll bet you married Greg Hardesty, right?"

"Yes, I did, about six months after he graduated from Trinity, and just before he enlisted."

"That's terrific, Kate. How is Greg? I'd love to see him again."

Greg Hardesty was one of the few friends I remembered from Granbury. His father had been an executive at my father's factory, and we used to play together all the time before I moved away. Kate had been a year behind us in school, but she always tagged along. At the time, I considered her something of a pest. I remembered that Greg and Kate used to fight like cats and dogs when we were kids; it was inevitable they'd get married.

Kate looked wistfully at me, but it was Susan who spoke. "My daddy died fighting the Nasties in Italy during the war. I wish he didn't, 'cause he was a hero."

I looked at Kate and clutched her hand in mine. "I'm so sorry."

"That's all right, Jamie. It's been nearly three years, now. At least he was home when Susan was born. That was something."

Susan didn't seem troubled by our exchange. She ran over to the counter, hopped up on one of the revolving stools and began spinning around. Kate and I each took a stool on either side of Susan, and Kate placed her hands on the little girl's shoulders to make her stop spinning.

A white-jacketed counterman came over and said, "What'll it be, folks?"

Susan asked, "Can I have anything I want, Mummy?"

"That's up to Mr. McCoy, Susan. He's treating. But don't be greedy."

"How about a hot fudge sundae?" I said.

"Yay! I'll have a hot fudge sundae with one scoop of vanilla and one scoop of chock-lit and a cherry."

Kate ordered a dish of pistachio and I ordered the same. Kate and I each got a Coke and Susan asked for a strawberry soda.

We ate our ice cream and sipped our sodas in between amiable small talk, watching Susan make a considerable mess of her sundae. Kate wiped her daughter's hands and face periodically, and we began talking more personally, getting reacquainted and comparing notes about our lives since I left Granbury. I told her a little about life in Boston and my years at Groton and Harvard, but I avoided the subject of my war service.

Greg and Kate had gotten married on the day before the Pearl Harbor attack; they were on their way to a honeymoon in Florida when it happened. Greg enlisted in January of '42 and was sent for training at Fort Benning, Georgia; after basic, he went to Fort Dix in New Jersey, so they were able to see each other on weekends for quite awhile. He was originally scheduled to be in the North Africa campaign, but a typical military SNAFU sent him off to Washington instead for three months. He eventually went to Italy where he was killed by a land mine.

Kate had been living with her in-laws for about a year by then—her parents and kid sister had moved to Long Island when her father landed a job with Grummann Aircraft. Susan was already a year old and very attached to Greg's parents, so Kate decided to stay in Granbury. During the war, she worked in the claims department at Aetna Insurance in Hartford, but now, with so many GIs returning, she was forced to give up her job to a man. I commented that it didn't seem fair, but she just passed it off as the way the world worked. Now she was employed about three days a week at the Granbury Savings Bank, making a little more than half of what she had earned at Aetna.

I asked about her father-in-law. "What's Mr. Hardesty doing now? I remember he had an important job working for my father, but I don't know what he did exactly. I'm pretty sure it had something to do with bookkeeping."

Kate laughed. "It was probably a little more involved than bookkeeping. He's back in his old office at your father's plant, only now it's owned by Pratt & Whitney. He's Vice President and Plant Controller. That makes him in charge of all the money."

"I'd love to see him again." I was thinking of more than just catching up with the father of an old friend. I wanted to ask him about what funny business might have taken place with my father's books back in 1934.

"I'm sure he'd love to see you. Write down your phone number and I'll ask him to give you a call."

I wrote it on a napkin and passed it along the counter to her. "Actually, I was thinking of asking you for your phone number," I said, a little sheepishly.

Kate blushed. She borrowed my pen and wrote it down for me on another napkin. "You never would have called me in the old days."

"I was just a kid. I thought all girls had cooties." We both laughed.

Just then, the front door burst open and a boisterous swarm of teenagers came in and rushed for the soda fountain. School had obviously let out for the day. We were immediately surrounded, and the only reasonable option was for us to beat a hasty retreat outside. I paid for our ice cream and sodas, leaving a generous tip, and I picked Susan up off her stool and the three of us nudged our way through the crowd.

"We should probably say goodbye," Kate said. "Our walk home is a bit far for Susan, and she needs a nap."

"Please, let me drive you," I offered.

"Oh. That would be lovely." She looked down at Susan. "What do you say to riding in a car instead of walking home, dear?"

"Yippee!" Susan exclaimed. She clapped her hands together and then hugged my leg, almost knocking me down.

Kate scolded her good-naturedly. "Susan Jean Hardesty. You are being too forward. A simple 'thank you' will do."

Kate smiled at Susan to show that she wasn't really angry and took her by the hand. Susan took mine in her other hand and we walked down Albany Road past the Noll Tavern to my car. Kate admired the Mercedes as I held the passenger door open for her. I picked up Susan and planted her on her mother's lap, then walked around and got in behind the wheel. As I backed the car out of its space, I noticed Hank Dietz's truck was no longer parked in front of the Police Station.

Kate and Susan lived at Greg's parents' house about a mile and a half away in a section of town called Gallows Hill. Despite the somber name, Gallows Hill was a charming neighborhood with tree-lined streets and colonial style houses. I dropped them off, and Kate promised to have her father-in-law call me.

"I'd like to see you again, too, Kate."

Susan piped in, "You can see *me* again if you buy me another sundae."

I burst out laughing. "It's a date, Susan."

"Kate rolled her eyes and said, "I can see I'm going to have to teach her better manners." She turned to Susan and said, "Say thank you to Mr. McCoy, sweetheart."

"Thank you, Mr. McCoy sweetheart."

At that, we both burst out laughing.

I knelt down and gave Susan a kiss on her cheek, which she seemed to enjoy. "I'll tell you what, Susan. My friends call me 'Jamie,' and I'd like you to call me that, too, if it's all right with your mother, of course."

Kate nodded, and Susan kissed me back. I wished it were the other way around.

I got back into the car and waved goodbye as they walked up the footpath to their front door. They both smiled at me. I drove up Gallows Hill to the end of the road, where it intersected with the Old Hartford Turnpike and I turned right, heading toward home.

What a glorious, top-down day it was. The wind whipped through the car. It felt wonderful, and I felt wonderful. The thoughts I had about Kate Hardesty, née Wellnett, were disloyal to my old friend's memory, but I tried hard to suppress any guilt. She was magnificent, and I wanted to see her again and again. And her little girl, Susan, was a pure delight.

I drove along, taking in the beauty of the rolling hills, oblivious to the car behind me until I heard a siren. I looked in the rear view mirror and saw a black and white patrol car with its blue dome light flashing on the roof.

I pulled my car over to the shoulder of the road and shut down the engine. The police car slowed to a stop directly behind me. I sat there for a full minute before the cop got out of his car, put on his peaked cap and walked over, carrying a small black notebook in one hand and a pen in the other. I saw in the mirror he was young, about my age, and dressed in a crisp, neatly pressed pale blue uniform that would have been appropriate for the royal court of Ruritania. I mentally compared his attire to that of Chief Eberhardt, who'd worn a rumpled tan shirt and wrinkled black slacks, with no indication of his office other than a silver badge pinned to his shirtfront. I kept both hands on the leather-covered steering wheel as the officer approached.

He was businesslike. "Good afternoon, sir. Do you know why I stopped you today?"

"Frankly, officer, no. I wasn't speeding."

"No, you weren't, but your car's license plates are about twelve years out of date."

I groaned.

"May I see your driver's license and car registration, please?" he said crisply.

I unlatched the glove compartment, where I presumed the registration certificate must be, and I came up with a yellowed piece of paper dated 1928 that had six renewal stamps for each of the following years, ending in 1934. I handed it to the cop and reached into my back pocket for my wallet. At least my military driver's license was still good. I had ninety days from the date of my discharge to transfer it to my state of permanent residence, and there was still several weeks left before the deadline. I fished the license out of my wallet and handed that over as well.

He examined both documents and said, "Jameson, I'm going to cite you for operating an unregistered motor vehicle. You should also transfer your military driver's license as soon as possible."

I blanched at his use of my proper first name; I realized he did it to place me at a psychological disadvantage, and I resented it. I debated whether or not it was worth demanding that he address me as "Mr. McCoy" and risk alienating one of Chief Eberhardt's cops. In the end, I decided a tactical retreat was in order.

"My friends call me Jamie," I said.

He wrote up the ticket without acknowledging my friendly overture. He said, "Your permanent address isn't listed on your military license."

"It's the same as the one listed on the registration certificate—179 Old Hartford Turnpike."

If he recognized the McCoy name or the address of my father's estate, he showed no visible sign. He handed me the citation book and his ballpoint pen.

"Sign on the bottom. It's not an admission of guilt. It's just to acknowledge receipt of the citation. And bear down so the carbon paper can record it."

Without saying a word, I signed where he indicated and handed the book back to him. He signed his name next to mine, tore off the ticket and handed it to me. I looked at his name; it was Charles Eberhardt.

"Is Chief Eberhardt your father?" I asked.

"He's my uncle." He didn't even change his expression. As he turned to walk back to his patrol car, he said, "Drive straight home and leave your car there. I don't want to see this vehicle on a public road again until you have it properly registered with new plates."

I waited until Officer Eberhardt restarted his car and drove away before I started mine. All I could think about was how the hell Hank Dietz could have maintained my father's car so meticulously for twelve years and failed to have registered the damned thing. What an idiot.

I turned into the driveway of the estate, still mentally cursing Dietz's stupidity, when it suddenly occurred to me that Officer Eberhardt might have been waiting for me to drive by on the Old Hartford Turnpike. After all, my car had been parked in front of the police station all morning, and the Chief could have easily noticed the out-of-date plates. I was sure he must have peppered Hank Dietz with questions about me. It would have been a simple matter for him or one of his officers to have cited me in town, but then it probably would have been a lesser fine because they wouldn't have caught me actually operating an unregistered vehicle. I considered the possibility that Chief Eberhardt sent his nephew out to trap me while I was driving the car.

As I came to a stop under the *porte-cochère*, I concluded that I was being paranoid. The police chief was certainly a jerk, but it didn't seem likely that he'd go out of his way to harass me.

CHAPTER 8

The next morning, Friday, Hank Dietz came by. When I told him about the ticket, he apologized for having failed to register the car.

"What did the police chief say about the guns?" I asked.

"Nuthin' much. He jes' said you was in earlier and you already told him about it."

I still had my suspicions about what happened on the Old Hartford Turnpike and, out of a nagging sense of paranoia, I asked, "Did he say anything to you about my car?"

"Nah. Chief Eberhardt didn't say much at all. He never pays no mind to me and I do my best to steer clear a him."

I thanked Hank and started on some of the odds and ends I needed to accomplish before heading back to the public library to start my research. I sat down at my father's desk and began making phone calls. The first one was to my father's attorney in Hartford, E. Biddle Franklin, Esq., who, I learned, went by the name of Ed (for Edmond) despite the fact that he had signed his earlier correspondence using his first initial and middle name. He was delighted to hear from me and assured me there would be no problem arranging a transfer of the automobile title from my father's estate to me. It should already have been taken care of; it had been an oversight he regretted. He advised me that I would, nonetheless, have to apply for a new registration and a transfer of my military driver's license at the Hartford office of the Department of Motor Vehicles, and he offered to prepare the necessary documents for me. I made arrangements with him to come into Hartford in a couple of days to file the paperwork at the DMV.

In the meantime, I still needed a car to get around town. I asked Hank for suggestions, and he said that Ernie Thayer's cousin, Nobbie Griffin, owned a Packard dealership out on Route 20, and that he could probably rent me a car for a few days. I called Ernie over at the Noll, and he said he'd have Nobbie call me back.

Next, I tried calling my father's old friends Roger Willoughby in Wallingford and Theodore Derwent in Chicago. I dialed Willoughby directly, but got no answer. I had to use the long distance operator for the call to Chicago, and she informed me that there was no answer there as well. I decided instead to send telegrams, so I called Western Union and dictated the following message to both men:

HOPE YOU WILL ATTEND CEREMONIES HONORING MY FATHER ON DECORATION DAY [STOP] PLEASE COME DAY BEFORE AND STAY OVERNIGHT AT MY HOME [STOP] REPLY BY RETURN WIRE COLLECT 179 OLD HARTFORD TPKE GRANBURY CONN [STOP] JAMIE MCCOY

I also sent a telegram to Mrs. Glendenning in Boston asking her to pack and mail one of my class-A uniforms, together with my ribbons and decorations.

Next on my list was a call to John Barrow—Uncle John. He and my father had been as close as brothers, had known each other since they were schoolboys, and he was the closest thing I had to family left in the world. He was a federal judge in New York City, and I knew I would at least be able to reach someone in his office by telephone. I dialed the long distance operator again and she put my call through to New York.

There was some static on the line at first, but it cleared quickly after two rings. I heard a click, and a nasal female voice said, "U.S. Court of Appeals, Second Circuit. What party are you trying to reach?"

"I'd like to speak with Judge John Barrow please."

"One moment, please." She pronounced the word "please" with two syllables. "I'll put you through to his clerk's office."

There was a second click on the line and a different ringing tone. Another female voice answered, this one more pleasing to the ear. "Edgar Hamilton's office, Miss Shanahan speaking. How may I help you?"

"Hello, my name is Jamie McCoy. I'm trying to reach Judge John Barrow. I'm not sure if I've reached the right office."

"This is Judge Barrow's clerk's office, Mr. McCoy. The judge is in chambers right now, but if you tell me what case this is regarding, I can put you through to Mr. Hamilton, who can assist you."

"Actually, my call is of a personal nature. I'm an old family friend of Judge Barrow's. Perhaps you can leave a message for him to call me back at his convenience."

"I'll be happy to, sir. Is that spelled M-C-C-O-Y?"

"Yes, Ma'am. The phone number is COlumbia 5-1984 in Granbury, Connecticut."

"I'll give Mr. Hamilton the message for Judge Barrow."

I thanked Miss Shanahan and hung up. Within minutes, the telephone rang, and I thought it might be Uncle John calling me right back. I was wrong. It was Ernie Thayer calling to tell me that his cousin Norbert—Nobbie—was on his way over to my place with a car, and I should expect him at any moment. I thanked Ernie and looked out the window to see if there was anyone coming up the driveway. Sure enough, there were two cars just pulling into the circular drive in front.

I went outside and met Nobbie Griffin and his son Larry. They had come in two cars so they could leave one with me. Both men were outgoing and pleasant, just like their cousin, and I expressed my gratitude for their assistance.

"This here's a real cream puff, Mr. McCoy," Nobbie said, pointing at the first car, a sleek maroon touring sedan with a split windshield, white-wall tires, vertical chrome grille and suicide doors. "She's a 1939 Packard Super Eight, a hundred and thirty horse-power, Safe-T-Flex suspension and only about nineteen thousand miles on her. Yes, sir, she's a real beaut."

Larry said, "I took this baby in trade two months ago from an insurance executive in Hartford. Been driving it myself now and then—she rides like a dream. Got four re-tread tires, too."

I got the feeling that Nobbie and his son were trying to sell me the car rather than rent it to me, and I wasn't wrong. As I looked the car over, Nobbie kept right on with his pitch.

"Eight cylinders, dual down-draft carburetor and automatic choke. Notice how she still shines. That's the original factory paint job—Loyola Maroon—and not a scratch on her. Her original list price was $1,750, including the Motorola radio. Seein' as you're Ernie's friend, and your daddy was Colonel McCoy, I can let it go for $650."

I had to admit Nobbie was right. The car was indeed a beauty. Nonetheless, I resisted the pitch. "Thank you for bringing it out here, Nobbie, I appreciate it a lot, but I already own a car. I just need a rental for a couple of days until I can get the title and registration on mine straightened out."

Larry looked over at my father's Mercedes SSK parked under the *porte-cochère*. "That's a sweet car, too, Mr. McCoy, but it's only got two seats. The Packard seats six easily and can squeeze in seven if they're small. We could take your car in trade."

"I don't have a family, Larry. I really don't have a need for more than two seats. And besides, it's kind of a family heirloom."

Nobbie said, "Tell you what, Jamie. I'll leave the dealer plates on her. You give me three dollars a day for the Packard, you pay for gas—she uses ethyl 76, nothin' less. Drive her around for a few days, and if you decide to keep her, well, I'm sure I can work with you on the price."

I chuckled to myself. This guy didn't know when to quit. In a way, I admired him for it. "You got yourself a deal, Nobbie." I took out my wallet and peeled off a ten and a five. "Here's five day's rent in advance. That should be plenty of time for me to decide."

We shook on the deal and Nobbie handed me the keys. Larry pointed out a few things I needed to know about the car, and then they left.

As I walked back up the front steps of the house, Mrs. Hanratty opened the front door and called out to me.

"Mr. McCoy—there's a telephone call for you. He says it's Judge John Barrow."

"Thank you, Mrs. Hanratty," I said. I went inside and took the call.

Uncle John was thrilled that I had called him. He immediately offered his condolences about my mother and told me he'd gone to the funeral in Boston. I was grateful. We talked about my mother some, and a little bit about the war, and he told me he'd lost his oldest son—an eighteen-year-old Marine—at Iwo Jima. I offered my condolences to him in return. I met a Marine lieutenant on the troopship home who'd been at Iwo and, from what he told me, it was the grisliest battle of the war.

I brought up the subject of the Decoration Day celebration in honor of my father, and asked him if he would come a day early and spend the night. He hesitated, and his tone of voice changed slightly, becoming more businesslike.

"Jamie, I'd love to see you, but I really can't come up there just now."

"Well how about just for the day, then?" I asked. "Mayor Gibbons was hoping you'd say a few words at the dedication. After all, you were my father's dearest friend."

"No, no, I really can't. I hope you'll understand." Now his tone sounded almost evasive. "I've just been asked by Justice Jackson to consult on the Nuremberg War Crimes trials. I need to spend every moment over the next several weeks clearing my calendar in preparation. I have to be ready to leave for Germany by the end of July."

"I see," I said. But I didn't see. It was only a three-hour train ride from New York, and Decoration Day, Thursday, May 30, was a holiday. Surely he wasn't working on a holiday.

I told him I was thinking of writing a book about my father, and I wanted him to share some of his memories with me. Instead of the enthusiastic response I expected, however, he hemmed and hawed, and finally said that the newspapers and magazines already lionized my father enough back in the thirties, and the public wasn't interested in stunt flyers anymore, especially after Lindbergh had made his pro-Nazi speeches before the war.

I was hurt. Uncle John had been my father's best friend. Not only had they roomed together at Choate and Yale, my father had been best man at his wedding.

Uncle John said, "Look, Jamie, I really do want to see you. How about if you come down here to New York and we'll get together? Why don't you come down one day during the first week of June?"

"Sure, Uncle John," I agreed. "I'll call you again and pick a date."

We said goodbye and hung up. I felt unsatisfied and somewhat nonplussed, not because his excuse for not coming to the Decoration Day ceremony wasn't important—working on the War Crimes trials would put

John Barrow's name on a world stage—but because I thought Uncle John should have been honored to pay tribute to my father's memory.

I tried to put it out of my mind as I made my last telephone call. I reached into my pocket, withdrew the paper napkin from Berry's Drugstore and dialed Kate's number. My hand trembled. I felt like a freshman calling my first date.

She answered on the first ring. "Hello?"

"Hi, Kate. It's Jamie."

"Hi, Jamie." She sounded excited to hear my voice.

"Are you free for lunch today?"

"Sure. I'm not working again until Monday. I'll leave Susan with my mother-in-law."

"I'll pick you up at noon," I said.

"No, no, that's all right. I'll just meet you downtown. If Susan sees you pull up in that car of yours, she'll insist on coming along."

I chuckled. "You won't have to worry about the car until next week sometime. After I dropped you off yesterday, I got a ticket for driving with an expired registration. I rented a stodgy old Packard sedan from Ernie Thayer's cousin until I can straighten everything out."

Kate laughed out loud. "Home only two days, and already you're a criminal."

I laughed, too. "Seriously, though, Susan is welcome to join us. She's an absolute delight."

"You say that now, but just you wait—she can be a hand-full. I appreciate the offer, but I'd like to have a grown-up day, and my mother-in-law loves being a grandma and having Susan all to herself."

"All right then," I said. I'll be at the library. I'll meet you in the Reference Room at noon."

CHAPTER 9

When I arrived at the library, it was empty except for Miss Marker and Dulcie Patch. Dulcie met me at the circulation desk and led me to the periodical archives, located in a low-ceilinged alcove at the back of the Reference Room. She demonstrated how to use the periodical card catalogue and showed me the lateral file cabinets—oak, of course—that held the back issues of the *Granbury Mercury.*

The *Mercury* had been published as a daily beginning in January 1861 and then became a weekly, published every Monday, in 1900. The first publisher was Jasper Crowell, Freddie's great-grandfather; it remained in the Crowell family ever since, with Freddie taking over from his uncle William in 1938. I started with the issues dating back to America's entry into World War I, where there was an article about my father going overseas. After reviewing three or four issues, I realized that the *Mercury* was a typical community paper. The writing was crisp and thoughtful, but it was heavily slanted and not up to the standards of the *Boston Globe* or the *New York Times.*

Dulcie remained with me for nearly an hour, returning issues I read and took notes on, and retrieving others I wanted to see. Her close attention made me uncomfortable. She touched me at every opportunity—a little pat on the forearm, a caress of my shoulder, a touch of my hand. Even her words were suggestive.

"Your father was very special to me. I hope you and I will become special friends, too."

I didn't know what to say. I took a pack of cigarettes from my pocket and was about to light up when she stopped me.

"Oh, Jamie, I'm sorry. But there's no smoking allowed in the periodical archives. We only allow smoking in the main reading room. Less chance of fire there, you know."

I told her that I understood, but that I needed a break. I excused myself and went into the main reading room, taking two back issues of the *Mercury* with me. As I walked past the circulation desk, Miss Marker smiled at me and I smiled back. She was a pretty girl, but much too young for me, just as Dulcie was much too old.

I sat in a large brown leather chair toward the back of the room, fired up a Lucky, and began flipping the pages of the paper's September 3, 1928 issue. On page three, there was a story about the McCoy Machine Works being sold to Marcus and Richard Pinkman, two entrepreneurs from the Bronx who arranged the financing through the National Bank of Hartford. The article pointed out that all company executives, except my father, and all the employees were expected to retain their jobs. Kate's father-in-law, Arlen Hardesty, was also mentioned as being promoted to Executive Vice President and Chief Financial Officer. The article went on to describe the Pinkman brothers, successful businessmen who previously ran an aircraft parts manufacturer in New York they later sold to Grummann.

I finished my cigarette and read through the September 10 edition before I returned to the periodical archive. Thankfully, Dulcie had left, and I was able to look through the back issues on my own. When I got to the October 2 edition, I was even more grateful she wasn't there. It had a front-page article about a fatal car accident on Route 20 that took the lives of Mr. And Mrs. Alexander Patch, Dulcie's parents. The story noted that Mr. Patch had been president and principal owner of the Granbury Bank, and that Mrs. Patch had been a member of the DAR. They were survived by their daughter, Dulcinea, and her older brother, Alexander Jr., both of Granbury.

By 11:30, I'd made it all the way through the rest of 1928, 1929, 1930 and the beginning of 1931. The research was easy, largely because the paper was no more than twenty pages an issue. I recorded the dates of editions I planned to read later and took notes from a few interesting articles. I intended to cull the significant facts and return to copy the stories verbatim if the need arose. There were some great stories and photographs about my father's early aviation exploits, including his record-breaking flights to Miami and Rio as well as an altitude record he held until Amelia Earhart broke it. There were wire service photos of him with Miss Earhart, Charles Lindbergh, Wiley Post, Jackie Cochran and Beryl Markham, all pioneers of early aviation.

I was starting to grow impatient for my luncheon date with Kate, but I decided I had enough time to look through at least one more issue. I opened the March 9,

1931 edition to the largest headline I'd seen in the *Mercury* since the Armistice in 1918. It read simply:

McCOY WORKS TO CLOSE

The story took up three columns of the front page and continued on the inside. It described a history of troubles at the plant beginning with a significant fall-off in orders starting in early 1930 due to the weak economy, and diminished demand for aircraft parts by the major manufacturers, Grummann, Lockheed, Hughes, and Martin. There had been a series of layoffs for more than a year, with many skilled workers being replaced by cheaper "Negro" labor from both Springfield and Hartford. Because the plant was non-union, the local workers had no recourse.

The article went on to say that auditors hired by the bank uncovered financial mismanagement, and the company petitioned the court for protection from creditors under the bankruptcy laws. But bank officials saw no hope for reorganization, and they predicted the company's assets would be liquidated. The same officials also hinted that they expected the Pinkman brothers to face criminal charges stemming from alleged misappropriation of funds.

I pondered the story, hoping Kate had asked her father-in-law to speak with me about my father and the McCoy Machine Works. I was so preoccupied with the story about the Pinkmans and the company, that I almost failed to notice another article, also on page one, but below the fold. The headline, smaller than the one about the McCoy Machine Works, read:

PATCH HEIR SUCCUMBS

Alexander Patch, Jr., president of the Granbury Bank, had been found in his home on the previous Friday, suffering from a gunshot wound to the head. He died the following day, without ever having regained consciousness; he left a suicide note addressed to his wife, Adele, and his sister, Dulcinea. Neither the police nor the family had released the contents of the note, but "sources close to the family indicated that Mr. Patch had been distraught that the bank over which he presided, and which had been controlled by his family for several generations, was in danger of failing."

The second paragraph dealt with the funeral arrangements, and the final two paragraphs reported that "Mr. Jameson (Harry) McCoy, a major shareholder of the bank, along with other investors from Hartford and New Haven" had announced plans to recapitalize it. The final sentence read, "Mr. McCoy wishes to assure the public that all deposits are safe."

I replaced the newspaper in the file drawer and walked back into the Reference Room where I planned to meet Kate. She was already waiting, sitting at one of the long writing tables, reading a back issue of *Life Magazine*. I was once again struck by her beauty when she stood to greet me. She had tied her hair back in a ponytail. She wore a pale yellow short-sleeved blouse, pleated shorts and wide-strapped sandals. She was dressed for a picnic, and she looked spectacular. I had worn a sport jacket and tie, planning to take her to the dining room of the Noll Tavern. Either I was overdressed or she had made other plans.

"You look very smart today," she said with a grin.

"And you look, ah, well—"

"Lovely? Thank you very much, kind sir. You are *so* gallant." She stressed the last syllable with a broad "a."

"You look beautiful," I said sheepishly.

She enfolded her right arm in my left and led me out the front door. I could feel Miss Marker staring at our backs from her enclosure behind the circulation desk.

"We're dining *al fresco* this afternoon on the village green," Kate said.

There was a hamper packed to the brim and a folded plaid blanket sitting on a bench in front of the portico. I picked them up, tucked the blanket under my right arm and carried the hamper in my right hand as we strolled across to the green. Kate spread out the blanket under the boughs of a towering maple as I set the hamper down and unpacked it.

"This is nice," I said. "What made you think of it?"

"I don't know. It was just such a lovely spring day. I thought we'd enjoy a picnic."

I looked across at the pedestrians and automobiles on Albany Road—Ferry Street was empty—and said, "Isn't this a little public?"

She winked at me. "An un-chaperoned young lady needs some protection, you know."

Kate poured lemonade from a thermos bottle, and we enjoyed a terrific lunch of deep-fried chicken, potato salad, pickles, and homemade apple cobbler for dessert. From the sidewalk across the street, people stared at us, making me feel self-conscious. But Kate and I were soon deep in conversation about my research on my father, and that distracted me. I described the article about the first closing of the McCoy Machine Works, and asked her if she'd had a chance to ask her father-in-law about meeting with me.

"Not only will he speak with you, he and my mother-in-law have invited you to dinner tomorrow evening if you're free."

"Of course," I said, almost too eagerly. "I'd love to come." I was happy at the prospect of speaking with Mr. Hardesty, but I was thrilled about the opportunity to spend more time with Kate.

"Why don't you stop by around six-thirty for cocktails? We usually dine early because of Susan." She arched her left eyebrow conspiratorially. "If you want to make a good impression on Arlen, bring him a cigar."

"Will do," I said. "What do I have to do to make a good impression on Mrs. Hardesty?"

"If you mean my mother-in-law, don't worry. Gwen is easy to please."

"I was, in fact, referring to your mother-in-law, but now that you mention it, how do I make a good impression on the other Mrs. Hardesty?"

She lowered her eyelids almost imperceptibly and said shyly, "You already have." Catching herself, she looked away quickly and then back at me again. "And as for Miss Hardesty, well, my daughter has already informed her grandparents that you are her boyfriend, and that she's going to marry you when she grows up."

I laughed. "Would that I could wait."

We spent a pleasant hour and a half relaxing and talking about nothing and everything. We finally got around to discussing Greg and how difficult it had been for her becoming a widowed mother at twenty-two. She said Greg had always planned to become a history teacher. He knew the pay wouldn't be very good, but he loved the idea of shaping young minds, and he had a particular love for studying the past. She missed him, of course, but the job of raising Susan without a father had kept her occupied. The Hardestys had been wonderful, helping her through it all.

Kate shifted the conversation back to me. She wanted to know why there wasn't a woman in my life. I told her that after I left Granbury, I had a difficult time feeling connected anywhere. After a couple of years in a Boston day school, my mother sent me to an all-boys boarding school. With every summer spent with my grandparents on an island in Maine, I hardly had any contact with the opposite sex until I went to college, and even then, I never met anyone who really appealed to me. Then the war came, and the South Pacific jungle wasn't the best place to meet girls.

It was almost two o'clock when we repacked the hamper and the blanket. I glanced at the library, and I thought I saw Dulcie Patch staring at us through the Palladian window of the Reference Room.

I asked, "What's the story with Dulcie Patch?"

"What do you mean?"

"Ernie Thayer and Freddie Crowell told me she has a fixation on my father. And, well, I don't know... She makes me feel uncomfortable."

Kate said, "When I was a kid, my friends and I used to call her 'Patches' behind her back. Nowadays, the kids in town refer to her as Madame Chiang."

I laughed, picturing the imperious and exotic Madame Chiang Kai-Shek, wife of the generalissimo of China. "It's an apt comparison," I said.

"She's pretentious, and she runs the library with an iron fist. If she doesn't like a book, no matter how good it is, it'll never find its way into the collection."

"Why doesn't the town just get rid of her?"

Kate gave me a quizzical look. "Oh. I just assumed you knew."

"Knew what?"

"The town council doesn't run the library; the library board does, and Dulcie is head of the library board. Your father put her there."

I shook my head, not understanding. "What did my father have to do with it?"

"The McCoy family donated the library to the town—"

"I know. My great-grandfather did."

"Yes, but he also established an endowment fund to run the library, controlled by a board of trustees, free of any political influence from the town. The chairman of that board was your great-grandfather; he was succeeded by your grandfather and then by your father."

"So?"

She furrowed her brows. "You really don't know, do you?"

I just shook my head and held my hands out, palms up.

"Dulcie's brother ran the bank in town that managed the endowment fund."

"I just read that he killed himself when the bank almost failed."

"That's right. And it's common knowledge that Alex Patch killed himself because he was looting the library endowment fund to cover the bank's losses. He was about to be discovered by the bank examiners, and he couldn't handle the disgrace. Your father stepped in with some of his rich friends and rescued the bank, but the endowment fund was almost gone.

"Dulcie and her brother lost everything of course. Alex's widow took her daughter back to Farmington and never spoke to anyone from Granbury again, but Dulcie had nowhere to go. Your father came to her rescue by re-establishing the endowment fund on the condition that Dulcie be appointed head librarian for as long as she wanted the job. He also put her on the library board, and eventually made her the chairwoman."

"I don't get it. Was my father beholden to her somehow?"

"I don't know. I suppose they must have been close friends, or he wouldn't have done what he did."

"How do you know all this, Kate? I mean, I was still in town back then and I sure don't remember any of this stuff."

"We were just kids, Jamie. It's not the kind of thing grownups share with children. I learned about it years later, from my parents and their friends. It's one of those small town scandals that never goes away."

I escorted Kate across Ferry Street to the Packard and held the passenger door open for her. I walked around to the other side, placed the hamper and blanket in the back seat and then got into the driver's seat. Kate slid across the large bench seat, close to me. I drove her home feeling better than I had in years. Nobbie and his son hadn't exaggerated about the car—it handled like a dream.

After I dropped Kate off, I returned to the library. I didn't want to see Dulcie again, but I wanted to read more back issues of the *Mercury*. Happily, Dulcie was otherwise engaged when I arrived, and I managed to slip into the periodical archives undisturbed.

I made it through the rest of 1931 and into April of 1932. The April 11 edition announced that my father had repurchased the McCoy Machine Works from the bank and would reopen the plant by the end of May. The article reported hiring preferences for local employees who had worked for McCoy before the shut-down.

There were a few other relevant stories in the June editions, including coverage of the Decoration Day parade and the Granbury Road Race. One of the July papers had a photograph and story about my father having won the Cleveland Invitational Air Race in his modified Lockheed Vega, but all five August issues were pretty thin, with nothing about either my father or the factory.

I went back to the file drawers looking for the September 1932 editions, but the hanging folder marked September was empty. I looked back at the table to see if I'd taken them already, but they weren't there. I spent half an hour checking the other drawers and hanging folders, but the missing issues were nowhere to be found. Puzzled, I walked out to the main circulation desk and asked Miss Marker if someone had checked out the missing issues of the *Mercury*. She informed me that newspaper archives were not allowed to circulate and special permission was needed to view any back issues more than two years old. She checked the periodical card file and said no one had requested access to the *Mercury* archives in more than a year, and the last person to do so had been Mr. Crowell, the publisher.

I asked her if I could speak to Miss Patch, and she told me to go right back to her office. Dulcie had left instructions that I have access to her whenever I wanted.

I groaned to myself and went through the Children's Library to Dulcie's office. The door was open.

"Hello, Jamie. How is your research coming along?"

"It's fine, Miss Patch, but—"

"Oh, heavens, Jamie. Call me Dulcie. You're almost family."

"Yes, Dulcie. There are several missing issues of the *Mercury*, and I was wondering if you might know what happened to them."

She smiled sweetly. "I wasn't aware of that. What issues?"

"All of September 1932."

"Really? That's unusual. Did you check at the front desk to see if anyone else has them? They don't circulate outside the library, you know."

"Yes, Miss Marker told me that, but no one except me has requested back issues in over a year."

She leaned back in her chair and touched the eraser tip of her pencil to her cheek. "Well, that *is* unusual," she said. "I suppose they could have been misfiled. Did you check some of the other drawers and file folders?"

"That's the first thing I did. They weren't misfiled."

"Well then," she said, putting her pencil down. "Perhaps someone stole them. Unfortunately, that sort of thing occurs from time to time in a public library."

I had feared that might have happened. "I see. Is there anywhere else I might find the missing issues? Perhaps the *Mercury* office?"

Dulcie shook her head. "Unfortunately, no. During the Depression, when Fred Crowell's uncle still published the *Mercury*, he moved the presses into a smaller building in order to save money. He didn't have room to store the archives, so he made permanent arrangements to keep them here. Sadly, if the issues you're looking for are gone, I don't think there's much hope of finding them."

I was disappointed, but there was nothing I could do. I decided I'd had enough for the day and left. When I got home, I found two telegrams waiting for me from Roger Willoughby and Theodore Derwent, both saying that they'd be happy to stay with me overnight for the Decoration Day ceremonies.

CHAPTER 10

On Saturday morning, I went back into town to do a few errands. My first stop was the tobacconist next door to Berry's Drugstore, where I asked the man behind the counter for a couple of his best cigars.

"That would be the Humberto Grandes, made in Havana using the finest Connecticut shade wrappers. Two dollars each."

"Fine. I'll take two, and a couple of packs of Lucky Strikes."

He went toward the back of the store and into a walk-in humidor, coming out with the cigars, which he wrapped in tissue paper for me. He handed me the cigars and the two packs of cigarettes and said, "That'll be four dollars and forty-eight cents."

I chuckled to myself, thinking that forty cigarettes cost less than half a buck, yet two imported cigars were more than eight times the price. I was glad I smoked cigarettes instead of Havana cigars. I gave him a five-dollar bill and he made change for me.

From there, I walked over to the stationery store to buy a typewriter. The storekeeper was a woman who appeared to be in her mid-thirties. She attended to me in a businesslike manner, showing me her small selection of new Royals and a few used Smith Coronas. I picked out one of the new Royals, only because it weighed a lot less than the older machines did, and I stocked up on typing paper, carbons and typewriter ribbons. The whole order came to forty-two dollars, but I only had thirty-five in cash, so I took out my checkbook and prepared to write a check.

The woman said, "I hope that's a local check, sir. I can't accept it otherwise."

I was stumped. My checking account was with the First National Bank of Boston. I hadn't yet opened an account in Connecticut.

"I have identification," I said. "And I live right here in town."

She was unbending. "I'm sorry, sir, I just work here, and that's store policy. If you'd like, I can hold the typewriter for you until Monday, and you can cash a check at the bank here in town."

I remembered my stock portfolio included a hefty chunk of shares in the Granbury Bank, but I didn't tell her that. I couldn't have been more frustrated. I wanted to get some of my notes typed up over the weekend. I decided to do a little name-dropping. "Look, ma'am, how about if I give you some references? Ernie Thayer over at the Noll Tavern is a friend of mine, and so is his brother-in-law, Freddie Crowell. The head librarian, Dulcie Patch, is also a good friend, and I'm sure I can get Mayor Gibbons to vouch for me, too."

The woman's eyes went wide. "What did you say your name was, sir?"

"Jamie McCoy," I said, and handed her my military driver's license.

She looked at it, mouth agape. She excused herself and went toward the back of the store where I saw her pick up the phone and dial, probably to her boss. She muffled her voice in the receiver, but I managed to hear the last part of her side of the conversation.

"Yes, Sir. I'll take care of it. No, Sir. I understand."

She came back to the front and handed my driver's license back to me. Giving me a weak smile, she said, "I'm sorry for the delay, Mr. McCoy. I spoke to my boss, and he said I could accept your check."

My last stop was the florist shop down by the railroad station. There, I picked out two identical bouquets of purple irises for Kate and Gwen Hardesty, and a small wrist corsage for Susan. I thought she'd like that.

I spent the rest of the day typing up the notes I'd taken at the library the day before, and sorting through some of my father's old papers I'd found in the attic. There was no semblance of order to the attic material— just boxes filled with yellowing letters, student papers, old bills and some ancient financial records dating back to the turn of the century. I'd hoped the letters would be helpful, but I discovered they belonged to my grandfather and grandmother, and most pre-dated World War One.

At 5:30, I went upstairs and showered. I shaved extra closely, taking care not to nick myself, and donned one of the new shirts Mrs. Hanratty had pressed for me. I dressed in gray slacks, my new blue blazer, a silk foulard tie and a pair of black loafers. I was ready.

I arrived at Kate's house at 6:30, carrying the two bouquets, the corsage and Mr. Hardesty's cigars. I felt like a teenager calling for my prom date. Mrs. Hardesty answered the doorbell, but Susan was right there, dressed in a pale blue party dress, tugging at her grandmother's hem.

"Hi, Jamie," she squealed, before her grandmother could say a word.

"Well hello, Susan," I said. I knelt down, handing her the corsage and said, "This is for you, princess."

I placed it on her wrist and she ran off to show Kate. "Mummy! Mummy! Lookit! Jamie brought me a flower!"

Mrs. Hardesty smiled broadly and said, "Welcome, Jamie, and please come in. It's been too many years since we've seen you."

Honestly, I didn't remember her face, but hearing her voice brought back memories of her son, Greg. I handed her one of the bouquets. She thanked me with a kiss on my cheek and asked me to come in, insisting I call her "Gwen" instead of "Mrs. Hardesty."

Arlen Hardesty shook hands with me and, pointing to the other bouquet, said, "Are those for me, son?"

I laughed and said, "No, sir. They're for Kate, but I brought these for you." I reached into my breast pocket and handed over the two cigars.

He took them and examined the red and gold bands, holding his glasses out toward the tip of his nose. "Humbertos. You have good taste in cigars. I hope you'll join me in one of these later."

After giving Kate her irises, we went into the living room where Arlen poured gin and tonics for Kate, Gwen and me. He poured himself a double shot of Scotch on the rocks and served Susan a Shirley Temple.

We had a wonderful dinner and dessert, with much of the entertainment provided by a precocious Susan. After dinner, we sat in the living room and listened to the radio for a bit before Kate took Susan upstairs to read her a story and put her to bed. I offered to help with the dishes, but Gwen shooed me away, telling Arlen and me to go into the den and smoke our foul cigars.

Mr. Hardesty sat down in a comfortable old reading chair and I sat on a low sofa. There was a framed photograph of Greg in his Army uniform on the mantelpiece, and another one next to it of Greg and Kate on their wedding day.

Arlen expertly clipped the ends of both cigars and lit mine first, then his own. He took a long draw and exhaled a stream of gray smoke. "Fine cigar." He leaned back in his chair and said, "Kate tells me you want to know about your father and the factory. Where do you want me to start?"

"At the beginning, I suppose." I described to him what I'd read in the *Mercury* the day before about the Pinkmans, and I also told him what Arthur Wiseman had revealed to me in Boston.

Arlen Hardesty listened, and then, in a calm and deliberate tone, he told me everything, beginning with how he came to work at McCoy Machine Works. He was hired as a clerk by my great-grandfather back in 1901 when he was fresh out of high school. The old man immediately took a liking to him and sent him to the University of Connecticut to study business—tuition, fees and all expenses paid. He graduated just a month before my great-grandfather died, but my grandfather, who took over the family business, continued the patronage of Arlen by arranging for him to get a job with a public accounting firm in Hartford so he could learn his profession. After Arlen had spent a few years with the accounting firm, my grandfather brought him back to

McCoy Machine Works as head bookkeeper, later making him Vice President of Finance.

"Your grandfather was a great man," Arlen said. "I was in awe of him. He was both a sharp businessman and a brilliant engineer. A lot of people think the factory was the source of your family's wealth, and perhaps it was—originally. But it was your grandfather's engine designs and innovations that eventually made the McCoys all their big money. Your grandfather pioneered virtually every major advance in aircraft engines before, during and immediately after the Great War. He held over two hundred patents.

"As brilliant as your grandfather was, it was your father who was the true visionary. He took your grandfather's designs and improved on them to the point where aircraft manufacturing couldn't keep pace with McCoy technology. Then, he licensed the technology to all the big players in the industry, and the fees from those licenses made him millions. He made even more millions by requiring the licensees to lock in exclusive production contracts with McCoy Machine Works.

"Then, your father did something truly amazing—and I'm not talking about his damned stunt flying escapades—he sold the company to the Pinkman brothers for twenty-five million dollars."

"I don't understand," I said. Why was selling the family business such a brilliant move?"

Arlen Hardesty puffed on his cigar and smiled at me. "Because, Jamie, he sold the company, but he kept all the patents, the designs, the license agreements and their associated fees. The Pinkmans got the factory and the production contracts—nothing more."

I was confused. "I understand the patents, designs and license fees were valuable, but the Pinkman brothers didn't buy a pig in a poke. You said the production contracts were worth millions."

"They were," he said, "until demand fell off. The contracts were good as long as there was demand for aircraft engine parts. As long as Lockheed, Grummann, Hughes and Martin were making and selling airplanes, they had to buy certain parts exclusively from McCoy Machine Works. But if the aircraft manufacturers weren't selling airplanes, they weren't building them, and if they weren't building them, then they didn't have to buy parts from anyone."

"Didn't the fall in demand affect my father's licensing fees, too?" I asked.

"Not as badly as it hurt the Pinkmans. You see, they had to spend money to make money—they had to produce parts and sell them. Your father didn't have to do anything but collect license fees whenever one of the manufacturers used one of his or your grandfather's designs. When demand for airplanes fell, your father's income slowed some. The Pinkmans' revenues stopped altogether."

"What happened to the Pinkmans? Did they go to jail?"

Arlen laughed. "Hell no. Marcus and Richard Pinkman weren't crooks. They were just victims of a bad economy and worse business judgment. They overpaid for the company and they didn't understand the fundamental source of the company's profitability. When the economy was good and profits were high, their error was of no consequence, but when the Depression hit, everything collapsed."

"But the newspaper article said—"

"I know what the article said, and it's a bunch of horse dung. Come on, Jamie, you're a smart fellow. You don't believe everything you read in the papers, do you?"

I shook my head no.

"First of all," he said, "There was no misappropriation of funds. Old Bill Crowell, the publisher of the *Mercury*, was a goddamn bigot who hated the Pinkmans because they were Jews. He just wrote that garbage in the paper to make them look bad. He was lucky they didn't sue him for libel.

"The fact is, I liked the Pinkmans and tried to help them. But they couldn't afford to keep me. When your father sold the company, he gave me a bonus of a quarter million dollars for helping to negotiate the purchase price, and he made the Pinkman brothers give me an employment contract for a year. My employment contract was up in 1929, and that was all there was to that.

"As to that baloney about the Pinkmans hiring low cost colored help to replace factory workers, that was more of Bill Crowell's bigotry. We had a couple of colored men from West Springfield working as janitors, but that was it. Thugs chased those poor bastards away after that article came out; lucky thing no one got killed."

I frowned. "What about afterwards—after the Pinkmans went bust?"

"I went to work for your father as his personal financial manager after I left the Pinkmans. I advised him to get out of the stock market in the middle of '29, and it's a good thing he did. When the factory closed in 1931, I helped your father buy it back from the bank for a fraction of what the Pinkman brothers paid. After your father regained control of the company, I went back on the payroll."

I was still puzzled. "But what caused it to fail a second time? What about all the things Arthur Wiseman told me? Was my father involved in something crooked?"

Arlen sighed. "I wish I could tell you, but the fact is I just don't know what happened."

I was floored. Arlen Hardesty had been the Chief Financial Officer. He was my father's personal financial advisor. He must have known the truth. I tried prodding him further, but he just shook his head.

"After I went back to work for the company, your father handled his personal financial affairs by himself. He cut me out completely. After he disappeared, I told your mother's lawyer and that detective she hired everything I knew; and all I knew was that your father got us production contracts when our competitors were starving. It wasn't until after he was gone that I discovered the customers were phony and the company was in deep trouble."

I asked, "But if my father was selling to phony customers, what happened to all the parts?"

"Who knows? Maybe he dumped 'em in the ocean." He looked up at the ceiling and shook his head. "The really stupid thing your father did—the one thing I never understood—was selling all the patents and license agreements to Pratt & Whitney about three months before he disappeared."

I didn't understand it either. "Why would he do that?"

"Who knows. Maybe he needed a lot of cash in a hurry. I suppose he used it to pay the company for all the parts the phony customers were buying."

Arlen finished his cigar and let the stub die out by itself in the ashtray. Mine had gone out long before. When I asked him what he thought my father had been up to, he shrugged and said he believed my father was trying to keep the factory open so the people in Granbury could get back to work.

"I thought the world of your father, Jamie. He took good care of me, and a lot of other people, too. He was a generous man who took his obligations to his friends and neighbors seriously."

"So I've been hearing," I said. I was skeptical, though. I decided to ask Arlen about my father's gun club, and that got a rise out of him. His demeanor changed abruptly, and what he said told me he knew more than he was willing to divulge.

"I don't know anything about it. Like I said, your father cut me out of his personal life after he repurchased the factory."

I let it go. It was no use pressing him. Besides, we'd been ignoring Gwen and Kate for over an hour. Arlen agreed, and suggested we return to the living room to sit with the ladies.

Later on, after I thanked Mr. and Mrs. Hardesty for a lovely dinner, Kate walked me to my car.

"I'm sorry I abandoned you for so long in there," I said.

"That's okay. I understand you needed to talk to Arlen. Did he tell you everything you wanted to know?"

"No, not everything."

"Well, maybe you can come by again and finish up."

"Kate, I'd love to come by again, but when I do, it will be to see you."

She kissed me on the cheek. We looked at each other for a long time, and then I kissed her—on the lips—and she kissed me back.

CHAPTER 11

On Monday morning, I boarded the 8:05 to Hartford. It was a commuter local—stopping at Windsor Locks, Windsor, and Wilson—and arriving at 8:33. When I arrived in Hartford's Union Station, I asked a redcap for directions to the Dowling Building. He directed me to walk four blocks up Asylum Avenue toward Trumbull Street.

The Dowling Building was ten stories high with a dour granite and brick façade. Through the revolving doors, I found a dimly lit lobby with a news counter and a shoeshine stand along one wall, and a bank of three elevators along the other. The building directory indicated that Selwyn & Macy occupied the top two floors; I boarded the middle elevator, and the elevator man closed the gate and whisked me up to the top.

Selwyn & Macy's offices were nothing like Arthur Wiseman's. Arthur's firm was comparatively new by law firm standards—only thirty years old—and the décor was modern. Selwyn & Macy traced itself back to Civil War days and was a pre-eminent New England law partnership that prided itself on its wealthy clientele. The décor bespoke permanence and Yankee respectability. The receptionist at Arthur's firm was young and pretty;

the receptionist at Selwyn & Macy looked like she, too, dated back to the Civil War. A gilt-framed painting of the firm's founders hung behind the receptionist. They reminded me of the Smith Brothers on the cough-drop boxes. A dozen photographs of distinguished gentlemen filled the other walls. One of them was of John Hughes Barrow—Uncle John.

I gave the receptionist my name and asked for Mr. Franklin.

She surprised me by asking, "Is your appointment with Mr. Franklin Senior or Mr. Franklin Junior?"

I shook my head. "I honestly don't know, Ma'am. His full name is E. Biddle Franklin, but he said he prefers to be called 'Ed' if that's any help."

"That would be Mr. Franklin Senior. Please have a seat, and I'll tell his secretary you're here." She got up from behind her desk and walked through a set of double doors on the left.

Rather than sit down, I studied the portraits adorning the walls. There were three Selwyns, a Biddle, two Macys, two Barrows—the younger was Uncle John— and several other impressive Yankee names.

The receptionist re-entered and informed me that Miss Finch would be along in just a moment to escort me to Mr. Franklin's office.

She saw me examining the photographs and said, "Those are the seventeen Selwyn & Macy partners who have been elevated to the bench over the years." She pronounced the word "been" as "bean."

"John Barrow was once a partner here?"

"Oh yes," she said enthusiastically. "Mr. Barrow was the youngest man ever admitted to the partnership. He went on to become Attorney General of Connecticut and a U.S. Attorney before he was appointed to the Federal Court. Do you know Mr. Barrow?"

"Yes," I said. "He was a close friend of my father."

Just then, Miss Finch entered and introduced herself, after which she escorted me to the inner sanctum. Ed Franklin's office was in a far corner with a spectacular view of Bushnell Park. It was larger than Arthur Wiseman's office, and more expensively furnished.

Ed Franklin wore a perfectly tailored charcoal gray three-piece suit with a gold watch chain across the front of his vest and from which dangled a Phi Beta Kappa key. His ash gray hair was combed back and thinning at the top, and his wire-rim glasses were more than a decade out of style. He appeared to be in his early sixties, about the same age as Arlen Hardesty.

Franklin extended his hand. "Delighted to meet you at last, young man. You're the very image of your late father."

I was getting tired of hearing that, but I smiled in response anyway. "It's nice to meet, you, too, Mr. Franklin."

"Please call me Ed."

"Thank you, Ed. And please call me Jamie."

He directed me to sit on a leather sofa near the south window, and he sat across from me in a captain's chair that bore the emblem of Yale Law School on its seatback. Miss Finch poured coffee and then left, closing the door behind her.

We chatted amiably for a few minutes while we drank our coffee, and then Ed produced the new title certificate for my father's Mercedes. I signed it and two other documents, and Ed gave me instructions on how to obtain my new registration and license plates at the Department of Motor Vehicles. He informed me that I could transfer my military driver's license at the same time.

"If you'll forgive me for saying so," I said, "this seems like a trivial matter for a senior member of this firm."

"Actually, I'm the managing Partner of Selwyn & Macy, and I confess that one of the junior associates handled it. The reason I wanted to meet you in person is that I have represented the McCoy family and its various business and personal interests for more than three decades. In fact, the firm has handled your family's legal matters since 1875, and I was hoping you'd permit us to continue in that capacity."

"I see no reason not to," I said. "I'll let you know if anything comes up that requires your help."

"Please feel free to call on me any time, Jamie. I'll write down my home telephone number in Farmington just in case there's anything you need outside of normal business hours."

He stood up and walked over to his desk, where he selected a business card from a silver tray and wrote his home number on the back with a large black fountain pen. He rolled an antique rocker blotter over the card and handed it to me.

I finished my coffee and said, "Come to think of it, there is something you could help me with." I explained my frustration in learning my father's activities before he disappeared—the company's business, the missing money and the mysterious gun club. I told him everyone I questioned claimed to know nothing.

Not surprisingly, Ed Franklin followed the same line.

"To be honest, Jamie, your father was very secretive about his affairs during the last years of his life, and he refused to follow my advice. In fact, I believe he used another attorney on some matters—someone from New York—but he didn't say who."

"Can you tell me anything he did confide?"

Ed Franklin hesitated. "I'm sorry, Jamie, but my communications with your father are privileged."

"My father has been dead for twelve years. I'm his sole heir. I think you can trust me."

"Legally, he's been dead only since December 1941. But living or dead, I'm not permitted to disclose anything he told me in confidence. It's not a matter of trusting you; it's a matter of legal ethics. If I breach lawyer-client privilege, I'll be disbarred."

"I see." But I didn't see. Inside, I was seething. "Look, Ed, I figure I'm worth somewhere in the neighborhood of ten million dollars. Having that kind of money means I'm going to need a lot of legal advice in the coming years. If you want Selwyn & Macy to represent me, I hope you'll be forthright about certain things."

Ed Franklin sighed. "Jamie, I wish I could help you, but my hands are tied."

"Isn't there anything you can tell me? What about the advice you say he didn't take? Certainly that's not privileged."

He pondered for a moment and said, "Well, within the scope of those limitations, there are a couple of things I can tell you. I advised him against selling his patents and licenses to Pratt & Whitney. I thought it was a colossal mistake, but he did it anyway. It was one of the last matters I handled for him."

"You said there were a couple of things."

He averted his eyes. "I advised your father to divorce your mother after she left him, but he wouldn't consider it."

I glared at him.

"I had nothing against your mother personally, Jamie; in fact, I thought she was a lovely woman. I gave your father that advice in order to protect *your* interests, because Connecticut family law stipulates a wife is entitled to half her husband's estate, irrespective of any will. In the end, at least, I persuaded your father to establish separate trust funds for you and your mother."

It was my turn to sigh. "As it turned out, Ed, it wouldn't have mattered. My mother inherited what was left of my father's estate, but she never touched a dime of his money. She left it all for me."

I left the offices of Selwyn & Macy and walked over to Main Street, where I stopped into the Hartford National Bank and spent an hour filling out the forms to open a checking account. That done, I crossed the street and headed toward the Department of Motor Vehicles. I passed the Hartford Athenaeum, City Hall and the Hartford Public Library, all impressive edifices. Just past the library, on my left, was a squat yellow brick building—home to the DMV and other State offices. It took more than two hours to negotiate the bureaucracy before I escaped with my new driver's license and plates. Mercifully, they told me that future renewals could be done by mail.

As I left the DMV, I contemplated grabbing a bite to eat before taking the train back to Granbury when it occurred to me that I might be able to find the missing issues of the *Granbury Mercury* in the Hartford Public Library.

I went in and asked for the periodical archives. Unlike the Granbury Library, the Hartford Public Library maintained its archived newspapers on microfilm. A pleasant young woman escorted me to the second floor and showed me how to look up past issues of all Connecticut newspapers. There was a large machine on a steel table with a sixteen-by-twenty-inch viewing screen. Across the top of the machine was a stylized brass nameplate with the name *Haloid-Rictograph* engraved in fancy script.

The woman showed me the drawers assigned to the various newspapers and selected a Bakelite film cartridge from the *Hartford Courant* to demonstrate.

"Each cartridge contains a month of issues for the daily newspapers, and six months of issues for the weeklies," she said. "All you have to do is insert the cartridge like this."

She placed the cartridge into a slot on the left side of the machine. "Turn on the viewing lamp like so."

She flipped a switch at the bottom, and a newspaper page appeared on the screen as a negative image. "You rotate this knob here on the right, forward or backward, to move through the pages. If you want to print out a particular page, you just center it between the black guidelines on the screen and press this red button here. It takes about sixty seconds for each page to print."

"May I try?" I asked.

I pushed the red button and the screen went black for a second. It whirred and clicked, and, after a full minute, a reduced positive image of the page emerged from a slot and fell into a receiving tray at the bottom. The surface was damp, so I picked it up by the edges.

"It takes about fifteen seconds for it to dry," she said. "When you're finished printing, just bring your copies to the desk over there." She pointed to a small gray steel desk in the corner. "The copies are five cents apiece."

I found the drawer for the *Granbury Mercury* and had no trouble finding the cartridge for the second half of 1932. I rotated the knob forward and came to the first week of September.

It didn't take me long to discover why someone might have wanted to remove the missing issues from the Granbury library. In the top left column on the front page of the September 5th edition was an article that read:

LOCAL WOMAN ASSAULTED
SUSPECT CAPTURED THEN ESCAPES

On Thursday evening at 7:00, Police Chief Victor Eberhardt responded to a call for assistance from a local woman in her home. The woman, whose name is being withheld to protect her privacy, indicated a Negro man broke into her house and assaulted her earlier in the evening. She identified her assailant as Paul Jefferson, a transient farm laborer employed at the estate of Col. Harry McCoy on the Old Hartford Turnpike.

Chief Eberhardt telephoned for Dr. Holcomb to come to the scene and attend the victim, and then called headquarters to alert the entire Granbury police force.

The Chief informed the *Mercury* that there were more than twenty Negro transient laborers at the McCoy estate and, because he feared resistance, he called on all six members of the police force as well as armed citizen volunteers to help apprehend the alleged assailant. At 7:30, Chief Eberhardt telephoned Col. McCoy to inform him of the situation and confirm the number of Negroes present on the estate. Col. McCoy suggested the police and the *posse comitatus* convene at his barn prior to attempting an arrest.

The police and volunteers assembled in Col. McCoy's barn at 11:30 and surrounded the Negroes' dormitories. After a brief confrontation, Jefferson was taken into custody shortly after midnight.

Chief Eberhardt escorted Jefferson to the barn in order to handcuff him and take him to the town jail, while the rest of the police officers and the posse maintained surveillance of the remaining laborers. According to Eberhardt, as he approached the barn holding the suspect at gunpoint, Jefferson seized the chief's weapon and escaped into the woods. The Chief immediately called for assistance, and two of the armed volunteers joined him and gave chase through the woods. Sergeant Peter Trask, who remained behind in command of the police officers and the remaining volunteers, reported hearing two, possibly more, gunshots, but it was unclear if the shots came from the pursuers or from Jefferson. Chief Eberhardt did not confirm the report of gunfire.

The pursuers failed to find Jefferson, who remains at large. Chief Eberhardt urged the community to remain calm, emphasizing his belief that the suspect had fled the vicinity. The Connecticut State Police were alerted on Friday afternoon. There was no reason given for the delay in notifying the State Police; however, it may have been caused by a miscommunication between Chief Eberhardt and his second-in-command, Sergeant Trask.

Henry Dietz, a foreman for Col. McCoy, described the alleged assailant, Paul Jefferson, as a light-skinned Negro of approximately twenty years of age, approximately six feet, two inches tall, and weighing about two hundred and twenty pounds. He is well muscled, has close-cropped curly black hair, and was last seen wearing shabby brown leather work-boots and faded blue denim dungaree overalls with no shirt. Dietz indicated that, to his knowledge, Jefferson had not caused any previous trouble on Col. McCoy's farm, and that the other Negro laborers remained calm despite the attempted arrest of their co-worker.

As a precautionary measure, Col. McCoy arranged for several armed men to remain on the estate, and asked all female members of his household staff to remain indoors for the time being. Col. McCoy also stated that his wife and young son were not present on the estate at the time of the incident, as both are presently away on an extended vacation with his wife's family.

Dr. Holcomb reported that the victim of the assault was in satisfactory condition, after having been treated for shock in her home. Dr. Holcomb did not consider hospitalization necessary.

I reviewed the article twice more looking for nuances I might have missed. Then it struck me. How could the victim identify a transient farm laborer by name?

I printed the article. Then I turned the knob to advance the pages; I wanted to see if there were any related articles in the rest of the paper. There was an interview with Hank Dietz on page three about the Negro laborers, but it offered nothing new. I printed it out anyway.

I advanced the pages to the September 12th edition. There were no other stories about the assault or the escapee on page one, but there was an article on page four reporting no progress by the State Police on apprehending Paul Jefferson. My father was quoted as saying he fired the other laborers, and he asked them to leave the estate. The workers packed their belongings into a truck and headed back to North Carolina; Granbury police officers escorted them to the town line.

After printing the rest of the September 12th edition, I advanced the roll of film to September 19th. On page two, I discovered who probably removed the copies from the Granbury library. In an interview with Dulcie Patch, it was revealed that she was the assault victim. She claimed she was recovering well and expected no lasting ill effects. I took this to mean that she wasn't pregnant.

She described the "horror of that night" in terms that left no doubt about what happened, although the word "rape" wasn't mentioned. I presumed she came forward because Granbury was a small town, and everyone had guessed her identity long before the story ever got to press. Dulcie must have removed the back issues the day I first went to the library. I printed this article, too.

There were two small items in the September 26th issue worth noting, both of them on the back page. The first was a one-paragraph report that Paul Jefferson had not yet been apprehended and was presumed to have left the state. The second was a longer story about the State Police investigation; they had questioned all members of the Granbury police force as well as the civilian volunteers who had been present that night. The article listed the names and addresses of the civilian volunteers, all from towns other than Granbury. Two were identified as leaders of the volunteers: Drazha Kunetz, a licensed pilot, and Lieutenant Boris Baransky, an Army reserve officer, both from Thompson, Connecticut. The others were identified as Otto Grebe, Carl Frank and Richard Green from Windsor; Ernest Lieber and George Crossman from Suffield; and Richard Kreuzer and John Hauser from Bloomfield. The story ended with the ominous line, "Colonel McCoy has not yet been questioned."

After printing the last page, I returned the film cartridge to its drawer and counted up the pages I printed. Including the sample page from the *Hartford Courant*, I'd printed seven pages. I handed the clerk thirty-five cents, and then I left. It was almost three o'clock, and I still hadn't eaten lunch.

The weather had turned while I was in the library. It was overcast and chilly and, as I walked out onto Main Street, I felt depressed. My research had raised new mysteries. I had a lot of questions and few ideas where to get the answers, but I'd begin with Hank Dietz. He was there on the night of the assault, and I intended to pump him hard.

I took the train schedule from the pocket of my sport jacket. There was a local leaving at 3:27. I decided to try for it and eat an early dinner at home.

CHAPTER 12

I arrived home shortly after four and immediately asked Mrs. Hanratty if she could prepare an early supper for me. She said that the fastest hot meal she could prepare was grilled steak and boiled potatoes, a suggestion I heartily accepted.

Hank Dietz was in the cellar repairing a leaky pipe. I waited in the study while Mrs. Hanratty went downstairs and asked him to join me. He knocked on the door a few minutes later.

"Mrs. Hanratty says you wanna see me."

"Come in, Hank. Have a seat." I remained standing.

"I really oughtn't to sit down. My overalls is pretty dirty from workin' in the cellar," he said.

"That's all right, Hank. Sit in the wooden chair over here." I indicated the side chair next to my father's desk. "I want to show you something."

Hank sat down. I handed him the copied pages from the *Granbury Mercury* and asked him to read them. After a few minutes, he finished and handed them back without saying anything.

"Well, do you want to tell me about it?" I asked.

"I don't get what you mean. What do you want me to say?"

I kept my cool. "I want you to tell me what happened that night and what my father had to do with it."

Beads of sweat formed at the edge of his hairline. He took a grimy rag from his pocket and dabbed his forehead, leaving a grease smear. "I don't know what to say, Mr. McCoy. It's just like it says there in the newspaper stories. There's nothin' else to tell ya."

I leaned against the mantel and folded my arms across my chest. It was like dealing with a goldbricking private.

"Last week, you said my father used the rifles we found to guard the Negro farm workers. Is this incident what you were speaking about?"

Hank fidgeted in his chair. "I suppose so. Yeah, I guess that's what I had in mind."

"And you didn't think it important to mention that one of the field hands raped a woman, an armed posse came here to arrest him, and he escaped into the woods?" I was fuming.

"Well, sir, it's just like it says in the paper. There weren't nothin' much more to it than that."

"Really? Perhaps you could tell me how Miss Patch was able to identify a Negro farm worker—a transient laborer—by name?"

Hank's fidget turned into a squirm. "That fella Jefferson wasn't like the others. He was different."

"How so?"

"First off, he was one a them light-skinned niggers. And he didn't know his place."

Hank tried to turn his head away, but I kept at him. "What else?" I said.

"He was a college boy. He had a year at one a them southern nigger colleges, and he was up here workin' to make money so's he could go back."

I raised my eyebrows in surprise.

Hank paused to collect himself. "Anyway, he was always readin' books. Back afore the war, the library used to stay open three nights a week, an' on those nights, Jefferson'd wash hisself up after work and walk into town to read at the library." Hank wiped his face with the rag again, leaving another grease stain. "Now that didn't make him none too popular with some folks, especially Billy Crowell and Chief Eberhardt. But Miss Patch, she said the library was open to the public, and the Jefferson boy had a right to go there."

"So she knew him."

Hank nodded. "Yes, sir, she knew him from the library. She claimed he followed her home that night, after the library closed."

"What about those 'civilian volunteers'? Who were they? None of them are local people. Why didn't Eberhardt call on Granbury men to volunteer?"

Hank dabbed his forehead again. He looked down at the rug, and when he spoke, it was barely a whisper. "Look, Mr. McCoy, all that stuff happened a long time ago. You was just a kid then, and you wasn't even around." He looked up at me. "Those fellas were your daddy's friends. Chief Eberhardt called your daddy that night, right about the time I was knockin' off work. He told your daddy what happened, and he said there might be trouble. He asked the Colonel to round up a bunch a men to help."

"But who were they? Two of them came all the way from Thompson. That's more than thirty miles away."

"Like I told you, they was yer daddy's friends—the same guys who came up here for meetins on weekends. That Baransky fella was the ringleader. The others called him the 'Count,' and his buddy Kunetz was a pilot like your daddy—I think that's how they became friends. Anyway, after the Chief called, your daddy telephoned the Count, and that Kunetz fella brought him here in his plane. I set out flares on the runway."

I could see Hank was uncomfortable, but I didn't want to let it go. "Jefferson—the one who hurt Miss Patch—how did he get away?"

"I swear to you, Mr. McCoy. I was upstairs in the barn with your daddy the whole time." He paused. "I never saw him get away."

"Did the State Police ever find him?"

Hank shook his head. "No, sir. Leastways, not that I ever heard."

I stood there, expecting him to say something more, but he just sat there blinking at me.

"Can I go now, Mr. McCoy? I still gotta finish up in the cellar."

"All right, Hank. If you think of anything else, come and see me right away."

Before he left, I handed him my new license plates and asked him to put them on the Mercedes before he went home for the day.

After Hank left, I went into the kitchen, where Mrs. Hanratty was putting my steak and boiled potatoes on a plate. She shooed me into the dining room, where she had set a place at the table and had already poured a glass of red wine. As I ate my dinner, I thought about Hank. Like Chief Eberhardt, Arlen Hardesty and Ed Franklin, it was clear to me that he knew more than he was telling. I decided to drive into town after dinner and talk about it with Ernie Thayer over a beer.

Before I left for town, I called Kate and invited her out for Tuesday night. At first, she protested it was a work night, but I heard her mother-in-law saying in the background, "Go on, Kate. I'll watch Susan." She finally assented. We decided to have an early dinner and a movie in Hartford, and I promised to pick her up at the bank right after work.

I arrived at the Noll Tavern just after 7:30. The dinner crowd had left, but a handful of regulars remained in the Tap Room. Ernie and Freddie Crowell were sitting at a small round table in a corner near the bar. I walked over to join them, and Ernie signaled the bartender to pour me a draft.

They were discussing baseball, so I sat back and listened. Ernie argued that Joe Cronin's Red Sox were a shoo-in for the pennant since Ted Williams was back in the line-up, and Freddie claimed that Detroit, which took the American League pennant in '45, was the team to watch with Hank Greenberg back for the whole season. They asked my opinion, but I pleaded ignorance on the grounds that I'd been away for four years and hadn't had an opportunity to follow baseball from New Guinea and the Philippines. Besides, I was a Braves fan. I let them go on for a little while, and then, after they exhausted the American League permutations and possibilities, I changed the subject.

I asked, "Do either of you guys remember this?" I unfolded my reprints of the *Granbury Mercury* and flattened them out on the table.

Ernie picked up a couple of pages and looked at them, and Freddie examined the others. Ernie put his down and stared at me. Freddie was still reading.

Ernie said, "I can't believe Dulcie showed you these."

"She didn't. Those issues of the paper weren't in the archives. I found them in the Hartford Public Library."

Freddie said, "I heard all about this, but I wasn't here when it happened. I was just starting my senior year at Amherst."

"What about you, Ernie?" I said.

"As a matter of fact," Ernie said, taking a pull on his beer, "I was in the Berkshires on a fishing trip when it happened. I didn't get home until the following Sunday."

"But you know about it, right?"

"Right." He sat there, holding his mug of beer, looking at me, daring me to say something.

Freddie broke the silence. "I don't get it. What's going on?"

Ernie's face fell. He said, "Jamie thinks his father was involved in something sinister. He's just trying to figure it out. What he doesn't understand is that his father was one of the greatest men this town ever produced, and that sometimes even great men get involved in things that don't bear the closest scrutiny."

"Was this one of those things?" I asked.

"I told you, Jamie, I wasn't here at the time, so I'm hardly the person to ask."

"Who are these men?" I asked, pointing to the page with the names of the posse. "Hank Dietz told me they were my father's friends."

Ernie shook his head. "I didn't know any of them. It's like I told you before; that was part of your father's life that didn't include me."

Freddie examined the articles again. He said, "Jamie, do you mind if I borrow this? A couple of these names seem familiar, and I might be able to track them down."

Ernie grimaced. "You guys oughtta leave this alone."

I ignored Ernie's suggestion and responded to Freddie. "Sure. Let me know what you find out."

Ernie shook his head in disgust.

"Maybe I should pay another visit to Chief Eberhardt and ask him about it again," I said.

"I wouldn't do that if I were you," Ernie said. "That night wasn't Victor Eberhardt's finest hour, and he won't be happy about you bringing it up again." He chuckled derisively. "Imagine—letting a prisoner steal your gun and run away."

I decided to beat a retreat and let Ernie and Freddie return to their discussion of baseball. I drove home and went to bed early.

On Tuesday, I spent the morning back at the Granbury library continuing my study of the *Mercury*'s back issues. Dulcie was as solicitous as usual, but after a warm greeting, she left me to my own devices in the periodical archives. I found a few stories about my father's last flight, and some terrific pictures. There was one of him at the last Granbury Road Race he attended, and another of him posing under the wing of his tri-motor plane with the glamorous Greta Huffmann. I wrote down the issue numbers, and decided to return to the Hartford Public Library and use the *Haloid-Rictograph* machine to make copies of them.

Not wishing to abuse my free-meal privileges at the Noll Tavern, I stopped into Berry's Drugstore for a light lunch at the soda fountain and, on the way out, I ran into Nobbie Griffin who was coming in to have a prescription filled. I was supposed to return the Packard later that afternoon.

"How do you like driving the Super Eight?" he asked. He wasn't about to give up on selling me that car.

"It's everything you said it was, Nobbie."

"If it's not, you just say the word and I'll fix you up with something else."

I thought about it. I realized I could use a good sedan for rainy days and cold weather. "I'll tell you what. You wanted $650 for the car; at three dollars a day, I could rent that car from you for the next five months for $450. How about if I give you $600 for it now and promise to trade it in on a new Packard when the '47 models come out?"

Nobbie scratched his chin. I could tell he liked the idea, but he was trying to drive a better bargain. Before he counter-offered, I took out my checkbook and a pen.

He flashed a broad grin and said, "Okay, you've got a deal." He offered me his hand and we shook on it.

"Just one more thing," I said. "You have to take care of getting the damned thing registered for me. I don't want to deal with those idiots at the DMV again."

"No problem. It's all part of the service. I'll send Larry out to your house with some papers to sign and we'll get you the new plates in a couple of days."

I wrote out a check on the spot, handed it to him, and we said goodbye. Nobbie walked away whistling.

That evening, I picked up Kate and we drove into Hartford for dinner at an Italian restaurant in the East End. Over dinner, I told her about my discoveries at the Hartford Public Library the day before. She listened attentively, but professed no knowledge of the incident. In fact, she seemed genuinely surprised.

I asked, "Why do you think nobody talks about it?"

"It's funny," she said. "The other day we were talking about small-town scandals, and how some stories take on a life of their own. Dulcie's brother committing suicide to avoid going to jail is like that. But this thing with Dulcie... I don't know. Maybe everyone just felt sorry for her."

After dinner, we drove to the Webster Theater in the South End where there was a movie Kate wanted to see. It was *To Each His Own*, starring Olivia de Havilland and Roland Culver, a real two-handkerchief tearjerker about a small-town girl who has an affair with a pilot during World War I and, after the pilot abandons her, she gives birth to an illegitimate son and puts the baby up for adoption. She ends up devoting her life to loving the boy from afar, pretending to be his aunt. It wasn't the kind of movie I would have chosen, but I didn't mind. Sitting in the dark with Kate, watching the flickering light from the screen illuminate her face, *Gone With the Wind* could have been playing and I wouldn't have cared.

Right after the newsreel, she moved closer, our shoulders touching, and I took her right hand in my left and rested them between the seats. Every so often, I gave her hand a squeeze, and each time she responded by squeezing back and nudging closer to me until the armrest became an annoyance. By the end of the movie, her head was on my shoulder, and my arm was around hers. I didn't want to leave the Webster Theater, ever.

Unfortunately, the house lights came up and it was time to go. She'd been crying, so I offered her my handkerchief. I started to laugh, but she cut me off with an elbow to my ribs.

"Men! You're all alike. I can't believe that didn't affect you." Then she laughed despite herself.

"I guess the story bothered me a little," I said. "After all, there's a World War One pilot who impregnates and then abandons Olivia de Havilland. The only World War One pilot I ever knew was my father, and I hope he was never that gutless."

"Oh, it's just a story. Next time, we'll go see a western."

That she said there would be a next time wasn't lost on me.

Kate took my arm and we strolled down New Britain Avenue. It was still early, so we stopped at a diner for a cup of coffee. I sat down next to her in the booth, rather than across the table, and her effortless acceptance of the seating arrangement made me feel like we were already a couple.

"Tell me," I said. "What do Gwen and Arlen think about you seeing me?"

She dipped her eyes coyly. "It's what I think that matters, Mr. McCoy."

"You know what I mean. They're Greg's parents, and you live with them. Aren't you worried they might think you're being disloyal to their son's memory?"

"Actually, they've been bugging me for months about getting out more and dating. I'm only twenty-five years old. They don't expect me to wear widow's weeds for the rest of my life."

"I suppose I'm relieved, but how do *you* feel about it?"

"Quite honestly, you're the first man I've dated besides Greg—ever—and so far, you've been rather sweet."

"I mean, how do you feel about dating at all?"

She looked exasperated. "Honestly, Jamie! Are all men as dense as you? I loved Greg Hardesty. I still love him, and I always will; but he's gone. It took me a long time to come to grips with the pain, and Arlen and Gwen have been swell—I couldn't have managed without them. In fact, we helped each other through it. But can't you see you're the first man I've wanted to be with since Greg died?"

I didn't know what to say, so I just blinked.

"Kiss me, you idiot," she said.

"What? In public?"

"Ugh!" She grabbed the back of my head and brought her lips to mine. We held the kiss for almost a full minute, and when it was over, I swear I didn't know or care where we were.

CHAPTER 13

Over the next several weeks, I saw Kate nearly every day, and we spent a lot of time with Susan. It was comfortable for all three of us. Gwen and Arlen Hardesty were more than supportive; in fact, they began treating me like a son. Kate and I were falling in love, and my concerns about loyalty to Greg Hardesty's memory began to fade. I drove the Packard more frequently, especially when I was with Kate, so we wouldn't have the roadster's stick shift between us.

One morning, I took a drive to visit the site of the McCoy Machine Works. The road leading to the factory was two miles north of town, right off the Old Hartford Turnpike. The factory consisted of a single rectangular red brick building, three stories high, topped with a steep slate roof, and surrounded by a ten-foot high chain-link fence. The sign at the entrance of the parking lot read, "Pratt & Whitney Aircraft Engine Plant Number 3— Security Clearance Required." At the far side of the parking lot was a gate through the fence with an enclosed guard's booth blocking the entrance.

I pulled into the parking lot, as far away from the guard booth as possible, and sat there in my car, staring at the building beyond the fence. I contemplated asking the plant manager for a tour, but, upon seeing the guard booth, decided it wasn't worth the trouble of explaining my lack of security clearance. Instead, I re-started my car and headed back home, thinking that, if things had been different, if my parents hadn't separated, if my father hadn't disappeared, running this factory might have been my life's work.

My visits to the Granbury library became fewer, as I spent more time at home in my father's study organizing and typing my notes, and looking through articles in back issues of magazines I found in his library. I searched my father's desk, file cabinets, bureau drawers, old suitcases, trunks and attic boxes, and, although I discovered plenty of material on his public exploits, I didn't find anything about his personal life. There were only a few inconsequential papers—old bills, ticket stubs, and a few letters from friends filled with banalities and trivial observations.

On Wednesday, May 22, I went back to the library and noticed a work crew on the green directly across the street installing my father's monument. They spent the better part of the day positioning a granite slab, atop which they placed a six-foot tall granite obelisk. When they were through, they covered it with a canvas tarpaulin and secured it at the base. Over the next several days, the work crew returned to set up a reviewing stand and a speaker's platform.

Later in the week, I ran into Freddie in the periodical archives. He was looking at old articles from the *Hartford Courant* and the *Hartford Times*. He motioned me over to his reading table, where he had several back issues of the papers spread out.

"I traced the names of your father's friends. I remembered reading about Baransky a few years ago. Here, take a look at these."

He indicated the front pages of the June 11, 1942 issues of the two papers. A sub-headline over an article on the far left column of the *Courant* read:

FIVE NAZI SPIES INDICTED

The *Times* ran a story in a middle column with the sub-headline:

FEDERAL GRAND JURY INDICTS FIFTH
COLUMNISTS

I read both stories. On June 10, 1942 a Federal Grand Jury in Hartford indicted five men for conspiracy to violate the Espionage Act of 1917. The men named were Gerhard Wilhelm Kunze, Dr. Otto Willumeit, Dr. Wolfgang Ebell, Reverend Kurt E. B. Molzahn and Boris Nicholaeivich Baransky.

Kunze was the leader of the German-American Bund in the United States, charged with conspiring to furnish vital information to the German and Japanese governments. Willumeit was the former head of the Chicago branch of the Bund. Ebell's part in the alleged conspiracy was serving as a contact man for Kunze and Baransky. Reverend Molzahn's participation was based on his relationship with Kunze and the fact that his home was used as a mail drop. The *Times* article also noted that Molzahn's brother-in-law was the Gestapo chief of the German province of Schleswig-Holstein.

The articles described Baransky, a naturalized American citizen and formerly a reserve officer in the United States Army, as a White Russian nobleman variously known as "B-B" and "Count Boris." The *Times* article said, "For many years, he headed the Russian National Party of Fascists, also known as the Russian Fascist Party, which he founded.... From his national headquarters at his palatial country estate in Thompson, Connecticut, he carried on fascist propaganda activities, principally through a publication known as *The Fascist.*"

On the inside pages, the *Courant* ran an extensive profile of all the conspirators. It said Baransky led a training camp in Thompson where he taught young people Nazi philosophy and military tactics. It alleged that he "maintained an arsenal of approximately ten thousand rifles and assorted pistols in a stone building on the estate." On May 8 and 9, 1942, the FBI searched Baransky's Thompson property and "vast amounts of contraband and illegal material were obtained." Among the articles seized were "file cabinets containing hundreds of documents relating to Baransky's fascist party, numerous weapons and ammunition, a large silk banner with the swastika emblem, two military style coats with swastika emblems on the left arm sleeve, and one box of swastika arm bands."

The *Times* article also listed more than forty other individuals arrested by the FBI in connection with the conspiracy. Among those on the list, Freddie pointed out the names of Carl Funk, George Crossman and John Hauser, all named in the *Mercury* article about the night of the assault on Dulcie Patch.

I was still reeling from all of this when Freddie handed me another edition of the *Times* dated June 15, 1941.

"I also came across this item," he said.

It was a story about an airplane crash in the hills of Barkhamstead in which the pilot and two passengers were killed. The pilot was identified as Drazha Kunetz of Thompson, and the passengers were identified as "Otto Grube (AKA Otto Grebe) and Rikhard Groën (AKA Richard Green), both of Windsor."

I felt claustrophobic sitting in the windowless periodical archive. I loosened my collar and sagged in the hard wooden chair.

Freddie looked at me. "Are you all right?"

I didn't know what to say.

"Jamie, there's a story here, you know."

I was horrified. "Jesus, Freddie, you can't. This will destroy my father's reputation." I hung my head in shame. "I can't believe my father associated with these people. That so-called gun club of his was a front for the Nazis." I felt sick.

Freddie put his left hand on my shoulder and said, "Look, kid, I know what you're thinking, because I'm thinking the same thing. It looks pretty bad, but I won't write anything yet. There's a lot more research to do, and you never know what will turn up."

"But you'll write it eventually, won't you?" It was more a statement than a question.

"Let's see what we can find out first."

"Do you think Ernie was involved in this?"

Freddie shook his head emphatically. "Not a chance. Ernie's one of the few Democrats in town. He bawled like a baby when Roosevelt died. There's no way he'd be mixed up with characters like that."

"I'll bet my life that Eberhardt's in on it. The night of the assault on Dulcie Patch, who does he call but the local Bund Führer—my father. 'Eberhardt' is a German name just like some of the others."

Freddie thought about it. "Could be. Eberhardt's sure mean enough to be a Nazi, but he was born here in Granbury. His ancestors are German, but the family's been here for at least eighty years."

"What about Hank Dietz?" I asked.

"Hank? Nah. He's from western Pennsylvania. I used to assume it was an Amish family, but he once told me that one of his ancestors was a Hessian mercenary during the American Revolution who decided to stay in America after the war was over." Freddie paused. "If Hank knows anything, it's only because he ran your father's farm, but I can't imagine him being actively involved. If I were a Nazi spy, I sure wouldn't trust him. He's too unreliable."

"What do you think I should do?"

"Don't do anything until we find out more. Maybe it isn't what we think. Maybe there's an innocent explanation."

I agreed, but I was skeptical. I started wondering if good old Arthur Wiseman and his private detective friend, Goddard MacFarlane, had held something back. It didn't seem possible that any detective worth his salt could have missed discovering my father's fascist associates, but there was no mention of it in the file Arthur gave me. I decided to re-read the report and track down MacFarlane. And I would confront Arthur Wiseman, too.

CHAPTER 14

During the next several days, I tried to put my dark suspicions about my father out of my mind. The day before Decoration Day, Ted Derwent and Roger Willoughby arrived. They were a Mutt and Jeff pair. Derwent was short and stocky, built like a fire-plug and still looking like a tough Marine despite his fifty-six years. He had played football for Amos Alonzo Stagg at the University of Chicago in the team's glory days. Willoughby was tall and thin with curly blond hair and a winning smile. He looked like a vaudeville comedian rather than the successful automobile dealer he was. He told me later that my father staked him to the money that got him his first Buick dealership in Wallingford in 1922. Derwent was a widower who lost his wife to cancer in '43; Willoughby was twice divorced and apparently very happy about it.

Kate, Susan, Gwen and Arlen Hardesty joined us for dinner, along with Ernie Thayer, Freddie Crowell, Mayor Gibbons and their wives. Dulcie Patch came, too. I had debated whether or not to invite her, but when Mayor Gibbons informed me that she and Roger Willoughby were old friends, I decided it would be rude not to ask her.

The weather was magnificent and, with the days getting longer, I decided to serve cocktails on the terrace before dinner. Hank Dietz acted as bartender and waiter, looking freshly scrubbed and uncomfortable in a white jacket and black tie, and Susan entertained everyone with her rendition of the alphabet song, collecting a penny for her troubles from her indulgent grandfather. Despite the presence of our four-year-old princess, Dulcie made herself the center of attention, flirting shamelessly with both Roger and Ted, and going on about how "glorious" it was to see my father's house restored to its former grandeur.

At 7:30, we were seated in the dining room, and Mrs. Hanratty served a thick vegetable soup followed by roast duck, roasted potatoes and asparagus. Ted regaled us with stories from his football days at the University of Chicago, and Roger talked about my father's student days at Choate and Yale. Over dessert, we chatted about the program for the following day and, after coffee, we moved into the front parlor for cigarettes and after-dinner drinks.

By 9:30, Susan was falling asleep in her mother's lap, so Kate and her in-laws took her home. Dulcie and the Gibbonses, the Thayers and the Crowells left soon after; it was still early, so my father's two old friends and I decided to have some brandy in the library.

Ted and Roger sat next to each other on a sofa near the fireplace, talking, laughing, drinking brandy and smoking cigarettes. I sat opposite them in a leather armchair, separated from the sofa by a low coffee table.

I'd been quiet throughout the evening, leaving much of the conversation to my guests. I wanted to absorb the reminiscences about my father objectively, but ugly thoughts haunted me. Every fond remembrance by Ted and Roger contradicted my belief that my father was involved in something tawdry. I waited for an opportunity to contribute something to the conversation, but each time I thought of something to say, Willoughby or Derwent would break into another story. I finally got a rise out of them when I announced I was writing my father's biography.

Derwent said, "That's wonderful. Maybe I can help. I've got a load of material about the time we spent in France."

"I'd appreciate that, Ted."

Not to be outdone, Roger Willoughby volunteered his support as well. I thought I could shock him by asking about Dulcie Patch and her relationship with my father. Instead of being shocked, he burst out laughing.

"Miss Dulicnea Patch? Isn't she something? Damn if she doesn't look better today than when we were kids—and she was a real looker then, too."

I hadn't realized Roger Willoughby knew her before college, but it turned out that Dulcie had attended Rosemary Hall, Choate's sister school in Greenwich, before going to Connecticut College for Women.

"It sounds like Dulcie was following my father to school."

"Hell, boy, she would've followed your daddy to France if she could've gotten away with it. She threw herself at him every chance she got."

Ted Derwent, who got to know Dulcie following World War One, agreed. "It always seemed to me she'd do anything to get your father's attention."

I said to Roger, "She was flirting with *you* quite a bit tonight."

Roger smiled wistfully. "I used to have a thing for Dulcie when I was a kid, and she sometimes let me think I had a chance with her. But I was just a poor scholarship student from Wallingford. Your father and Johnny Barrow were Yankee aristocrats who had it all, and believe me, Dulcie wanted it all. She just used me to make your father jealous, but it never worked."

"Someone told me she expected to marry my father before he went off to war, and she was upset when he came home married to my mother. Is that true?"

Roger shook his head in amusement. "I can't say what Dulcie thought or didn't think, but I know your father never did anything to encourage her. The Patches were just small town bankers. Sure, they knew your family, but your grandparents had greater aspirations for your father."

He said my father had been shy around women as a teenager, and even as a college student. I could identify with that.

Ted Derwent said, "I don't know what Harry McCoy was like in college, Roger, but when he got to France he sure didn't have any trouble with the ladies—at least not when I knew him."

Ted spoke about my father's army career. He already knew how to fly a plane before he joined up, so he was assigned to the 27th Squadron of the American Air Service First Pursuit Group, along with an Arizonan by the name of Frank Luke, who later became famous as the "Balloon Buster." Captain Luke, along with my father and Captain Eddie Rickenbacker of the 94th, were the only American airmen to win the Medal of Honor in the Great War.

My father arrived in France in April 1918, just before the Royal Flying Corps downed the infamous Red Baron, Manfred von Richtofen. Like Luke and Rickenbacker, he routinely struck out on his own to engage the enemy and, also like them, he irked his commanding officer with his recklessness.

Derwent said, "I was leading a company of Marines on a reconnaissance patrol, trying to find a soft spot in the enemy position, when we walked smack into a pocket of German infantry." He took a long drink and looked me right in the eyes. "You've led men behind enemy lines before, Jamie, so you know what I'm talkin' about. Those Hun bastards caught us by surprise and started ripping us to pieces. Flamethrowers, machine guns, everything they had. We were doomed, and we knew it.

"Then a flight of enemy planes came out of the clouds and began strafing the hell out of us. Suddenly, your father arrived out of nowhere and blasted the hell out of everything in sight. He was a whirlwind—the wrath of God coming out of the heavens to save us. The next thing I know, he's forcing the last Kraut plane to land in a field behind us, and then he's back up again, letting the enemy infantry have it. Your father saved my company's collective ass."

This was how I wanted to remember my father, and I promised myself to keep that image of him in my mind during the ceremony on the green.

* * *

The next morning, I put on the dress uniform Mrs. Glendenning sent down, complete with campaign ribbons and the Distinguished Service Cross. Roger Willoughby wore his old AEF field uniform, which still fit him reasonably well, and Ted Derwent barely squeezed into his old Marine Corps dress uniform.

We drove down to the cemetery at the foot of Gallows Hill, where the parade was assembling. After a brief ceremony during which the American Legion Post Commander said a few words, Reverend Hopewell said a prayer. Next, a bugler played Taps, and the members of the American Legion decorated the veterans' graves with American flags. Several people placed wreaths or bouquets of flowers on gravesites, and Kate, Susan, Gwen and Arlen placed a wreath on Greg's.

After the ceremony, the crowd moved off toward the center of town. The high school band formed up and led the parade out of the cemetery, past the schoolhouse and up Albany Road toward the head of the green. As honorary Grand Marshall, I led the American Legion, closely followed by Sergeant Willoughby and Major Derwent. After the Legionnaires came the local Boy Scout troop, the town's ten police officers, and the sixteen members of the Granbury Volunteer Fire Department. The whole town turned out to cheer as we marched along Albany Road. I saw Ernie and his family, and Freddie and his wife at the curbside in front of the Noll Tavern. Nobbie and his son Larry were there with their families, as were Hank Dietz, his wife and two boys.

When we reached the reviewing stand, the band formed ranks in front of the library, and the American Legion formed up opposite. The crowd lining the streets slowly assembled on the green in front of the reviewing stand. I was pleased to see Kate, Susan, Gwen and Arlen close to the front.

Mayor Gibbons was waiting, dressed in a double-breasted blue suit, and he motioned for Roger, Ted and me to join him on the reviewing stand, along with Dulcie Patch and the town council. Chief Eberhardt, who did his best to ignore me, stood on the lawn near the podium. The Boy Scout troop was given the honor of raising the colors on the flagpole, after which Dulcie led the crowd in the singing of "God Bless America." She was no Kate Smith, but she did a good job nonetheless.

Mayor Gibbons stepped up to the podium and tapped the microphone to draw the crowd's attention.

"Fellow citizens of Granbury," he began. "As we do every year on May 30, we are gathered here today to pay tribute to the memory of the soldiers, sailors and airmen who have given their last full measure of devotion in the service of their country and in the cause of freedom. We give our thanks to God for the peace that so many of them paid the highest price to achieve, and we beseech God's blessing on their immortal souls."

There were quiet murmurings of "amen" from the crowd.

The mayor continued, "We have another purpose today, and that is to dedicate a memorial to one of Granbury's, and indeed one of America's, greatest heroes. Harry McCoy was commended for action above and beyond the call of duty in the First World War, earning the Medal of Honor, this nation's highest military award for valor. After the Great War, he continued to serve his country as a reserve officer, rising to the rank of Colonel. He went on to distinguish himself as one of the world's preeminent aviation pioneers, and he became Granbury's greatest benefactor before losing his life in search of new frontiers to conquer.

"We are privileged to have with us today two of Harry McCoy's dear friends: Theodore Derwent and

Roger Willoughby, both decorated veterans of World War One." The crowd applauded. "I call on them now to unveil the Colonel Jameson Hale McCoy, Jr. Memorial."

Roger and Ted stepped up to the canvas tarpaulin and released the ropes securing the bottom. They pulled it back to reveal the obelisk. On its face was a bronze plaque with raised lettering and the image of my father's tri-motor plane carved at the bottom. On the very tip of the obelisk was a bronze replica of the Medal of Honor. I was overcome with emotion; it was beautiful in its simplicity.

Mayor Gibbons said, "I now call upon our town librarian, Miss Dulcinea Patch, to read the inscription."

The mayor stepped aside and Dulcie read the words.

"Dedicated to the memory of Colonel Jameson Hale "Harry" McCoy, Jr., 1893 – 1934, late of this town and forever in the hearts of its citizens. Soldier – Aviator – American Hero."

The crowd burst into applause, and the band struck up "Columbia the Gem of the Ocean."

Mayor Gibbons returned to the podium after the band finished and tapped the microphone again for attention. "We are honored today by the presence of Harry McCoy's son, Captain Jameson Hale McCoy, III. Jamie has returned to Granbury after having been fourteen years away. Like his father, he returns a hero, holder of the Distinguished Service Cross for conspicuous gallantry in the face of the enemy at great risk to his own life. Jamie's action in the Philippines saved the lives of over three hundred American prisoners of war. Ladies and gentlemen, I give you Captain Jamie McCoy."

Again, the crowd burst into applause. Kate clapped and smiled, and Susan, my personal one-girl fan club, jumped up and down with glee.

I stepped up to the podium and removed my note cards from my pocket. I had agonized for days over what to say.

"I can't begin to tell you how wonderful it has been these past several weeks to be welcomed back to Granbury so warmly. This is my home, and it's good to be here again." The crowd interrupted me with their applause. "And I want to thank Mayor Gibbons for his kind words. You honor me by calling me a hero, but I think it's important to say that what I did in the Pacific was necessary, but it wasn't heroic, and it was no more than that done by millions of others in all of the far-flung theaters of the war. I say that, not out of false humility, but out of respect and admiration for those, like my friend Greg Hardesty, who gave so much more than I did, and who didn't live to see the fruits of their sacrifice." I looked directly at Kate and her family in the front row. Her lower lip trembled, and Gwen stifled a sob.

"You have chosen to pay homage to my father today, and to call him a hero. For this I'm also grateful. In doing so, perhaps you're thinking, not merely of his wartime exploits, but also of his post-war career as a flyer, or of his many generous actions on behalf of this community and its people. True, he was a daring flyer, and as an aviation pioneer, he showed dauntless courage. And it's also true that he gave unfailing support to Granbury. But it seems to me that my father's wartime conduct was the thing that most epitomized him as a hero, in that his actions were motivated by the finest ideals of chivalry and honor. As he so rightly proved, it is more than killing the enemy that defines a hero.

"All too often in the throes of mortal combat, soldiers are carried away by the death and destruction around them. Killing the enemy is the dreadful duty of every soldier, and the best of them hate the thought of killing, but recognize it's necessary to achieve victory and peace. I believe the real heroes in war are those who do that awful duty when they must, yet show mercy when it is theirs to give. That's why my father is a hero, and that's why it's fitting that you honor him today."

Those last words almost stuck in my throat. As I spoke them, images of San Rafael prison camp flashed in my mind, and I thought of that terrible order I gave my men to shoot our Japanese prisoners. No, I really wasn't showing false humility when I asked the crowd not to regard me as a hero. As long as the memory of that terrible day remained with me, I could never think of myself as heroic.

Mayor Gibbons stood up and led the crowd in an ovation, as the band played "The Stars and Stripes Forever."

The program ended with Mayor Gibbons announcing a concert in the band shell at the other end of the green, and giving a one o'clock starting time for the Granbury Road Race. He requested that all race participants assemble at the train station parking lot by twelve-thirty.

CHAPTER 15

I hadn't planned on running in the Granbury Road Race, but Kate and Susan talked me into it. Although I was still in good shape, I had never been a fast runner, and I was loath to embarrass myself by finishing poorly. Roger and Ted agreed to compete despite their age, but they confided that they planned to do a slow jog for most of the way and walk up Gallows Hill rather than knock themselves out trying to run it. They recommended I pace myself early in the race and save my energy for a final burst at the end.

Close to a thousand people gathered on the green to watch the start of the race. Families spread blankets and picnic lunches on the lawn, creating a carnival atmosphere. Shortly before one-o'clock, two hundred eager runners gathered at the train station and advanced as a group to the starting line in front of the library. Kate and her family staked out a spot near my father's monument, and they all waved as I took my position. A member of the high school band climbed atop the roof of the bank and sounded "Call to the Post" on his trumpet. At precisely one o'clock, Chief Eberhardt fired a starter pistol and the runners took off.

The five-mile course went down the north side of the green on Ferry Street, turned left in front of the firehouse, and meandered along a winding road south of the cemetery. Then it turned east through the cemetery, and up Gallows Hill all the way to the Old Hartford Turnpike, and then north back to the center of town. The finish line was directly in front of the bank on Albany Road. Police officers and civilian volunteers were stationed along the route at every intersection to block traffic and watch for accidents among the runners.

I started out well, maintaining a steady pace at the front of the pack with a group of lean and muscular teenagers from the high school track team. At the first turn, I was in sixth position and gaining on the youngsters ahead of me. When we turned up Gallows Hill, I was in second place, pumping hard and ignoring Ted and Roger's advice to pace myself. All I felt was the pulsating rush of adrenaline driving me to compete, and I thought it was possible for me to win.

About a hundred yards up the hill, I began to tire and drop behind; I noticed many of the other runners were just getting their pace and passing me without even breathing hard. Foolishly, I poured it on even more, straining to regain my position at the front, but by the time I came within sight of Kate's house, I felt myself running out of steam. I slowed to a trot, trying to regain my breath, but I continued falling behind.

As I struggled up Gallows Hill, I noticed Chief Eberhardt's nephew standing in Kate's front yard with his arms folded across his chest. His icy stare followed me as I jogged by. I nodded to him, and he responded by resting his left hand on the butt of his sidearm and pointing at me with his right index finger, flicking his thumb like he was shooting. As I passed, I thought I saw him raise his middle finger, but I couldn't be sure. I looked back, but he had already turned away. I put it out of my mind.

As more runners passed me, I struggled to advance up the now oppressive hill. Sweat gushed from every pore in my body, and my leg muscles tightened up. No matter how hard I tried, I couldn't make myself run faster. Finally, I slowed to a fast walk, noticing others ahead of me were doing the same. As I approached the crest of the hill at the Old Hartford Turnpike, I glanced at my watch. About thirty-five minutes had elapsed since the start of the race, and there was still a mile to go. When I reached level ground, my breathing steadied and I picked up speed again. I approached the corner of Albany Road, oblivious to the throng of onlookers cheering as the runners went by. Turning the corner, I managed a final burst of speed heading toward the finish line and crossed the marker. The official timekeeper allotted me thirty-ninth place and posted my time at forty-three minutes and ten seconds. The winner was an eighteen year-old track team member who clocked in at twenty-nine minutes and fifty-one seconds.

I collapsed in a heap on the grass, breathing hard and soaking with sweat. Kate and Susan ran up and hugged me.

"Did you win? Did you win?" Susan squealed.

"No, dear," I said gently between shallow pants for air, "but I sure gave it a go."

Kate handed me a thermos of ice water. I took a long slow drink and then dumped the rest all over my head, causing Susan to laugh hysterically. I sat there, lazily watching the other runners finish, and waved at Ted and

Roger as they crossed the line together near the end of the pack. They came over to join us, both of them far less winded than I was, despite the fact that they were twice my age.

We didn't wait around for the presentation of the win, place and show medals. Instead, Kate helped me up, and the five of us walked back up the hill to the top of the green and over toward the train station where I had parked my car. I plopped into the front passenger seat, and Roger and Ted got into the back with Susan in between them. Kate drove us back to my house.

CHAPTER 16

Later that day, after Roger and Ted left, Susan curled up for a nap on a couch in the front parlor. Kate and I sat together on a rug in front of the fireplace on the other side of the room and talked quietly so as not to wake her.

"I liked your speech today," she said.

I thanked her, but I knew there was something else she wanted to say.

"You were troubled today, Jamie. I could tell, not just from what you said at the ceremony, but from the way you said it."

She already knew me too well. I felt like a hypocrite for standing at the podium and extolling the virtues of chivalry in battle while my own wartime behavior haunted my soul. I could pretend that coming back to Granbury was about trying to rediscover the past, but it was just as much about running away from it. And now that I was learning the truth about my father's conduct, I didn't like it. How could I tell Kate that the great hero of Granbury had consorted with Nazis?

"What if my father wasn't a hero? What if that monument and all it stands for is a fraud?"

She looked confused. "But he *was* a hero. Everyone knows what he did in the last war. And his flying records, and everything he did for this town..."

I was frustrated by my own doubts and my inability to convey my meaning to Kate. "I know, I know. But what if he did something else, something shameful? Would he still be a hero?"

"I don't know what you mean, but I don't see how it would matter. He did what he did, and he was who he was. Nothing you do or say or think can change that." She looked at me tenderly and touched my cheek with her hand. "If you're trying to compare yourself to your father, or live up to an image you have of him, it's not worth it."

She completely misunderstood me. I tried to tell her. "No, I—"

"Shh," she said, and touched my lips with her finger. Then she kissed me.

Later that evening, after Kate and Susan went home and I was alone, I sat at my father's desk and re-read Goddard MacFarlane's report, hoping to find something I'd missed before. As I flipped the pages, I found it difficult to read the white type on the black background of the photo-static copies. Some of the pages slipped onto the floor, and as I bent down to pick them up, I noticed something unusual. Pages 2 and 36 lay together, and the out-of-sequence juxtaposition revealed that different typewriters had printed them.

I examined the other pages more closely; several of them had been retyped and inserted with the originals. As I re-read the report for the third time, now looking for the differences in typeface rather than reading for content, I realized the incomplete sentences I earlier

THE REAL McCOY • 181

ascribed to sloppiness were the result of deliberate alterations.

I retrieved my address book from the top drawer of the desk and found Arthur Wiseman's home telephone number in Brookline, Massachusetts. I dialed the long distance operator and asked her to connect me. When Arthur answered the phone, I did my best to suppress my growing anger.

"Arthur, it's Jamie McCoy. We need to talk."

I related what I discovered about MacFarlane's report, about my father's Nazi friends, and about the 1932 incident involving Paul Jefferson and Dulcie Patch. When I finished, there was silence at the other end of the line, and I thought for a moment we'd been disconnected.

"Arthur? Are you still there?"

Finally, he spoke. His voice was calm and controlled. "I don't know what to say. Some of this is news to me, too."

I was seething. "Really, Arthur? Only *some* of it is news? What did you choose *not* to tell me?"

"Listen, Jamie, you don't understand. It has nothing to do with you. It was your mother's wish—"

"Don't give me that baloney. Did you deliberately alter the detective's report? Just answer me—yes or no."

"Look son," he said. "I'm not in the witness stand here, and I won't be cross examined."

"I'm not your son, Arthur. I'm your client, and you owe me the truth."

My belligerent tone wasn't lost on him, and he responded with his own burst of anger. "Not to put too fine a point on it, but your mother was my client, not you."

"Damn it, I have a right to know everything, no matter how ugly it is. Are you going to tell me the truth or not?"

Again there was silence.

"Arthur? Speak to me."

His anger transformed into resignation. "All right, Jamie. If you insist, I'll tell you everything I know. But please, not on the telephone. I think we should do this face to face."

"Okay. When can you get down here?"

"Absolutely not," he said. "I'll never set foot in that town again. You come here—to my home."

"I'll drive up tomorrow."

"No," he said. "I have appointments all day. Come up on Saturday."

I agreed. I decided driving would be faster than taking the train, and Arthur gave me directions.

The next morning, I telephoned Uncle John and made an appointment to see him in New York the following Wednesday. I offered to meet him at the federal courthouse in Foley Square, but he insisted on a different venue, suggesting instead the Oak Room Bar at the Plaza Hotel.

I also tried to reach Goddard MacFarlane at the phone number listed on his letterhead, but the operator said it was disconnected. I called long distance information, but struck out there too. There was no listing for Goddard MacFarlane, either home or business, in any of the five boroughs.

I thought about calling Arthur back and asking if he knew how to contact the detective, but I decided I didn't want him to know what I was doing. Instead, I telephoned Ed Franklin and told him I was trying to track down an Army buddy I'd lost track of, and asked him if he could recommend a private detective to help me out. He suggested Amos Drayton, an investigator his firm used for litigation support, and gave me the number to call in Hartford.

I called Drayton, and was immediately put through by his secretary when I explained that Ed Franklin of Selwyn & Macy had referred me. I told Drayton the same lie I told Ed Franklin about the missing army buddy.

"You say this fella MacFarlane was a private investigator from New York and a former T-man? Well, there's always the possibility he's dead—that would explain why there's no phone listing—but if the guy's still alive, it shouldn't be too difficult to track him down. P.I.'s are licensed, so the cops'll have a record of him. And I know a few guys at Treasury who might've known him. Ya never know. How soon ya need this?"

I told him I wanted it by Monday if possible, and he agreed to do his best.

"It's twenty-five bucks a day," he said, "plus expenses. Thirty-five a day on the weekends if I have to go into Saturday and Sunday to make your deadline."

"Not a problem," I said. "But I want to make sure you keep this just between us. I don't want anyone else to know I'm looking for MacFarlane. Okay?"

"Don't worry about it, Mr. McCoy. That's why they call us *private* detectives."

Next, I gave Kate a call. I wanted her to come with me to New York.

"I don't know, Jamie," she said. "I really shouldn't."

"If you're worried about appearances, we can get separate hotel rooms. We can get separate hotels, if you'd like."

She laughed. "No, silly, that's not what I was thinking, although I probably should have. It's Susan. I have no one to stay with her. Gwen and Arlen are leaving for Virginia Beach on Saturday for a two-week vacation."

"Then let's take Susan with us. She'll love the city, and we'll get tickets for a matinee. We can take the train on Wednesday morning and spend the night; I have a business meeting on Wednesday evening, but it shouldn't take more than a couple of hours. What do you say?"

"Jamie, you're a better salesman than Nobbie Griffin. We'd love to go."

I reserved a two-bedroom suite at the Plaza Hotel for Wednesday night. I picked the Plaza, not only because it was where Uncle John wanted to meet; the hotel was a New York landmark I knew Susan and Kate would enjoy.

I drove up to Boston in the Mercedes on Friday afternoon so I could spend the night on Van Houghton Row and be fresh for my meeting with Arthur Wiseman the following day. The newest road map in the glove compartment was a B. F. Goodrich touring guide of southern New England dated 1929, and many of the roads had changed since then. The Goodrich map didn't even have numbered routes. I took the Old Hartford Turnpike north toward Springfield, stopping at an Esso station in Suffield to get a fill-up and purchase a new map. While the attendants topped off my tank and checked the oil, I spread my new map out on the counter next to the cash register and plotted my route to Boston. Route 5-A north, on the west side of the Connecticut River to West Springfield. From there, I could cross the Founders' Bridge and pick up U.S. Route 20 east all the way to Boston. At an average speed of forty-five, and allowing for a couple of stops, I figured I could make the trip in no more than three hours.

I telephoned Mr. and Mrs. Glendenning the night before, not wishing to surprise them like I did in March. When I arrived, they both went out of their way to make my second Boston homecoming more pleasant than the first. That evening, after dinner, Mr. Glendenning confided that his wife's earlier attitude was due to her fear that I would sell the house and put them out. I promised him I'd keep the house in Boston, and they could stay as long as they desired. I decided I could reassure them better by asking Arthur Wiseman to arrange a retirement fund. My mother would have wanted me to do that.

CHAPTER 17

On Saturday morning, I got up early and drove to Brookline. Arthur lived on Asbury Road, a broad tree-lined street just outside the Boston city limits. It was an affluent neighborhood with large well-maintained homes; Arthur's house was at the very end of the street—a two-and-a-half story Georgian colonial with white shutters and a detached two-car garage. As I pulled into the driveway, I saw Arthur sitting in a wicker chair on his back porch reading the morning paper and smoking a pipe. He wore a cardigan sweater and an open-collar shirt. He put the paper down and gestured for me to come in through the back door. Together, we went into the kitchen, where we sat down and had a cup of coffee.

Stirring a teaspoonful of sugar into his cup, Arthur looked at me and said, "What do you think of the neighborhood?"

"It's very nice," I said. I fidgeted in my chair; I hadn't come for small talk.

"It *is* nice, isn't it?" He re-lit his pipe and gave me an avuncular smile. "You know, my wife and I bought this house in 1921, when our boys were still little. Of course, Leah's gone now, and the boys are grown men with families of their own."

I thought he was still making small talk, but he seemed to have a purpose in what he was saying.

"My friends think I'm crazy for staying in this big old house by myself," he continued, "but, you know what? They'll have to carry me out of here."

I lit a cigarette and let him go on.

"We were the first Jewish family on Asbury Road. When we tried to buy the house, we were told the neighborhood was restricted."

"Restricted? How?" I asked.

"The other homeowners signed a covenant not to sell to Jews. They were afraid the neighborhood would go to hell if one of us moved in."

I nodded my understanding, still wondering what his point was.

Arthur took another draw on his pipe and blew the smoke in my direction. "Anyway, I took 'em to court and broke the covenant. As you can see, the neighborhood hasn't gone to hell."

"Why are you telling me this?" I asked.

He took a small metal object from the front pocket of his sweater and used it to tamp the tobacco in his pipe. He then re-lit the pipe with a kitchen match. "Let me ask you something." He blew another puff of smoke. "How many Jewish boys went to Groton with you?"

I didn't even have to think about it. "None."

"And how many were at Harvard when you were there?"

"I'm sure there were some."

"But you didn't know any of them, did you?"

"Well, no."

"What about Catholics? Did you know any Catholic boys at Groton or Harvard?"

"Sure," I said immediately. "There were several at Harvard. There were Ambassador Kennedy's two boys—I knew Jack a little."

"Two of them, huh?" He smiled. "Any Negroes?"

I was becoming exasperated. "What's your point, Arthur? Am I a bad person because I went to schools that didn't have a lot of Jews or Catholics or Negroes?"

He took another draw on his pipe. "No, not at all. But humor me for a moment more."

"All right," I said impatiently.

"Tell me about Granbury. Any Jews in Granbury? Any Catholics?"

"I don't know." His questions were annoying me. "I've only been there about a month. I haven't met everyone in town yet."

"That's okay, Jamie. I know the answer. Granbury is as homogenous a town as you'll find anywhere in New England. The closest Jewish family is in Hartford, and the only Catholics probably work for rich folks like you."

I thought about Mrs. Hanratty. "Fine. I still don't understand what all of this has to do with what we discussed on the phone the other day." I jammed my cigarette into the ashtray, sending sparks flying.

Arthur tapped the bowl of his pipe into the ashtray and rested it on the table. "I merely want you to have a sense for the kind of world your family comes from—so you'll understand what happened to me in Granbury."

"Fine. I get the point. I come from a family of rich Yankee bigots. But aren't *you* pre-judging *me* now? I'm not responsible for decisions that were made for me about where and how I was raised or where my parents sent me to school." I glared at him. "My mother was your friend, Arthur, and I always liked you, too. She wasn't a bigot and neither am I."

"I know, Jamie. That's why I should have told you everything about MacFarlane's report before."

"Then why didn't you?"

"I wanted to, but I couldn't. Long ago, I promised your mother I'd never disclose the report's contents to you, but I felt compelled to break that promise, at least partially. I agonized over it for days, but in the end I concluded that if you were planning to return to Granbury, you needed to know why your mother would be disparaged."

He looked sad. I started to speak, but he held up his hand and continued.

"I'm no coward, Jamie—I served in the trenches in 1918—but I was unprepared for what happened to me in Granbury. If it hadn't been for God MacFarlane, I probably would have been killed."

Then he told me the whole ugly truth.

After my father disappeared in 1934, Ed Franklin visited my mother in Boston to disclose the irregularities with my father's affairs. Because my parents were separated, he recommended she engage her own counsel to represent her interests.

Arthur said, "She came to me, of course, but I was reluctant because it wasn't my specialty and I knew I wouldn't be welcome in Granbury. But your mother was distraught, and, to be honest, I found it difficult to refuse her anything."

"Were you in love with my mother?"

He looked at me over the rims of his glasses. "I suppose I was. But the feeling wasn't mutual, Jamie. She loved your father until the day she died."

"Then why did she leave him?"

"I can only guess. As I told you once before, she never discussed it with me. I think she became terrified of what he was becoming."

"Was he a fascist?"

"I don't know for sure, but your mother believed he was."

Arthur then related what happened to him in Granbury in April and May of 1934. He drove down there, not knowing what he would find, and was confronted with an enigma. He spent almost a week at my father's house and at the factory, sifting through my father's private papers, but nothing he found solved the mystery.

"When someone dies suddenly, they usually leave a mess of loose ends with a complicated paper trail for their heirs to unravel. But your father left almost nothing behind. Either he destroyed his personal papers before he left on his last flight, or someone else cleaned it all out after he disappeared."

When Arthur visited the McCoy Machine Works, he found the employees close to panic. There were no new orders and there was no money in the company's bank account. Ed Franklin and Arthur obtained a court order to open my father's safe deposit box at the Granbury Bank. Inside, they found detailed instructions providing for the dissolution of his affairs.

Each member of his household staff received $2,500 in cash from my father's personal accounts, as did every employee of the McCoy Machine Works—the sum came to three quarters of a million dollars. Trust funds were established for my mother and me, and a special trust was created for the preservation and maintenance of my father's property in Granbury, to be turned over to me when I reached my twenty-fifth birthday. A provision of the preservation trust guaranteed Henry Dietz a job as caretaker at an annual salary of $4,000; if I were ever to sell the property, Hank would receive a lifetime payment of $2,500 per year from the income of the trust.

"Except for the Dietz provision, none of it seemed unusual for someone like your father," Arthur said. "He'd always been generous to a fault with his employees, but your mother thought Hank Dietz was one of the most unreliable employees on the estate, and she didn't understand your father's loyalty to him."

The real problem was that much of the McCoy family money had disappeared. A check of the bank records—a bank my father had controlled since the suicide of Dulcie's brother—revealed that he'd liquidated most of his fortune over the previous two years. Additionally, the company books and records exposed operating losses for every month during the same period. There was no working capital left, and the company couldn't meet another payroll. Arlen Hardesty was desperately concerned that people would think he embezzled the company's funds; he willingly opened up the records to the lawyers, but they realized they needed the help of an outside auditor.

It was the auditor who suspected tax fraud. It appeared that my father created the two fictitious companies through which he funneled money from his personal accounts. He used those companies to purchase aircraft engine parts from McCoy Machine Works at a price below fair market value.

I didn't understand how tax fraud could be involved.

Arthur tried to explain. "Your father's money was invested in income-producing assets, creating a large personal income on which he had to pay high taxes. As he liquidated those assets, the income and his tax obligation diminished. We suspected he funneled his personal fortune through the dummy companies to purchase products that he then re-sold at a profit, making the source of the profits difficult to trace. The two dummy companies never paid taxes, and, if what we suspected was true, your father hid about seventy million dollars—probably in foreign bank accounts—the income from which wasn't taxable in the U.S. We assumed his death prevented him from completing the scheme, and we wanted to find the missing money."

On behalf of my mother, Arthur obtained receivership of the company and he shut it down. He decided they needed a private investigator with experience detecting tax fraud schemes, and the auditor recommended Goddard MacFarlane, a former Treasury agent from New York who had once worked with Elmer Irey, the T-man who had nailed Al Capone for tax evasion.

At that point, Ed Franklin recused himself because he represented my father's interests, and he wanted no part of uncovering potential wrongdoing. MacFarlane came to Granbury and interviewed everyone who ever had contact with my father. He then hired an army of accountants to re-examine the books in greater detail.

Arthur said, "Goddard MacFarlane was an imposing man—built like a linebacker and twice as tough. His colleagues referred to him as 'God.' As long as he was around Granbury, no one bothered me."

But MacFarlane soon went back to New York to trace the phony companies, leaving Arthur behind to wrap up the affairs of the factory. Arthur stayed at my father's house, waking up one morning to find his car painted with red swastikas.

"I called the police, but Chief Eberhardt merely said it might be best if I left town."

"Eberhardt's not the most charming personality in Granbury," I said.

Arthur grimaced. "He's a lot worse than that, Jamie." He stuffed his pipe with tobacco again and lit up. "I told God MacFarlane about it, and he suggested I move out of your father's house and into a hotel, so I got a room at a motor lodge in Suffield a few miles up the road. One evening, when I was working late at the factory, I looked out the window and saw my car ablaze in the parking lot."

Eberhardt responded by accusing Arthur of having set the fire himself.

"I was pretty shaken up," he said. "I telephoned for a cab and offered them fifty bucks to pick me up at the factory and drive me to Suffield. About fifteen minutes after I got to the hotel, there was a knock at my door, and four hooded goons hauled me out of the room and into the parking lot." Arthur trembled as he told the story. "They dragged me into the woods, tied me to a tree and pistol-whipped me. I would have died that night, but God MacFarlane showed up and saved me."

As the four men were beating Arthur, MacFarlane arrived on the scene with a shotgun and fired a blast into the air. The goons froze in their tracks, and MacFarlane made them untie Arthur and remove their hoods. One of them was Chief Victor Eberhardt. MacFarlane made them lie down while he checked the driver's licenses of the other three; they were Otto Grebe, Ernest Lieber and George Crossman, three of my father's Nazi pals.

Eberhardt suddenly went for his gun, but MacFarlane was too quick for him. He fired the shotgun, taking the chief's left foot off just above the ankle.

"I was in agony, but I managed to pick up Eberhardt's gun and hold the others at bay," Arthur said. "Then God MacFarlane astonished me. He told the other three men to take Eberhardt and get him to a hospital. Eberhardt was writhing on the ground, and MacFarlane said to him, 'We'll keep our mouths shut about this, and you do the same. No one ever finds out what happened here tonight.'

"I spent the next ten days in a Springfield hospital, recovering from three broken ribs, a punctured lung and a bruised kidney. A few days before I was released, MacFarlane came to see me and told me the investigation was over."

Goddard MacFarlane had driven up from New York on the night of Arthur Wiseman's attack to tell him that a former colleague from the Justice Department advised him to back off the case. If he refused, they'd see to it that his license was revoked.

I asked, "Why would the Justice Department interfere with MacFarlane's investigation?"

Arthur retrieved a large accordion envelope from one of the kitchen drawers. He removed some old newspapers and handed them to me. "I didn't find much at your father's house, but these arrived in the mail for him after he disappeared."

They were issues of the Baransky's newspaper, *The Fascist*.

Arthur snarled, "They're disgusting—the worst kind of racist garbage. And your father was a subscriber." He handed me a sheaf of typed papers from the envelope. "These are the missing pages from God MacFarlane's report to your mother. He discovered that your father had organized a group of German-Americans allied with Boris Baransky's Russian Fascists. The Justice Department was investigating both organizations, and they didn't want MacFarlane to interfere."

I felt like crying. I thought Arthur Wiseman couldn't tell me anything worse, but then he did.

"God MacFarlane suspected your father was illegally selling contraband aircraft engine parts to Germany. He also believed your father didn't die in the flight to Africa. In fact, he suspected from the beginning that the flight was an elaborate cover story for him to flee the country."

My head throbbed. I massaged my temples with my thumb and index finger, trying to dull the pain. "Are you saying my father might still be alive?"

"I don't know for sure, but MacFarlane thought so. He believed your father set up the dummy companies to get his money out of the country in advance of the flight, and that he'd been planning it for more than a year before he disappeared. It's all in the report."

"This is incredible. But where did he go?"

"MacFarlane thought Germany; but he was told to back off before he could prove it. Needless to say, your mother was devastated, and she didn't want you to know the truth."

Arthur couldn't have hurt me more if he'd hit me with a bat. I was aghast; at last I understood why my mother never again spoke of my father. He was a defector—a traitor. I didn't think I could bear anymore, but I asked, "Why would my father betray his country? It doesn't make sense. He was a war hero. He was famous."

"So? Lindbergh was a hero, and more famous than your father. He was a Nazi sympathizer, too."

I felt ill. I just wanted to leave—to get in my car and drive away and never stop. I didn't know how I'd find the strength to return to Granbury.

CHAPTER 18

Amos Drayton telephoned me Monday morning with news about the mysterious Goddard MacFarlane.

"MacFarlane's a tough guy to track down, but I discovered a lot."

Richard Goddard MacFarlane was born in Newburgh, New York on August 8, 1895. He attended public primary schools and went to high school at the New York Military Academy in nearby Cornwall-on-Hudson; he went on to Columbia University, where he played both varsity football and baseball and graduated second in his class. During the First World War, he served as a first lieutenant in the 165th New York Infantry Regiment—the famous "Fighting 69th"—under Colonel William "Wild Bill" Donovan. Upon his return from France, he attended Columbia Law School, again graduating with distinction. After passing the Bar in 1922, he spent a year and a half serving as a deputy assistant U.S. attorney under Donovan in Buffalo.

In 1924, President Coolidge's Attorney General, Harlan Stone, went on a campaign to rid the Justice Department of the corruption left over from the Harding Administration. Stone appointed J. Edgar Hoover acting director of what was then called simply the Bureau of

Investigation; Stone appointed Wild Bill Donovan as Assistant Attorney General with direct authority over Hoover and the Bureau. Goddard MacFarlane followed Donovan there, working as a Special Investigator under Hoover. When Donovan left the Justice Department in 1929, MacFarlane requested and received a transfer to the Treasury Department.

Drayton's sources at the Justice Department revealed that the transfer was a result of a conflict with Hoover; Donovan and Hoover were archrivals, and MacFarlane was a Donovan protégé. MacFarlane's work with Elmer Irey in the Capone investigation arose from his feud with Hoover. Hoover wanted nothing to do with investigating bootleggers, partly because it was Donovan's idea. It was MacFarlane who sold Irey on the notion of going after the gangsters on tax evasion charges.

In early 1933, when the new Roosevelt administration loaded the Treasury Department with Democratic appointees, MacFarlane quit and became a private detective in New York.

"He was a brilliant investigator and his colleagues liked him a lot," Drayton said. "The only one who didn't was Hoover."

"Where is he now?" I asked. "How can I get in touch with him?"

"That might be difficult. He's fallen off the face of the earth."

"What do you mean?"

"MacFarlane closed his office in July '41 and didn't renew his private dick's license. He disconnected his phone and moved out of his apartment. I checked the

New York Bureau of Vital Statistics, but they have no record of him after 1941, not even a death certificate."

"What about family—wife and kids?"

"No record of a marriage."

"He couldn't have been drafted; he would have been too old," I said.

"I already checked. Other than World War I, there's no military record." Drayton lowered his voice. "The only thing that makes sense to me is intelligence work—the OSS. Wild Bill Donovan ran intelligence operations in '41, and he might have recruited his former pal MacFarlane to go along. Anyway, I checked for telephone listings in Washington, Virginia and Maryland. No luck."

My initial thought was naive. "Have you tried calling the OSS?"

Drayton laughed. "I would, but President Truman disbanded it last year, right after the war ended." He paused. "One of my contacts told me the War Department absorbed a few of the old OSS departments. I called the federal personnel administration office, but they had no listing for MacFarlane—or at least none they'd tell me about."

"What can I do then?"

"Try calling the War Department switchboard and ask for him."

"That's it? That's all you've got for me?" I was annoyed.

"I don't know what else to tell you, Mr. McCoy. Your man has either flown the coop, he's dead, or he's a government spook. I can't think of any other alternatives."

I thanked Drayton and asked him to send me a bill. As preposterous as it sounded, the only thing left was to telephone the War Department. I got the number from long-distance information and placed the call.

A woman with a southern accent picked up on the first ring. "War Department. May I help you?"

"I'm trying to locate Richard Goddard MacFarlane." I spelled the last name for her.

She asked if he were civilian or military, and I said I didn't know. "One moment, sir, and I'll try to find a listing."

The operator put me on hold, and about a minute later, she came back on the line. "I'll put you through to an information officer, sir."

The line clicked and buzzed, and then rang through. A man answered. "Captain Wallace speaking. How may I help you?"

Once again, I explained whom I was trying to reach. Captain Wallace hesitated, almost imperceptibly, and then asked me to identify myself. It was my turn to hesitate. I decided to use my old military rank.

"Captain Jameson McCoy, U.S. Army Reserve."

Captain Wallace said, "There's no listing of the name Richard Goddard MacFarlane in the War Department, Captain McCoy. But I'd be happy to check further and get back to you if you'd care to leave a telephone number."

I left my number, but I doubted I'd hear back from Captain Wallace anytime soon.

I spent the rest of the day moping and worrying, trying to rationalize my father's behavior but not succeeding. Other people in Granbury must have known. Certainly Chief Eberhardt, Hank Dietz, Kate's father-in-law and Dulcie Patch knew. And I wondered how much Ernie Thayer knew. Freddie Crowell expected me to tell him what I found out, but I didn't want to see my father's name sullied in the newspaper.

My image of Granbury and its people had changed, and I didn't know whom to trust. There was only one person I felt sure of, and that was Kate. I telephoned her at home after work and asked her to have dinner with me. She was home alone with Susan and couldn't go out; instead, she asked me to the Hardesty house for dinner, an invitation I gratefully accepted.

Kate couldn't help seeing I was upset. Susan, however, was her usual chatty self and didn't noticed anything wrong. After we put her to bed, Kate mixed cocktails, and we sat in the living room, nestling on her mother-in-law's camelback sofa.

"What's wrong, Jamie? You seem distraught."

"I hardly know where to begin," I said.

She put her hand on my knee and looked deeply into my eyes. "Just start at the beginning and keep talking. I promise to be a good listener."

So I told her everything. I tried to be dispassionate—neutral in my choice of words—because I didn't want to influence her opinion. When I finished, she poured more drinks. I lit two cigarettes and passed one to her.

Kate was an inexpert smoker—she picked up the habit from her late husband, and she didn't smoke often. After a few half-hearted puffs, she stubbed it out in the ashtray.

"What are you going to do now?" she asked, stroking my hair.

"I don't know whether to scream everything to the world or keep it quiet and pretend nothing happened."

Kate sipped her drink. "At least one man would want you to keep it quiet—Chief Eberhardt." She took another sip. "I never liked him."

"What about Arlen?" I asked. "What do you think he'd want?"

She lowered her eyes. "I can't believe he knew anything about this, Jamie. He'd never allow himself to get mixed up with people like that. Arlen Hardesty is one of the kindest men I've ever met. He's been like a father to me."

I lifted her chin in my hand and said, "Don't get me wrong, Kate, I like Arlen, too, but he clammed up when I asked him about my father's weekend visitors."

She turned her face away and then looked back at me. "If Arlen knew anything about your father's activities and didn't tell you, he was only trying to protect you."

I told her about my plans to meet John Barrow in New York on Wednesday. I'd decided to tell Uncle John everything I knew and ask him for advice. There was a good chance that he, too, knew about my father's activities. I asked Kate if she and Susan still wanted to come with me under the circumstances.

"Of course I do, Jamie. I want to be there for you, and Susan is so looking forward to it."

I was grateful for her support. We talked long into the night, and Kate suggested I sleep over, but, as much as I wanted to stay, I insisted on going home. I didn't want the neighbors talking.

Early Wednesday morning, I picked up Kate and Susan, and we drove to Union Station in Hartford where we caught an express to New Haven. We changed trains in New Haven, getting on the Yankee Clipper to Grand

Central in Manhattan. From there, we took a taxi to the Plaza Hotel at Fifth Avenue and 59th Street.

Kate was excited, and Susan was wide-eyed with wonder. This was her first trip to New York, and she greedily ogled every building and passing car, not wanting to miss anything. Kate and I reveled in her enthusiasm.

We registered as J. H. McCoy and Family, getting a two-bedroom suite. The rooms were palatial—fifteen-foot ceilings with crown moldings and towering windows overlooking Central Park. The living room was magnificently appointed, complete with a working fireplace and a full bar setup. I'd promised the girls a Broadway show, and Susan fidgeted in anticipation.

"When are we gonna see the show, Mummy?"

I suggested the matinee performance of *Pygmalion* with Gertrude Lawrence and Raymond Massey, but Kate vetoed the idea.

"You obviously don't have much experience with four-year-old girls," she said. "A movie musical is a better idea."

The concierge suggested we see *The Harvey Girls* at Radio City Music Hall, starring Judy Garland and Ray Bolger. I tipped the man five dollars, and he made the reservations for us, arranging will-call tickets at the box office.

The movie was hokey, but Susan loved the singing and dancing—and she thought the Rockettes show after the movie was the best thing she'd ever seen. After the movie and the Rockettes, we strolled down Sixth Avenue and ate lunch at the outdoor café in front of the Hotel St. Moritz, followed by sundaes at Rumplemeyer's next door.

By three o'clock, Susan was ready for a nap, but Kate and I had a difficult time convincing her to lie down, succeeding only after I promised her a horse and buggy ride through Central Park for the following morning.

There was a console radio next to the fireplace, so I tuned in a popular music station, keeping the volume low so it wouldn't disturb Susan. I removed my jacket, loosened my tie and mixed myself a Scotch and soda while Kate got Susan settled, and then poured one for her when she joined me a few minutes later. Kate removed her shoes. She took the drink and curled up next to me on the couch.

"What are you going to tell Judge Barrow?" she asked.

I looked at my watch. It was already ten after three, and my date with Uncle John downstairs in the Oak Bar was for four o'clock. "Everything, I guess. I'll bet there's more he can tell me than I can tell him."

We cuddled on the couch for a while, not saying anything, just slowly sipping our drinks and listening to the music on the radio. At last we kissed, holding it for a long time. I desperately wanted to make love to her, and I sensed she was ready, but time was short and I had to head down to the lobby.

I stood up and put my jacket on. Kate stood also and leaned against my body, kissing me again. Then she smiled and straightened my tie.

"I'll be waiting here, my darling. Be strong."

"I love you," I said.

She kissed me, slowly and sweetly. "I love you, too."

* * *

When I arrived at the Oak Bar, Uncle John was waiting for me in a corner table by the window. Though I hadn't seen him in years, I recognized him from his trademark blue polka dot bowtie. He recognized me, too; he stood up and walked over, extending his hand and grasping my shoulder.

"Jamie, my boy. You look great. The Army must have agreed with you."

"Hardly, Uncle John."

He was fifty-three, but he looked younger. He was a good inch or two taller than me, still slender, and without a trace of gray in his wavy brown hair. He looked me up and down like a long-lost son.

We sat down and ordered drinks from the waiter. I had another Scotch and soda, and he ordered a dry martini.

For almost an hour, I told him everything I knew—except Arthur Wiseman's suspicion that my father might still be alive. We had two more drinks, and I must have gone through a dozen Luckies. Uncle John asked a few questions, nodding at every new revelation.

When I was all talked out, he sighed and averted his eyes. He said, "I didn't come to Granbury last week because I felt your father's memory wasn't worth honoring."

"Because he was a fascist?"

He shook his head. "No, that wasn't it. To be honest, before today I didn't know the half of it." He lit a cigarette and took a sip of his martini. "I knew about his unsavory friends, but I didn't think he was a fascist. I had other reasons for distancing myself." He drained his glass.

In September 1932, while Uncle John was Connecticut's Attorney General, the state police received an all-points-bulletin from Granbury to be on the lookout for Paul Jefferson—wanted for rape, resisting arrest, and fleeing to evade prosecution.

A pair of state troopers stopped a truck carrying my father's Negro laborers on the Boston Post Road, but Jefferson wasn't with them. They all had a similar tale to tell, and even when questioned separately, none of them wavered. They described the Granbury police and the vigilantes surrounding them on my father's estate. The Negroes swore that Jefferson was in his dormitory when the alleged rape occurred; but the Granbury police ignored the alibi.

The Negroes watched Chief Eberhardt cuff Jefferson's hands and lead him to the barn; they watched him shove Jefferson inside and close the doors. And moments later, they heard four gunshots. The next day, the workers packed up and left.

When he received the state police report, Uncle John ordered an investigation, but nothing came of it. All the white witnesses, except my father and Hank Dietz, corroborated Chief Eberhardt's version. My father and Hank claimed they were upstairs in the barn and hadn't seen or heard anything.

Uncle John said, "Later that fall, your father and I went to the annual Harvard-Yale regatta on the Thames." He lit another cigarette and blew the smoke toward the window. "I asked him what happened that night, but he got angry and refused to discuss it. His silence told me all I needed to know."

"Are you suggesting my father was an accessory to murder?"

"I don't know if he was an accessory, but I'm almost certain he was a material witness," he said. "I never found out, because a few weeks later, two FBI agents came to my office and asked me to drop the whole thing. They said your father was involved in a more serious federal case, and my investigation was interfering."

"And you agreed?"

"Not at first, but the pressure from Washington was relentless. Finally, the Governor ordered me to back off. I had no choice. My consolation prize was an appointment as U.S. Attorney for the State of Connecticut."

"They paid you off with a plum job." I was disgusted.

Uncle John swirled his martini in the glass and puffed on his cigarette. Then he lowered his voice and said, "I was on President Hoover's short list for the appointment anyway, but yes, they bought my silence."

I shook my head sadly. "I used to think you and my father were great men."

"No, Jamie, we were just men. For all I know, your father told the truth and he didn't witness the murder; but in the end, it didn't matter. After the regatta, I never heard from him again. He disappeared over the Atlantic a year and a half later, and I saw no point in destroying his reputation."

"What about now? You're a federal judge with a lifetime appointment. No one can stop you from reopening the case."

"It doesn't work that way. It's not a federal matter, and judges don't decide what cases to pursue. Even if I could convince the Connecticut A.G. to reopen it, he'd have to find witnesses to corroborate the Negroes' story."

"So that's it? My father flies off into the sunset, and Chief Eberhardt gets away with murder."

"Eberhardt's a bully, Jamie, and my advice is to steer clear of him."

"What about Dulcie Patch? She must know something."

He shrugged. "She refused to cooperate when it happened; I doubt she'd start now. I've known Dulcie for as long as I've known your father, and she was always strange. You never know what she's capable of doing."

"Would you have thought my father capable of consorting with Nazis and murderers?"

"No, not in a million years."

I was exasperated, and I didn't know what I wanted anymore. The thought of Eberhardt getting off scot-free turned my stomach, but the price of justice would likely include ruining my father's name too.

Uncle John looked at his watch. "I've got to go."

He had to review briefs from Nuremberg in preparation for the trials of the lesser war criminals.

"I was hoping to be one of the judges, but I'll probably end up prosecuting," he said.

Uncle John insisted on paying our bill, and he left me with promises to see me again before he left for Germany.

* * *

It was after six when I returned to the suite. Kate was reading to Susan from a storybook, and I walked over and kissed them both. I suggested we go out for dinner, but Kate said it might be better to order from room service. Susan was exhausted; Kate thought she might fall asleep in the restaurant and we'd be stuck having to carry her back to the hotel.

I ordered a prime rib dinner for Kate and me, and a hamburger with French fries for Susan. As we waited for our order to arrive, Kate distracted Susan by giving her a Minnie Mouse coloring book. As Susan settled down at the coffee table with her crayons, I took Kate aside and told her about my conversation with Uncle John.

"This is terrible," she said. "What are you going to do?"

I put my hand on the small of her back and drew her close to me. "There's nothing I can do right now, but when we get back to Granbury, I'm going to confront Hank Dietz and beat the truth out of him if I have to."

She rested her head against my chest and whispered, "Be careful, Jamie. I'm afraid of what Chief Eberhardt might do if he finds out you're poking into this."

After dinner, we listened to *The Lone Ranger* and *The Green Hornet* on the Mutual Network. Susan was delighted with the shows, but I noted that Kato, the Green Hornet's faithful valet, had somehow become a Filipino. He'd been Japanese before the war.

Kate put Susan to bed at eight o'clock, and at eight-thirty, she emerged from her bedroom wearing a low-cut, long blue negligee that sent my heart racing. I tuned the radio to the *Bayer American Melody Hour* on CBS, where a female singer gave her rendition of "Till the End of Time." I scooped Kate into my arms, and we danced until the song was over. I took her by the hand and led her into the other bedroom; we melted into each other's arms and onto the bed, where we made love.

We were tentative at first, each of us trying to please the other, but it soon became natural, and it felt like we'd been lovers for years. This was unlike anything I'd experienced in my college days, with the attendant guilty rush of surreptitious passion in cheap hotels. Instead, I felt only pleasure and an overwhelming need to please her.

Later, sometime after midnight, Kate put on her nightgown and returned to the other bedroom. Before she left, she kissed me on the forehead.

"I'd better be there when Susan wakes up in the morning," she said. "I don't want her to be frightened."

I looked at her with longing eyes. "Marry me," I said.

She knelt by the bed and kissed me again, this time on the lips. "Yes, my darling," she whispered.

CHAPTER 19

I didn't waste any time before confronting Hank Dietz when we returned to Granbury. Mrs. Hanratty informed me he was working in the barn; I drove out there and found him on the lower level replacing the hasp and lock on my father's gun locker.

He was surprised to see me—even more so when I revealed the purpose of my visit. I held nothing back. I demanded he tell me everything he knew about the assault on Dulcie Patch and the disappearance of Paul Jefferson.

His face went white. "I swear to you, Mr. McCoy. I already told you everything. I didn't see nothin' that night—honest."

His hands trembled and his mouth twitched.

I decided to bluff. "Look, Hank. I'll make it easy for you. I already know Jefferson didn't escape. He was murdered." Hank started to shake his head violently in denial, but I cut him off. "Don't bother, Hank. I know my father was involved, so there's no use trying to lie about it. I'm not interested in what you did or didn't do. I'll never tell anyone. I just want to know the truth about my father."

He hung his head, staring at the stone floor. "Please, Mr. McCoy, don't ask me about this no more."

I gave him no quarter. "Either you tell me everything, Hank, or you're fired. And I'll stop your annuity, too."

Hank looked at me, puzzled. I realized he didn't know what an annuity was.

"The yearly payment my father arranged for you," I said. "I'll cancel it."

That he understood. "You can't do that. Your daddy promised me. I got it in writing."

"I can and I will." I was lying, but he didn't know that. There was no legal way to break my father's trust. "I have the best lawyers in the state—Selwyn & Macy— and they can do anything. So talk."

Hank dropped the screwdriver he'd been holding in his right hand. He turned away from me and sat down on his toolbox, holding his forehead in his hands. He was a defeated man.

Hank reached into his jacket pocket and pulled out an envelope. He handed it to me and said, "I lied to you about your father's friends. It was more than a gun club."

I opened the envelope and found a dozen snapshots of my father with a group of men dressed in black military uniforms with Sam Browne belts and red armbands. On the armbands, there was a silver lightning bolt—exactly like the so-called water stain over the front door of my father's house.

"Where did you get these?"

"They was in the gun locker, under a box of ammo."

"Okay, Hank, spill it. Tell me about Paul Jefferson's murder."

"It didn't happen zactly like I told you before, Mr. McCoy," he began, almost in a whimper. "That night, when Chief Eberhardt called your daddy, I wasn't here. I just got home, and my wife, Maggie, she got a phone call from Doc Holcomb. He wanted her to come over right away." He looked up at me and said, "Maggie was the Doc's nurse. Anyway, I says to her, 'What's wrong?' and she says, 'Doc Holcomb claims someone raped Dulcie Patch and I gotta go over and help.' Then your daddy called and told me to come over to the house right away, so I dropped Maggie off at Doc Holcomb's and I met the Colonel here at the barn."

Hank trembled as he spoke, frightened, not only of what he was telling me, but of what I was going to do about it.

By the time Hank arrived at the barn that night, it was already eight o'clock. My father was waiting for him at the gun locker with Chief Eberhardt and his deputies. Eberhardt was afraid the Negroes would resist, and he wanted an armed posse surrounding them. My father then telephoned Boris Baransky, who alerted his cohorts.

Baransky's men arrived in small groups; they were instructed to drive to the back of the barn with their lights out so they wouldn't alert the Negroes. At ten o'clock, my father told Hank to light up the airstrip for Baransky and Drazha Kunetz, who were flying in from Thompson. By eleven, all the vigilantes had assembled in the barn and my father passed out the guns; Chief Eberhardt took his own revolver and led the men to the dormitories.

Hank said, "Your daddy and the Count and me stayed in the barn on the upper level, watchin' through the window."

It was a warm clear September night, lit by a three-quarter moon. Hank saw and heard everything. Eberhardt called out through a megaphone for Jefferson to surrender. There was a commotion inside, the door opened and three Negro laborers came out onto the grass to confront the posse. Jefferson wasn't among them.

Chief Eberhardt ordered the posse to aim their weapons at the three men and announced that, if Jefferson didn't surrender, he'd order his men to fire. Upon hearing the chief's threat, Jefferson came out with his hands up, bare-chested and dressed in denim overalls and work boots. Eberhardt handcuffed him and marched him into the barn at gunpoint.

Hank said, "The three of us—your daddy and Count Baransky and me—we went over to the top of the stairs and started to go down. We made it about halfway, when the chief—he opened up and shot the nigger fella right in the back. Three times. That nigger went down on the stone floor like a sack of dirt. Then the chief shot him again in the back of the head. I never seen so much blood."

Hank started sobbing into his hands. I didn't say a word.

"The chief was cussin' him out and kickin' the body. He was crazy. I thought he was gonna shoot the body again, but your daddy ran over and pulled him off." Hank looked like he was going to throw up.

Two of the cops outside the barn tried to come in, but my father shooed them away. Hank and Baransky disarmed the chief, and my father took command. He told Hank to wrap the body in a canvas tarp, and he ordered Baransky to go outside and keep the others away. Chief Eberhardt finally calmed down, and he and Hank removed the body and took it in Hank's truck out to the lake, where they tied it, weighted it down with cinderblocks, and dumped it into the deep.

Hank said, "I was scared and I was ashamed, Mr. McCoy, but no one had to tell me to keep my mouth shut. I didn't wanna go to jail."

I looked at him, hating what they'd done to that poor man and sick at heart about my father's complicity. But Hank was nothing more than a poor simpleton who was coerced by his boss and a crooked cop. "It wasn't your fault, Hank. They made you do it. The Chief might have killed you, too, if you refused."

Hank looked at me with pleading eyes. "You don't get it, Mr. McCoy. The whole thing—it was all for nothin'. When I got home that night, it was after three. Maggie was at the kitchen table drinkin' coffee, waitin' for me. She says, 'Doc Holcomb and me examined Miss Patch, and there wasn't a scratch on 'er.'"

"I don't understand."

Hank said, "Miss Patch wasn't raped." He shook his head. "There weren't no bruises or scratches or nothin' else. My wife and Doc Holcomb examined her—her privates, ya know what I mean? She was still a virgin. I swear, my wife said she was still a virgin."

I stared at him in disbelief. "But why, Hank? Why would Dulcie say she was raped?"

He shook his head again. "I don't know, Mr. McCoy. I plain just don't know. But that nigger fella got killed fer nothing."

The enormity of it seared my mind. I lost my balance and staggered back, but I broke my fall with my right hand against the stone wall. I steadied myself and reached into my jacket pocket for a cigarette. When I brought the match to the tip, my hand shook so much that it went out. I lit the cigarette on the second try and took three long drags, hacking as I exhaled the smoke into the barn.

Hank said, "When I told your daddy what Maggie said about Miss Patch, he ordered me never to tell no one, and I ain't till now."

I stammered, unsure of what to do next. "I don't...I don't know what to say. You can't just let these people get away with it. It's wrong, Hank, it's just plain wrong."

Hank stood up and begged. "No, Mr. McCoy. You can't say anything. I don't wanna go to no jail. I didn't kill that poor fella. I was just followin' your daddy's orders."

When he said that, I froze. He was just following orders—my father's orders. I'd seen newsreels about the concentration camps; the Allies were still trying to count the millions of nameless dead. The Nazi leaders were about to go on trial in Nuremberg, and their sickening refrain was, "I was just following orders."

Hank said, "You can't tell no one about this, Mr. McCoy. Not just for my sake, but fer yours, too. Chief Eberhardt's a powerful man around here, and he won't take kindly to anyone interferin' with him."

I stared blankly, my senses dulled from shock.

Hank looked down at the stone floor and absently kicked some loose hay. He said, "That nigger fella's dead, and there ain't no one can bring 'im back. Best you just leave it alone like I been doin' all these years."

I told Hank to go home. I needed to be alone and figure out what to do. I stood there in the barn for a long time, perhaps on the very spot where Victor Eberhardt gunned down Paul Jefferson right in front of my father. Almost without thinking, I examined the stone floor for bloodstains, but in the dim light, I couldn't discern any discoloration. If there were any ghosts in that place, they were sleeping, and my presence could only disturb them.

A noise at the top of the stairs startled me. I snapped my head around and looked up, not knowing what to expect, but I saw it was only Buster the cat, hunting for field mice in the loft.

I drove back to the house, poured myself a double Scotch, and shut myself in the library where I could think. By the time I passed out later that night, the bottle was empty.

CHAPTER 20

The next morning I spent nursing a hangover and contemplating everything I'd learned in the past several days. I couldn't bear to sleep in my father's bedroom anymore; instead, I'd slept on the couch in the library, fully clothed. I had to call Kate—after all, she just accepted my marriage proposal—but I had no idea what to say to her.

Despite everything I'd learned from the newspaper stories, from Arthur Wiseman and John Barrow, I wanted to hope there was a reasonable explanation for my father's behavior. But after hearing Hank Dietz's story, my hope evaporated. My father was a fascist, an abettor of murder, a traitor, and, for all I knew, he was still alive somewhere enjoying his millions.

I telephoned Kate at noon, trying desperately to sound cheerful. At first, I kept the conversation about us, but she could tell I was hiding something. Rather than press me for more information, she told me she'd be there for me whenever I wanted to talk about it. The only hint I gave her was a question about how she and Susan might feel about moving away from Granbury.

"Whither thou goest, I will go," she said.

I smiled for the first time since I'd kissed her goodbye the day before. "I love you, Kathryn Wellnett Hardesty."

"And I love you."

We decided to get together the following day and talk about our future. In the meantime, I contemplated my past. I wanted to call Uncle John and again raise the possibility of charging Chief Eberhardt, knowing it would destroy my father's reputation forever. I had to face the choice of living with a lie or living with disgrace.

I thought about Charles Lindbergh giving speeches as a champion of America First and the isolationists before the war. His anti-Semitic remarks at national rallies, and his open admiration for the Nazis cost him not only the public's adoration, but also any residual sympathy over his first-born son's kidnapping and murder. Lindbergh had been guilty of prejudice and bad judgment. The evidence against my father was far more damning.

I gave Mrs. Hanratty the day off, so when the telephone rang shortly after three, I answered it immediately. It was Dulcie Patch, and her voice sounded grim. Hank Dietz had been to see her and he confessed what he'd told me.

"Henry Dietz is a fool," she said. "You can't believe anything he tells you."

I had no desire to argue. "I'm sorry, but I do believe Hank."

"Then you're a bigger fool than he is," she hissed. "You mustn't speak about this to anyone." It was a command, not a plea.

"Look, Dulcie, I haven't decided what I'm going to do." I wanted to call her a self-involved, delusional woman, but I held my tongue.

"Where is your sense of loyalty, Jamie? You can't permit your father's reputation to be ruined."

"Whose reputation are you really worried about?" I asked. "My father's or your own?"

There was silence at the other end of the line for a moment, and then Dulcie released all of her venom.

"I won't permit you to destroy your father's memory. I'm warning you not to say a word to anyone, or—"

I cut her off. "Or what? Are you going to charge me an overdue library fine? Christ, Dulcie. Get a life for yourself, and stay the hell away from me." I slammed the telephone receiver down on its cradle.

My hangover was getting worse, not better, and Dulcie Patch's ranting hadn't helped. I went upstairs to the master bathroom and found a bottle of aspirin in the medicine cabinet. I took three tablets and washed them down by placing my mouth directly on the faucet and turning on the cold-water tap. I badly needed to sleep it off, so I buried my compunctions about my father's bed, kicked off my shoes and curled up under the covers, still wearing my clothes.

I slept fitfully, and when I awoke it was dark. My headache was gone, but I still felt groggy. I switched on the bed-stand lamp and looked at my alarm clock, but it had wound down. It read three-thirty, but I knew it couldn't be early Saturday morning—I couldn't have slept that long. My wristwatch had wound down, too, just after four o'clock, presumably on Friday afternoon. I stumbled into the bathroom and examined myself in the mirror. My eyes were bloodshot and I desperately needed a shave. When I was in combat, I'd gone days, even weeks, without bathing, but I always shaved in the field, if only out of pride. I brushed my teeth, then lathered my face with Barbasol and scraped off two days of stubble. I undressed and poured myself into the shower, soaking for twenty minutes, allowing the steam to revitalize my body and my spirits.

Still not knowing the time, I got dressed. I was famished, and I planned to go down to the kitchen and see if there was anything in the new refrigerator Hank had installed for me. As I was lacing up my shoes, I heard a noise downstairs. It was subtle—not the random creaks and groans old houses make at night, but more like someone moving slowly and deliberately. The bedroom door was ajar, but I couldn't see into the hallway, so I listened carefully and thought I heard someone climbing the staircase.

At first, I thought it might be Kate coming to surprise me, but a remnant of my Ranger training must have made me wary. If it were a burglar, I wouldn't let him get away without a fight. I looked around the room for a weapon, but there was nothing handy. I retreated behind the door and waited. Despite the hallway carpeting, I heard footsteps approaching my room. I steadied myself, prepared for anything, but hoping it was Kate or Mrs. Hanratty coming to check on me. The door moved slightly, opening into the room but still concealing my view. In the dim light of the bed-stand lamp, I saw a hand grasp the edge of the door; then an arm extended into the room followed by the form of a large man. The intruder held a revolver in his hand and wore a baseball cap low over his face.

Without waiting to see who it was, I leaped from behind the door and tackled him high on his back, bringing him down on the edge of the carpet. He grunted and raised his hand to club me with the pistol, all the while trying to kick me away. I ducked the blows and grabbed for the man's wrist, keeping the gun at bay. I punched at his jaw and, despite his attempt to parry my jabs, I connected twice, finally sending his head crashing to the bare floor on the other side of the rug. I scrambled over and grabbed the gun, but he rolled over and punched me on the side of the head. He must have been wearing a ring, because his blow cut a gash on my right temple, and I felt blood streaming down the side of my face.

As I went down, the revolver flew out of my hand and onto the floor beside my attacker. He scooped it up, cocked the hammer and fired at me—too hastily—and the bullet went wide, striking a bureau on the far wall. As he got up and staggered back, I recovered and tackled him again, this time wrestling him to the ground, all the while forcing his gun hand aside. He lay on his stomach. I wriggled up the back of his body and grabbed him by the hair, smashing his head onto the oak floor until he lost consciousness.

I switched on the overhead light and turned him over. It was Charles Eberhardt, the chief's nephew. The cheekbones under his eyes were black and swollen. His broken nose bled into his mouth and his cracked eyebrow bled down his cheek. I ripped a sash cord from the window curtains and used it to hogtie Officer Eberhardt wrists-to-ankles behind his back.

I retreated to the bathroom, where I splashed cold water on my face and cleaned the blood from my own head-wound. As I came out drying my face with a towel, I heard Eberhardt moan. His nose had stopped bleeding, and I used the towel to dry the blood off his face.

"You son of a bitch," he said.

I felt like hitting him again, but I didn't. "You break into my home and threaten me with a gun, and *I'm* a son of a bitch? That's rich."

I couldn't call the Granbury police, so I decided to telephone the state police and let them sort it out. I dialed the operator from the telephone on my nightstand and asked to be connected to the state police. The dispatcher was skeptical, insisting I call the Granbury police, and I had to insist that he put me through to an inspector. Once I explained things to the inspector, he agreed to send help.

When Officer Eberhardt heard me calling the state police, he laughed. "Your ass is in a sling, McCoy," he said. "We can add charges of assaulting a police officer and resisting arrest to everything else we've got on you."

"Shut up, asshole," I said.

As I went downstairs to turn on the outside lights, I wondered about the "everything else." The downstairs was completely dark, so I switched on the lights in the front hall and went into the kitchen to grab a snack from the refrigerator. I realized I still had no idea what time it was, so I set my watch by the electric clock on the kitchen wall; it was five after ten. I grabbed a cold chicken leg from the fridge and started back to the foyer. I barely had time to wolf it down before I saw the flashing dome light of the state police car through the front window as it pulled up to the circular drive.

The two state cops were big men—bigger than either Eberhardt or me—and they wore tailored slate-blue uniforms with riding breeches and polished black jackboots. They looked like *SS* officers. They introduced themselves as troopers Gammon and Pease. I handed them Eberhardt's revolver and explained the situation. They followed me upstairs, where Charles Eberhardt lay trussed up on the floor.

Eberhardt spoke as soon as we entered the room. "Thank God you're here," he said. "I'm a police officer. I came here to arrest this man, and he assaulted me."

"What?" I yelled. "You lying sack of shit." I turned to the troopers. "This man broke into my house in the middle of the night, out of uniform and without a warrant. He snuck upstairs without identifying himself and came into my bedroom brandishing a gun. I don't care if he is a cop; I had every right to defend myself, and I intend to press charges."

Trooper Pease bent down to untie Eberhardt while Trooper Gammon positioned himself between me and the other two. "Relax, Mr. McCoy," he said. "We'll get to the bottom of this."

Pease helped Eberhardt to his feet. His face was an awful mess, and he was angry as a hornet. He showed the troopers his badge and said, "I came here to arrest McCoy for possession of unregistered firearms and to question him about the murder of his handyman, Henry Dietz."

I snapped my head around. "What? What happened to Hank?"

Both troopers looked at me now, ready to take action if I made any sudden moves. Eberhardt carefully took a .45 automatic from his jacket pocket and handed it over to Pease, butt end first.

Eberhardt said, "I found this on his nightstand when I entered the room. It may be the murder weapon."

I shouted, "He's a liar. He never got more than two feet into the bedroom."

Pease sniffed the barrel of the gun and said it had been fired recently. Over my loud protests, Eberhardt explained that Hank Dietz called the Granbury police to report that I had a cache of rifles and pistols hidden in my house. On their way out here to investigate, he and his uncle, the chief, found Dietz in his pickup truck, in a ditch on the Old Hartford Turnpike, with a bullet in the back of his head. Officer Eberhardt claimed he arrived here and found the house dark and the front door open. He entered and discovered the weapons in a crate in my library, and then he came upstairs to look for me when I attacked him.

I shouted him down. "Those guns belonged to my father. Dietz was my handyman; he turned them over to Chief Eberhardt more than a month ago."

The troopers drew their weapons and kept both Eberhardt and me covered. Gammon went downstairs to investigate the library and returned a few minutes later, confirming Eberhardt's story.

"That bastard is trying to frame me," I said.

Gammon and Pease decided to take us both to the Windsor barracks, but I was the only one in handcuffs.

We arrived at the state police barracks shortly after eleven. Gammon led Eberhardt to an interrogation room, and Pease was about to do the same to me. Once out of Eberhardt's earshot, however, I demanded to use the telephone; Pease reluctantly agreed, and took me to a pay phone in the lobby. I dropped a nickel in the slot and dialed Ed Franklin at his home in Farmington. I had to relate the story twice, eating up my three minutes. The operator chimed in demanding another nickel, which I dutifully deposited, but Trooper Pease tugged me on the arm, telling me my time was up.

"Just call John Barrow in New York," I told Ed. "Tell him Chief Eberhardt is trying to frame me for murder and I need his help." I knew Uncle John would take the call, not only for my sake, but because he and Ed Franklin were former law partners.

Franklin promised to do his best, and he advised me not to answer any questions until he could get there. Pease took the receiver from me and hung up before I could say goodbye.

The next few hours were both harrowing and disorienting. For the time being, they charged me only with possession of unlicensed firearms. They fingerprinted me and then took me to an interrogation room where a state police detective questioned me. I decided to ignore Ed Franklin's advice to remain silent, because if I failed to refute Charlie Eberhardt's story, I'd soon face charges of murder, assault, and resisting arrest. The detective repeated the same questions over and over again, trying to catch me in a lie. More than an hour passed and Franklin still hadn't shown up, or if he had, the police weren't allowing him to see me.

The detective, who never told me his name, kept prodding me. Occasionally, he'd leave the room and come back a few minutes later with more questions. I denied any knowledge of Hank Dietz's murder and repeated my assertion that Dietz had turned the weapons over to Chief Eberhardt more than a month before. I also repeated my account of Officer Eberhardt's break-in and the ensuing fight.

The detective asked, "Why would the police want to frame you?"

I shut up. The story was too complicated to tell, and I didn't think he'd believe me. I decided to wait until Ed Franklin arrived and I told the detective I was through talking.

"Fine by me, pal. I can hold you without a warrant for twenty-four hours."

He turned me over to Pease who escorted me to a holding cell in the basement. I was the only one in the lock-up; they must have released Officer Eberhardt.

The cellblock consisted of six cells, three on each side of a wide hallway. Pease put me in one close to the stairway and locked the door. It was small and spare, about eight feet square with three cinderblock walls and floor-to-ceiling bars on the fourth. A narrow cot hugged one of the walls, with a thin bare mattress and no pillow; a washstand and toilet in the back completed the decor. A bare incandescent bulb hung from the ceiling.

I desperately wanted a cigarette, but the police had confiscated my possessions. I paced the floor for awhile, hoping Ed Franklin would come to my rescue. Having already slept for much of the day, I wasn't tired, but I decided I'd better sleep anyway.

As I curled up on the bare mattress and closed my eyes, I tried to remember that I'd survived more miserable conditions in the South Pacific.

CHAPTER 21

At eight o'clock on Saturday morning, a guard brought me a cup of tepid black coffee and two pieces of cold buttered toast on a paper plate. I thanked him, and he left me to eat my meager breakfast alone.

The guard came back at eight-thirty and unlocked the cell door. "Come along with me," he said. "You're being released."

Without saying a word, I followed the guard upstairs where he led me to an office with a thick translucent glass door labeled "Detective Inspector Andrew R. Lipton." Inside, the man who interrogated me the night before sat behind a messy desk, and Ed Franklin was there as well, sitting in an armchair. Two other men, both dressed in dark summer-weight suits and wearing gray fedoras stood behind the detective. They looked like they were from central casting, but they introduced themselves as Special Agents Compton and O'Neal of the FBI without offering to shake hands.

I said, "Didn't I see you guys in a Humphrey Bogart movie?"

They ignored my remark.

Ed Franklin stood up to greet me, and Detective Inspector Lipton invited me to have a seat.

"You have some friends in high places," Lipton said. "I received a telephone call from Governor Snow early this morning, directing me to release you to the custody of these federal agents."

"What about the charges?" I asked.

Ed Franklin answered for him. "There won't be any charges, Jamie, but you have to go with Agents Compton and O'Neal."

Warily, I asked, "Where to?"

Compton answered, too politely, almost deferentially. I got the impression he was performing for my lawyer. "We're taking you to New York to meet with Judge Barrow. You're not under arrest, but you're a material witness in a federal case. We've explained everything to your attorney."

Ed Franklin asked that he and I have a few moments alone to confer, and we went, unescorted, down the hall to the interrogation room where I'd been questioned the night before. Ed shut the door, and he told me the G-men had explained very little. I did my best to summarize what I knew about Chief Eberhardt and the murder of Paul Jefferson, but I held back most of the damning information about my father and his involvement with the fascists. I didn't know how much Franklin knew, and, even though he was my lawyer, the less said the better.

Ed asked a few questions, and then he said accompanying the federal agents wasn't a condition of my release, but I should go anyway. He offered to come along, but I refused. I didn't need a lawyer to speak with Uncle John.

When we returned to Lipton's office, I asked what they were going to do about Charles and Victor Eberhardt.

Detective Inspector Lipton said, "We're holding Charles Eberhardt for questioning in the murder of Henry Dietz, and we've already sent troopers to arrest Victor Eberhardt for murder and conspiracy to commit murder."

"What convinced you?"

"Judge Barrow tipped us to Carl Frank, George Crossman and John Hauser. They're three of the mugs doing time at the Danbury Pen for espionage. All three agreed to testify against Eberhardt on the Jefferson murder in exchange for consideration at parole time.

"The ballistics test on the .45 isn't back from the lab yet, but I'll bet my pension it's the Dietz murder weapon. Charles Eberhardt's fingerprints are all over it. We also lifted his prints from Dietz's truck and the crate of weapons we found in your house."

I surmised that Charles Eberhardt planned to kill me, plant the .45 on my body and claim he'd shot me in self-defense while I was resisting arrest.

* * *

Shortly after nine, I left with Agents Compton and O'Neal in their Hudson sedan. O'Neal drove and Compton rode up front, leaving the back seat to me. I had a lot of questions, but they didn't give me any answers, so I stretched out and fell asleep before the car reached the turnpike.

We arrived in lower Manhattan around twelve-thirty, and I awoke with a stiff neck, feeling like I'd gone ten rounds with a middleweight. I looked around, but the neighborhood wasn't familiar. It was seedy and dark, even though it was midday. O'Neal pulled over at the curb and I asked, "Where are we?"

"Lower Mott Street. Edge of Chinatown," he said. "Judge Barrow's office is a few blocks away in Foley Square. We got a stop to make first. Someone wants to see you."

"Who?"

"Never mind," Compton said. "Just come with me." He got out of the front passenger seat and came around to open my door on the street side.

I didn't like the sound of it, but there were two of them and one of me, and I was in no shape to take on the FBI. I got out and tried to straighten the wrinkles out of my jacket.

Compton smirked and said, "You look fine. We're not going to see a dame."

O'Neal waited in the car while Compton steered me across Mott Street to the front door of the Celebrity Tavern, a dive that probably never saw a celebrity. He opened the door and shoved me inside, where the darkness was so complete I wondered if the place was open for business.

"Hold on," I said. "I can't see a thing."

Compton laughed. "You'll get used to it," he said. "Nothin' much to see anyway."

He led me deeper into the room. After a moment, my eyes adjusted and I saw that the Celebrity Tavern was not, in fact, open for business. The floor was strewn with trash and the bar was covered with a layer of grime that would have taken years to accumulate. All the way in the rear, past rows of abandoned high-backed booths, was a lone figure sitting at a cheap wooden table.

Compton pulled out a chair for me and then walked over to the back wall where he flipped a light switch. Once again, my eyes took time to adjust. Across the table from me was a broad shouldered man in a tailored blue double-breasted suit who looked like a Leyendecker painting of the Arrow Collar man. He had the shoulders of a linebacker; his skin was smooth and tanned; his face conveyed both serenity and confidence, and his posture was relaxed, yet somehow ready for action.

Compton raised a finger to the brim of his fedora and said to the Arrow Collar man, "I'll be outside in the car if you need me." Then he walked back toward the front of the bar and left.

"I give up," I said. "Who are you, and what is this place?"

He looked up and said, "I'm Brigadier General Goddard MacFarlane, Deputy Director of War Department Intelligence Services. Used to be known as the OSS."

I should have guessed. I was about to reach over and offer to shake hands, but something in MacFarlane's eyes told me the gesture wasn't necessary. Instead, I merely nodded. Had we been in uniform, I would have saluted.

He answered my second question next. "This is the world famous Celebrity Tavern."

"World famous?"

MacFarlane shrugged and said, "Well, New York City famous, anyway." He pointed to the bar. "The Mott Street Massacre happened right over there in '31."

"Never heard of it."

"No matter," he said. "You're from out of town."

I leaned back in my chair, trying not to betray my impatience. "Why are we meeting in an abandoned bar?"

"It's just a place the OSS and the FBI used during the war to make drops—contacts with informants and turned foreign agents. It's convenient and discreet. Besides, I like the joint. Used to hang out here sometimes in the old days—when it was a speakeasy."

I looked around. The Celebrity Tavern didn't have the glamour of the famous New York speakeasies of 52nd Street. It was a dirty hole and it reeked of stale piss and dead rodents.

"I got a message that you phoned me," MacFarlane said. "I was going to ignore it, but you went and dug up something that forced my hand. Since I don't have a choice in the matter now, I figured I ought to meet you before you saw Judge Barrow."

I nodded.

"We have an awkward situation here, Mr. McCoy."

"How so?"

"You and Judge Barrow have gotten yourselves mixed up in some government business a lot of people want buried. As it turns out, the judge would have gotten involved anyway, but you—I wish I knew what to do about you." He paused and shook his head. "By pushing the investigation of Chief Eberhardt, you've opened up a hornet's nest. After you met with the judge last Wednesday, he telephoned the Connecticut Attorney General and convinced him to go after Eberhardt by using the testimony of Baransky's stooges, Hauser, Crossman and Frank."

"How do you know all this?"

"You'd be amazed at what I know."

I thought about all that had happened in the past few days, and I realized that, unwittingly, I must have set in motion a deadly chain of events by forcing Hank Dietz to talk. "I assume your investigation into my father's disappearance years ago has something to do with this," I said.

MacFarlane answered, "That would be correct." Despite his businesslike demeanor, he forced what could pass for a smile. "Harry McCoy is one of the more interesting men I've ever encountered, although I confess I began with a low opinion of him."

"And now?"

"Well, now is what we're here to talk about."

He reached into his breast pocket and withdrew a leather cigar case. He peeled back the top flap and offered me one. "They're Havanas. Have one."

"No thanks," I said. "Those things'll kill you. I'll just have a cigarette."

"Suit yourself," he said. "I'd offer you a drink, but as you can see, the bar's closed."

I lit up a Lucky, and the general took his time with the ritual of clipping the end of his cigar and lighting up. The smoke rapidly filled the room, improving the aroma of the Celebrity Tavern.

"All right, MacFarlane," I said. "Is this where you tell me what you know about my father? That he was a fascist and a murderer?"

He blew a cloud of smoke in my face and laughed. "Son," he said, "what you don't know about your father could fill a book."

"I think I've already learned more than I want to know."

"I wish I could let you off that easy. If it were up to me, I'd let it go, but there are others involved who want your cooperation. You peeled back the first layers of the onion, and now you have to keep going till you get the whole stink."

"The whole stink? How can it get worse than treason and murder?"

MacFarlane considered my question, and then said, "I didn't say it was worse. It's just more complicated than what you might think."

"All right," I said. "Tell me."

He leaned back in his chair, trying to enjoy the cigar, but after a few more puffs, he let it die out. "When your mother and Arthur Wiseman first hired me," MacFarlane said, "I assumed your father was involved in something shady—that he'd dreamed up his last flight to escape prosecution. Cooking his books the way he did is a classic scheme I'd seen many times. It's called 'money laundering'—using a series of fraudulent transactions to make the funds untraceable. I needed only a few days with the accountant and your father's chief financial officer to figure out what was going on, but my problem was how to trace the money and your father."

MacFarlane reached down under his chair and brought a thin leather briefcase up onto the table. He unfastened the straps and removed a sheaf of papers that he passed across to me. "Take a look at this," he said.

It was the report he'd given my mother—complete with the pages Wiseman had altered. I flipped through it while MacFarlane re-lit his cigar. Everything was there: the sale of aircraft engine parts to the phony companies in New York, and their subsequent shipment to the warehouse in Perth Amboy. Shipping records from the warehouse listed "farm implements" on the receiving orders; and receipts for bills of lading indicated consignment to three German-registered cargo vessels over the course of a year and a half between late 1932 and early 1934.

I swallowed hard. MacFarlane was right—the stink was getting worse. I stubbed out my cigarette and lit another.

MacFarlane said, "It didn't take Sherlock Holmes to figure out that your father was selling contraband airplane parts to Germany."

Seeing the evidence in my hand was one thing, but hearing MacFarlane say it aloud was too much. It was cool in the bar, but I began to sweat. My head ached. I felt myself trembling and breathing hard.

"This place gives me the creeps, General. Can we go someplace else?"

He shook his head. "Not yet. We have an appointment with the judge in a little bit, but we have to wait for him to arrive at his office."

"All right then. What else do you have to say?"

MacFarlane spoke at length, reciting a story that pulled me deeper into the abyss of my father's degradation. "Before I could trace your father's money, or even begin to find out what happened to him, I had a visit from my former boss, J. Edgar Hoover. He showed up at my office unannounced, and gave me an ultimatum: drop the case or lose my license. He said the FBI was conducting an investigation involving Harry McCoy, and my inquiries were endangering it."

"What was Hoover investigating? The murder, my father's little fascist club, or selling contraband to the Nazis?"

MacFarlane gave me a wry smile. "It's not what you think, and it wasn't what I thought, either. It was years before I learned the truth. You see, I never let it go completely, and it was more than mere curiosity—I hated Hoover and his high-handed ways. So, in between other jobs, whenever time permitted, I worked on tracing the money and figuring out what really happened to your father on his last flight."

I saw where MacFarlane was heading with this, and I wasn't sure I was ready to go there with him. "Arthur Wiseman told me you thought he didn't go down over the Atlantic—that he flew to Germany instead."

He nodded. "That's exactly what I thought then and it's what I know now."

I groaned. MacFarlane chuckled and shook his head at me, telling me with this gesture that he thought I was hopelessly naïve.

He said, "I put myself in your father's place: If I was trying to escape the United States, and if my ultimate destination were Germany, I'd find a way to get my money there. From my days at Treasury, I knew a former T-man who worked at First Bank and Trust of New York, and he traced a series of large money transfers to bank accounts in Italy over the same period of time as the shipments from Perth Amboy. From the Italian banks, the money found its way to accounts in Switzerland and Germany.

"Tracing the flight was more difficult. Over the years, I questioned employees at small airfields all along the eastern seaboard. I suspected your father diverted his flight after crossing Montauk Point and landed somewhere on the mainland. I was wrong. The clue to Harry McCoy's disappearance came from the stated destination of the last ship out of Perth Amboy. The steamship *Holzmar* called on Hamilton, Bermuda within two days of your father's departure from Granbury and then sailed to Bremerhaven. I went to Bermuda and confirmed that a plane made an unscheduled arrival at a private airfield on the afternoon of April 2, 1934."

If what MacFarlane said was true, and deep down I knew it was, my father survived his final flight. He'd gone to Germany years before the war began. I was afraid to ask the obvious question, but I had to. "What happened to him?"

"Then or now?"

"Now? Is he still alive?"

MacFarlane nodded.

His silent confirmation rattled me, even though I sensed it coming. My initial reaction was a deep feeling of loss that surpassed any grief I once felt when I thought he'd died a hero. Knowledge of my father's betrayal was worse than believing him dead. Then the full horror of the situation struck me: with him alive, all of his dirty secrets would come to light; his name—my name—would become an eponym for traitor, like Benedict Arnold and Vidkun Quisling. I thought of Kate and Susan and what it would mean to them, to us. Even if I changed my name, the stain would follow me wherever I went.

Before I could comment, Agent Compton poked his head in the door and said, "It's time, General. The judge just arrived at the Federal Building."

MacFarlane said, "I guess we'll have to finish this in the judge's chambers."

We left the squalor of the Celebrity Tavern, but the stench of my father's treason still clung to me.

CHAPTER 22

Compton, MacFarlane and I walked in silence the two blocks to the federal court building at Foley Square, with O'Neal following us in the car. I felt queasy and disoriented, all the while fighting back the sensation that I was in a waking nightmare. MacFarlane had said there were more revelations to come. I wondered what they were and how Uncle John was involved.

It being Saturday, the courthouse at Foley Square was locked up tight, but we were expected. A court officer admitted us and signed us in at the reception desk. The officer escorted us up an elevator to the fourth floor and down a long corridor past a row of courtrooms. Our footsteps clacked on the granite floor, their echo magnified by the vastness of the deserted corridor. We came to an unmarked door. Compton knocked and opened it without waiting for an answer.

In the anteroom, a man in a suit identical to Compton's greeted us and told us to go through another door on the far wall into Uncle John's private chambers. Compton remained behind with the other suit; MacFarlane and I went inside.

Uncle John's private office was a book-lined sanctuary of dark wood and leather upholstery—the perquisites of a federal judge one step removed from the Supreme Court. In this setting, I expected to see Uncle John in black robes, but he sat behind a massive walnut desk in shirtsleeves smoking a pipe and reading documents.

Uncle John looked up and invited us to come in and make ourselves comfortable. MacFarlane sat on the sofa across from the desk, and I took a side chair.

Uncle John said to me, "I see you've met General MacFarlane."

"Yes, and he told me a lot about my dear father—things I suppose you already know." I turned to MacFarlane and said, "Harry McCoy was quite a heel, wasn't he, General?"

MacFarlane said, "Hold on, kid. I never said your dad was a heel."

"Then what would you call him?"

"There's a lot you don't know," MacFarlane said.

I ignored MacFarlane's remark and glared at Uncle John, but he lowered his head and averted his gaze. "I'm afraid I was guilty of underestimating your father, too, Jamie."

"How so? Did you underestimate his ability to betray his country?"

MacFarlane said, "Whoa, kid. You're jumping to conclusions. There's more to the story."

I was too upset to realize I was projecting my anger on Uncle John and God MacFarlane. "What else is there?"

"Quite a bit, actually," MacFarlane said.

"All right, then. Tell me."

MacFarlane said, "In the middle of 1941, I thought I had your father's disappearance figured out. I took my information to my old friend Wild Bill Donovan, who was then in charge of foreign intelligence. Donovan told me quite a tale.

"Way back in 1927, Franklin Roosevelt developed a keen interest in foreign intelligence. He and his cousin, Vincent Astor, formed a secret society of influential men including Teddy Roosevelt's son Kermit, banker Winthrop Aldrich, journalist Marshall Field III, publisher Nelson Doubleday, Donovan, and your father. Their purpose was to gather and discuss economic and military information about Germany, Russia, Japan and Italy—countries they considered threats to American interests."

"Why them? Why my father?"

"They were well-known celebrities who could travel the world without arousing suspicion. Even hostile governments welcomed them, giving them access to intelligence from Europe, Asia and the Far East. When Roosevelt was elected President, they became his private spy network. Then Donovan discovered that J. Edgar Hoover had created his own secret group within the FBI—the General Intelligence Division—to monitor fascists and Communist subversives.

"Your father knew a man named Drazha Kunetz, a former Tsarist officer and a celebrated pilot. Kunetz and his fellow White Russian, Count Boris Baransky, had formed an underground fascist network, and Kunetz invited your father to join.

"Donovan saw the invitation as an opportunity to infiltrate Baransky's group and use it to heal strained relations with Hoover; he wanted access to Hoover's intelligence. Donovan arranged a meeting between your father and Hoover, and Hoover proposed that your father join Baransky's fascists as an *agent provocateur*. He'd report directly to Hoover, but would also share information with Roosevelt's secret spy group. Your father agreed and soon became one of Kunetz and Baransky's closest associates."

As MacFarlane talked, everything I thought I knew fell away and reformed into a new picture, like the pieces of a jigsaw puzzle. My father was an undercover agent, not a fascist.

According to MacFarlane, my father's involvement with the Jefferson murder began when Chief Eberhardt telephoned him to report an alleged rapist at large on our property. Eberhardt asked my father to recruit a posse. The people who came to mind were Baransky's fascists.

As MacFarlane spoke about that night, Uncle John looked sad. He'd been silent throughout MacFarlane's recitation, but at last he spoke up. "The tragedy was that your father underestimated Eberhardt's potential for violence. A man like that leading an armed mob is a recipe for murder."

I told both men what Hank Dietz had revealed about Dulcie Patch—that Jefferson couldn't have raped her.

Uncle John shook his head in disgust. He said, "There's no excuse for vigilante justice under any circumstances, but when it takes the life of an innocent man for no other reason than a woman's vanity—"

"Why do you think Dulcie accused Jefferson of rape?" I asked.

"I told you before—she was obsessed with your father. As long as your mother was around, it never amounted to anything more than harmless flirting, but after your mother left, Dulcie must have thought the way was clear for her. When your father didn't respond, I can only guess that she tried to play the role of damsel in distress to get her hero's attention."

MacFarlane said, "After Jefferson's murder, your father asked Hoover to cover it up."

Uncle John interjected, "That's why he told me to drop my investigation."

"Unfortunately," MacFarlane said, "the Jefferson murder made your father vulnerable to blackmail."

By early 1933, Hitler was beginning his stranglehold on Germany, and his first agenda was rebuilding the Luftwaffe under Hermann Goering. Baransky and Kunetz informed Goering that my father had reacquired the McCoy Machine Works and was a potential source of aircraft engines for the Luftwaffe. The two Russians believed my father was truly sympathetic to the Nazi cause, but in case sympathy wasn't enough, they would resort to blackmail.

Uncle John said, "I don't know why your father didn't come to me, Jamie. I would have helped him."

"He couldn't," MacFarlane said. "He was in too deep." He turned back to me and said, "Your father's old combat foe from the First World War, Count von Sielau, asked him to sell parts to Germany. Your father refused, but then Baransky threatened to expose his participation in the Jefferson affair. Your father discussed the situation with Donovan and Roosevelt, and they decided your father's cooperation could get them an inside look at the Luftwaffe. Roosevelt convinced him to cooperate with the Nazis and report everything he learned to Donovan."

My father reluctantly agreed; he sold some obsolete parts to the Nazis, and everything worked well for a few months. But Kunetz and Baransky pressured him to do more.

"Then," MacFarlane said, "in July 1933, Rudy and Greta Huffmann crashed their plane in Bridgeport, supposedly attempting to set a new air speed record from Berlin to New York. But the true purpose of their flight was to convince your father to defect. They wanted him to prove his loyalty to the Nazi cause by taking his new aeronautics designs to Germany.

"It was too much for him. He was willing to be an *agent provocateur*, but not a defector. He demanded and got an audience with President Roosevelt, but Roosevelt thought it was a wonderful idea. He wanted your father to be a double agent—to defect openly and then spy for America. Your father refused. He was even willing to suffer the consequences of disclosing the Jefferson affair rather than subject your mother and you to the humiliation of seeing him betray his country."

"Donovan proposed a resolution that satisfied both your father and the president. Your father would defect, but not publicly. He'd stage a flight to Capetown and disappear en route; to the public, he'd be dead. The Nazis would give him a new name and promise never to reveal his true identity. In that way, he'd preserve his image as an American hero for his family and be free to spy on Germany without suffering the disgrace of treason."

"So my father was a spy, not a traitor?"

Uncle John and God MacFarlane nodded.

MacFarlane said, "Donovan helped your father arrange his last flight, and he helped him sell his best patents and designs to Pratt & Whitney. After all,

President Roosevelt didn't want that kind of technology falling into the hands of the Nazis."

With my father in Germany as a double agent, the president had his own private spy with access to top-level Nazis. Donovan became my father's principal contact, and he transmitted the information my father sent directly to the president. By the time war came, Donovan was running the OSS, with control of all American spy operations in Europe.

MacFarlane said, "I met General Donovan for a drink in the Army-Navy Club in Washington in early '41, and I started telling him what I suspected about your father. He almost spit up his drink. He hustled me out of the club and over to his office, where he locked the door and grilled me about everything I'd discovered. Then he gave me a choice—either join the OSS or go to jail."

So MacFarlane went to work for Donovan, and he took over as my father's principal contact. My father was living in Dresden under the name Oskar Jürgens, an industrialist who owned and operated seven aircraft engine factories in different parts of the Reich. Although he was well-connected with Nazis at the highest level, he lived a quiet life and rarely socialized. This, of course, was part of his cover.

The story seemed incredible. But each of MacFarlane's revelations restored the heroic image I once had of my father. "If only I'd known before," I said.

MacFarlane said, "He was the most productive spy the Allies had inside Germany. The Battle of Britain might have gone the other way if it hadn't been for the information your father provided to General Donovan, who, with President Roosevelt's blessing, passed it on to the British."

I didn't know what to say. My emotions had been on a roller coaster since MacFarlane began. I came in knowing my father was involved in murder and believing he was a traitor. Now he was a hero again.

"Thanks to your father," MacFarlane said, "we had access to every Nazi advance in aeronautics."

I felt happy and relaxed, more so than I'd been in days. I said to MacFarlane, "Back in the bar, you said my father was still alive. Is he coming home? When can I see him?"

MacFarlane didn't respond. Instead, he looked at Uncle John, who cleared his throat awkwardly and said, "Your father *is* alive. I just found out yesterday."

"Wonderful," I said. "When is he coming home? My God, I've only seen pictures of his parade from the last war. This time, they'll have fireworks."

Both Uncle John and General MacFarlane bowed their heads, avoiding eye contact with me.

"What is it? What aren't you telling me?"

Uncle John answered. "Your father may never come home."

"I don't understand. Why not? The war's over. When people find out what he's done, they'll give him another Medal of Honor."

Uncle John looked up at me. "I'm afraid not. You see, the Russians captured him in the closing days of the war, and they've accused him of war crimes. They want to put him on trial."

"War crimes? What war crimes?"

"They say his factories used slave labor."

"But if he was an American spy, he was just pretending, wasn't he? Why doesn't General Donovan tell them the truth?"

God MacFarlane said, "It's not that simple. We've already told the Russians he was one of ours, but we haven't disclosed that he's really Harry McCoy. We told them he was on active duty in our espionage services, but it didn't do any good." He paused. "There are three possibilities: the Russians want to embarrass the United States by exposing one of our agents as a war criminal; or they could be using the charges as a ploy to kidnap your father and force him to work for them. He designed the new rocket engines for Germany, and the Russians want the technology."

"What's the third possibility?"

"They could be sincere. Many of the slave laborers were Russian, and they're hot for revenge."

"That's how I got involved," Uncle John said. "Bob Jackson sent for me because your father wants me as his defense counsel."

My mind reeled. I thought of my mother and felt profoundly sad. "After all these years," I said, "and my mother died without knowing he was still alive."

MacFarlane said, "She knew. I told her."

"What? When? When did you tell her?"

"I'd been keeping tabs on her for your father, and when I found out she was terminally ill, I went to see her in the hospital just before the end. I couldn't let her die without knowing the truth."

Then MacFarlane told me what no one else could: my father's association with Baransky and Kunetz was the reason my mother left him. She couldn't accept that the man she loved was a fascist, and she confessed her feelings to MacFarlane. Now I realized the awful dilemma my father had faced—for her own protection, he couldn't disclose his real purpose to my mother, but the more active he became with the fascists, the more he alienated her.

"I want to go over there and see him," I said.

MacFarlane said, "That's not a good idea. Your presence could tip the Russians to your father's true identity, and they'd use it for propaganda."

"Besides, Jamie," Uncle John said, "the Russians aren't bluffing. From the briefing I received yesterday, it's possible there's some truth to their allegations."

"I don't understand. If he was a spy, he was working for the Allies. Surely the Russians appreciate that."

MacFarlane started to say something, but Uncle John cut him off. The general may have been known as "God" among his friends and colleagues, but this was U.S. Circuit Court Judge John Hughes Barrow's domain, and Uncle John let him know with a glance who was in charge.

"Jamie, your father was active in the Nazi party for eleven years. He used thousands of slave laborers in his factories—Russians, Poles and Jews—most of whom died." Uncle John focused his eyes on mine. "We've indicted other prominent industrialists for war crimes, including Gustave Krupp. The Russians are within their rights."

"But he's an American hero," I said. "He gave up everything for his country."

Uncle John sighed. "I know, son. I agree with you, but I'm afraid our Russian allies don't see it that way."

"Allies, my ass," MacFarlane grumbled.

"I still want to see him," I said.

General MacFarlane said, "I told you, it's not a good idea. It will harm America's position and it won't help your father's case."

Uncle John looked at MacFarlane and suggested, "The Russians don't know they have Harry McCoy in custody, and there's no connection between Jamie and Oskar Jürgens. He could accompany me as my law clerk."

The general said, "But he's not even a lawyer."

"It doesn't matter. He's a commissioned officer in the United States Army Reserve. Transfer him to the Judge Advocate General's Corps and I'll see that he's credentialed."

I interrupted them. "But I've already been discharged."

MacFarlane stroked his chin, thinking it over. "I suppose I could get him recalled." He looked at me, silently asking me what I thought.

Uncle John said, "If you want to see him, Jamie, it's the only way."

"All right," I agreed. I turned to the general and asked, "How long would I have to be back in uniform?"

MacFarlane shrugged. "Ask the judge. It's his case."

"Six months, I would imagine," Uncle John said.

"Well, if that's the only way to see my father, then so be it."

I didn't think about the charges my father faced; I felt confident Uncle John would clear his name. Instead, I considered the possibility of seeing him again after fourteen years, and I desperately wished my mother were alive to see him too.

I kept picturing in my mind a triumphant return to Granbury for my father, where the townspeople would hold a grand parade. Uncle John, Ted Derwent and Roger Willoughby would be there, cheering him as he led the parade, and I would march right alongside, both of us proudly wearing our uniforms and decorations.

I refused to believe the war crimes tribunal would find him guilty; but if they did, the results could be far worse than anything I'd previously imagined.

CHAPTER 23

It was almost four o'clock when we finished talking, and Special Agent Compton was still waiting in the Judge's anteroom. As I said my goodbyes to Uncle John and Goddard MacFarlane, I remembered I hadn't called Kate.

I asked Uncle John if I could make a long distance call, and he told me to use the private line in his chambers. Uncle John and MacFarlane went into the anteroom, and I dialed the operator and waited while she made the connection. It rang four times without any answer. I was about to hang up on the fifth ring, when she picked up.

"Hello?" she said.

"Kate, it's Jamie. I'm sorry I didn't call earlier, but I'm in New—"

"Oh, hello, Arlen."

"No, Kate, it's Jamie."

"Oh, yes, I know, Arlen. Susan's just fine. How's Gwen? Are you enjoying the beach?"

"Kate, it's Jamie. I'm calling from New York."

"Oh? You're stopping in New York on the way home? Well, no hurry. Everything's just fine here. You and Gwen take your time."

In addition to the nonsensical responses, her voice sounded strange, almost forced.

"Kate," I said quietly, "Are you in some kind of trouble?"

"Yes, I am. I have to run now. I have company. Bye-bye."

And she hung up.

I panicked and called out to the anteroom. "Agent Compton, I think there's a problem."

Compton came into the Judge's chamber, followed by Uncle John and Goddard MacFarlane.

"What is it?" he asked.

"I'm not sure, but I think my fiancée is in trouble."

All three men gave me a puzzled look. I explained what happened on the phone call, but they didn't understand.

"Look," I said. "I don't know what's going on, but Kate was trying to tell me she's in trouble." I turned to Agent Compton. "Are you sure the state police arrested Victor Eberhardt? If he was crazy enough to kill Hank Dietz, he's crazy enough to hurt Kate and her daughter just to get back at me."

Compton picked up the phone and called the Windsor barracks of the Connecticut State Police. They confirmed that Chief Eberhardt had indeed been arrested. He refused to talk, but his nephew confessed everything as soon as he saw his uncle in handcuffs.

Agent Compton held the receiver away from his face and asked me, "What do you want me to do?"

I hesitated, unsure of what to say. "I don't know," I said. I turned to Uncle John. "Could someone else be helping Eberhardt?"

Uncle John grabbed the phone from Agent Compton and spoke into the receiver. "This is U.S. Circuit Court Judge John Barrow speaking. Who is this?"

There was a pause.

Uncle John said, "Detective Inspector Lipton, I want you to dispatch two troopers to Mrs. Kathryn Hardesty's house immediately. I believe she's in danger. I'll put Jamie McCoy on the phone to give you the address."

I took the phone and gave Lipton the address, and then I asked Compton, "How long will it take us to drive back to Granbury?"

"I can get us a police escort, but it'll still take two and a half, maybe three hours at least."

General MacFarlane said, "I can get you a small plane out of Idlewild. That'll cut the time in half."

Compton telephoned for a police escort, and MacFarlane made two quick calls to arrange for the airplane.

Compton and I left Uncle John's chambers without saying goodbye. We ran down four flights of stairs and out the front door to find the Hudson waiting by the curb with O'Neal behind the wheel. Two motorcycle cops had positioned themselves in the front and rear of the Hudson and were ready to go. With sirens blaring all the way, we sped across the Brooklyn Bridge and across Rockaway Boulevard all the way to Idlewild, making it in twenty minutes. We drove right onto the field. The plane was a silver, twin-engine Lockheed 12-A, a smaller version of the airplane Amelia Earhart used in her last flight around the world that ended tragically in the Pacific. The irony wasn't lost on me.

The pilot introduced himself as Lieutenant Picard, and identified the plane as a government craft assigned to the Postmaster General. Compton and I introduced ourselves and boarded, followed by Picard, who instructed us to buckle our safety belts.

After Lieutenant Picard shut the cabin door, he turned to me and asked, "Are you any relation to the famous flyer, Harry McCoy?"

"Yes," I said. "He was my father."

Picard smiled. "Wow. That's something. When I was a kid, he was my hero."

"Yeah, he was mine, too."

We were airborne by quarter after five, flying over Brooklyn, Queens and Long Island Sound. The heater in the cabin was off and, despite the mild temperature at sea level, up in the air it was cold. I looked out the window at the landscape below; conversation with Compton was impossible due to the roar of the Pratt & Whitney Wasp engines. The wait was maddening. Picard flew northeast over the Sound along the coast and then turned due north, following the Connecticut River. The only landmark I recognized before we reached Hartford was the campus of Wesleyan University; about ten minutes later, I recognized Hartford in the distance from the tower of the Travelers Insurance Building, the tallest in New England.

From my front seat in the cabin, I saw Lieutenant Picard motioning with his hand for me to come into the cockpit. He raised his right earphone and shouted at me to help him locate the airstrip on my father's estate. We passed over Hartford on the port side of the plane, and I pointed north, just past the confluence of the Farmington and Connecticut Rivers. He spotted the Windsor Locks Air Base, built on the old American Sumatra Tobacco Company's Bull Run Plantation. It had just been re-named Bradley Field. Two miles north was Granbury.

Navigating by the Old Hartford Turnpike, the pilot came in low, aiming right for my father's airstrip. Up ahead, I spotted a column of dense smoke rising high into the still air; it was coming from somewhere on my father's estate. I buckled in and prepared to land. As we descended, I saw the house looming up beyond the tobacco barns. I tried to focus on the airstrip, but quickly looked back. The smoke we'd seen from the air billowed from under the eaves of my father's house. As we got closer, I saw three fire engines and two police cars in the circular drive. A dozen hoses connected like a tangle of snakes from a pumper truck to the fire-pond on the other side of the hedgerow; a score of firefighters poured water into the upper floors of the house from hoses linked to the pumper.

I frantically pointed to the burning house, trying to get the pilot's attention, but he waved me off and shouted at me to shut up and sit back. Seconds later, he set the Electra down on the grass strip and taxied toward the tobacco barn. I unstrapped myself and bolted back into the passenger cabin, where Compton had already opened the exit door.

We jumped down to the grass, and ran together toward the house. From fifty feet away, I saw Detective Inspector Lipton running toward us, waving his arm.

"Kate!" I yelled. "Where's Kate?"

Lipton reached me, sweating and out of breath. "She's okay," he gasped. "She's with your friend, Mr. Thayer."

"Thank God," I said. "What about Susan?"

"She's with them. She's fine."

Compton said, "What the hell is going on here?"

"Fire," said Lipton.

Compton and I said the same thing at the same time. "No shit!"

I said, "I see it's a fire. What the hell caused it?"

"Miss Patch. We have her in custody, but she's badly burned. The firemen pulled her out and there's an ambulance on the way." Lipton looked back at the house, shaking his head. "Miss Patch will survive, but I doubt your house will," he said.

I looked over at my father's house. Smoke poured out the second and third-floor windows, filling the air with an acrid stench. At first, I thought the first floor was okay, but as I looked closer, I saw through the library windows a solid wall of orange. The fire rose up through the center of the house, and the thick sandstone construction acted like a giant chimney, sweeping the flames upward.

Lipton regained his composure. "Right after you called from New York, we sent a car to Mrs. Hardesty's house." He pulled a spiral notebook from his breast pocket and flipped open the cover, consulting his notes. "When the troopers arrived, they saw Miss Patch running out the front door, her face covered in blood."

According to Lipton, Dulcie ran to her car and sped away. One of the troopers ran into Kate's house while the other chased Dulcie in the patrol car. Kate was hysterical, trying to get away from the state trooper so she could find Susan, who was nowhere in sight.

When Chief Eberhardt was arrested, word had spread through town quickly. Dulcie became frantic, realizing the sordid details about the Jefferson murder would surface. She raced over to my house, but when she discovered I wasn't home, she went straight to the Hardesty's, where she ranted at Kate to stop me from destroying my father's reputation. When Kate told her to leave, Dulcie pulled a gun and demanded that Kate get in touch with me.

Coincidentally, I called just at that moment. The ringing telephone awakened Susan from her nap, and she walked in on Dulcie aiming the gun at her mother. After Kate hung up with me, Dulcie began screaming. Susan was frightened, and Kate tried to soothe her, but Dulcie's behavior became more threatening. Kate lunged at Dulcie and shouted at Susan to run out of the house and "go see daddy." As Susan ran away, Dulcie struggled with Kate. Kate pushed her aside, grabbed a silver pie server from the dining room sideboard, and slashed at Dulcie's face, ripping open a gash in her cheek from the corner of her eye down to her upper lip. Dulcie ran out of the house just as the police arrived.

When Kate told Susan to "go see daddy," Susan ran down Gallows Hill to the cemetery, where Greg Hardesty was buried. She hid behind the gravestone until Kate arrived with the state trooper.

The other trooper chased Dulcie up Gallows Hill toward the Old Hartford Turnpike, but when he made the right turn heading south, he took it too wide and careened into a delivery van heading north.

Meanwhile, Dulcie drove back to my house, hoping I'd returned, and ran through the place calling my name and screaming that she was going to destroy me. When Mrs. Hanratty came to see what was going on, Dulcie tried to shoot her, but couldn't get the gun to fire. Mrs. Hanratty ran from the house, all the way down the gravel drive until she got to the turnpike. She waved down a passing car and got away.

The state police arrived at the house twenty minutes later, along with the fire department. From the driveway, they saw Dulcie through the windows, running through the upper rooms and screaming like a banshee. The first floor was a wall of flames, but two firemen got a ladder up to the second floor and hauled Dulcie out.

As Lipton finished telling us what had happened, the Fire Chief came over to inform me the house was a total loss. "It's beyond saving," he said.

I shook my head in disgust, not at losing the house, but at the calamity I'd caused by returning to Granbury and reopening it.

I turned to Lipton and said, "I want to see Kate and Susan. Can you drive me?"

Lipton agreed and drove me to the Noll Tavern, where I fell into Kate's arms and hugged her for what seemed like an eternity. I knew then I never wanted to let her go.

CHAPTER 24

I told Kate I didn't want to stay in Granbury. I begged her to take Susan and come with me to Boston, but she was reluctant.

"Whither thou goest..." I reminded her.

She smiled sweetly and said, "I know, but I have to think of Susan. She's so close to her grandparents— Gwen and Arlen would be crushed."

I sighed. "Kate, I can't stay here. After everything that's happened, after everything I've discovered about my father... It's too much."

"You're right, of course."

"But I can't leave you, or Susan either," I said. I looked at her, pleading. "Say you'll come with me. I love you, Kate, and I can't live without you."

In the end, she relented. Over the next week, I stayed with Ernie Thayer above the Noll Tavern and did my best to straighten out my affairs. I could have opened up the old saltbox on the estate, but I wanted to stay closer to Kate and Susan. I made Nobbie Griffin a happy man by selling him the Mercedes. I decided that a roadster wasn't appropriate for a family man, and I'd grown to like the Packard.

Freddie Crowell called on me, trying to elicit facts for his impending newspaper article. He was relentless, but I resisted disclosing anything he couldn't glean from public sources. God MacFarlane admonished me that everything we'd discussed was classified—subject to the National Defense Act of 1942—and I could go to jail if I revealed any of it.

I got Freddie off my back by promising something I would never deliver—the inside story on my father. It was of no consequence; I'd be long gone before Freddie could collect on the promise. In return, he assured me he would downplay my father's role in the Jefferson murder.

The state police dragged the lake on my property and found what was left of Jefferson's body. The skull was intact, and lodged inside was a slug matching the ballistics on Chief Eberhardt's revolver.

A week after the fire, Arlen and Gwen came home from Virginia Beach. We stayed on a few more days, then said our goodbyes and packed the car for the trip to Boston. I can't say they were happy about Kate and Susan leaving, but they were understanding and supportive, nonetheless. We promised there would be a wedding as soon as possible, but I didn't tell them it might be delayed for several months owing to my impending trip to Germany.

The Glendennings were actually thrilled to see us when we arrived in Boston. They never had children of their own, and Mrs. Glendenning doted on Susan. Within a few days, she was transformed from a sour old lady into a surrogate grandmother. With all her fussing over Susan and Kate, even her attitude toward me softened.

Kate felt awkward living in my house without the benefit of a marriage license; for appearances sake, she took my mother's bedroom, but we spent the nights together in my grandparents' room anyway. Susan took my old bedroom, and Kate and Mrs. Glendenning redecorated it for a little girl. Even with the prospect of my European trip and the expectation of seeing my father again hanging over me, I was a happy man for several weeks.

In July, I received my orders; I was reactivated and told to report to Washington for a briefing. General MacFarlane, Uncle John and I met in a nondescript conference room at the War Department. MacFarlane gave me the temporary rank of lieutenant colonel; the high rank was for the Russians' benefit.

"I would have made you a brigadier general," MacFarlane said, "but you're too young for them to believe that. Wear your DSC—they're impressed by medals."

My father was being held in Berlin, in a prison barracks on the grounds of Tempelhof Airport. American officers were permitted to inspect once a day, but they weren't allowed to question him. The Russians maintained a close twenty-four hour guard. Apparently, they had no idea of my father's true identity; to them, he was Oskar Jürgens, Nazi industrialist, exploiter of slave labor, murderer, and war criminal. To the inspecting American officers, he was Colonel Oscar Jergens, OSS operative and war hero.

The only Americans who knew my father's true identity, apart from the three of us, were President Truman, former Army Chief of Staff General George Marshall, Air Force Commanding General Hap Arnold, Generals Eisenhower and Bradley, Associate Supreme Court Justice Robert Jackson, who was America's chief prosecutor in Nuremberg, and General Wild Bill Donovan, former head of the OSS and now a special assistant to Justice Jackson.

Uncle John said, "General Donovan and Judge Jackson have tried negotiating your father's release, but the Russians refuse to cooperate. For once it appears as though they have no ulterior motive—they're sincere about prosecuting him."

"President Truman is personally concerned about this," MacFarlane said. "He wants to resurrect your father as an undercover war hero, but he can't permit a Medal of Honor winner to be disgraced as a war criminal."

Uncle John said, "I spoke to the President myself, and he said, quote, 'I don't want another damned Lindbergh on our hands. If the bastard's guilty, cut a deal with the Russians and let him hang. If not, kidnap him if you have to, and get him home.'"

"So what are we going to do?" I asked.

MacFarlane said the Russians agreed to let us meet with my father privately. We needed to be careful what we said inside the barracks, because the place was probably wired for sound, but it was possible to speak with him safely during his daily outdoor exercise.

"The Russians gave us a dossier on Oskar Jürgens," Uncle John said, "and it's damning."

He opened his briefcase and withdrew several file folders, all stuffed with photographs, copies of affidavits and legal briefs. He spread the material on the table for me to examine. There were photographs of my father's factories—some taken by the Germans during the war, others taken by Allied airmen, and still others by Russian occupation forces. They were identified, either by signage in the pictures themselves, or with labels at the bottom that said "Jürgens Maschine Fabrik Gesellschaft" or "JMF" followed by a factory identification number. The aerial photographs had date stamps, but the others were undated; some had explanatory remarks written either in German, Russian or in English. Some of the factories had serious bomb damage; others were relatively untouched.

Except for the bomb damage, the buildings looked nondescript—like ordinary factories one might see anywhere in America—but the interior photos told another story. The working conditions were beyond description, exceeding even my worst imaginings. Charles Dickens couldn't have conjured anything bleaker. I'd seen photographs in *Life Magazine* of the concentration camps, and these were no better.

My mouth went dry, and I experienced the same queasy feeling as when I first learned of my father's involvement with Baransky.

Uncle John showed me more. There were scores of affidavits—attested translations—from survivors who described unspeakable atrocities committed against them and their families while being forced to work for my father throughout the course of the war: starvation, rape, beating, torture, killing. There were more photographs of slave labor camps attached to each of the factories, where prisoners were crammed into lice and rat-infested barracks. The death rate was appalling; torture and starvation were routine.

"The Russians claim my father was responsible for all this?" I asked.

MacFarlane answered. "They do. And the evidence is overwhelming."

"But he was working for the Allies. He was one of us. Why would he commit war crimes when he was on our side?"

"Yes, he was on our side," the general said. "He was one of our best spies. In fact, he supplied more intelligence than any five other agents combined."

My father was also a saboteur. After his parts passed their field tests, he altered their specifications creating weaknesses in more than twenty-five percent of all German aircraft engines. That act alone ensured Allied air superiority at critical moments of the war. Little things, such as altering the diameter of a fuel intake valve by a micrometer, caused a Messerschmidt to stall in a climb. That he managed to get away with it for all those years was astonishing.

Uncle John said, "It's messy from a legal standpoint, and the Russians are shoving it in our faces. It was Bob Jackson who insisted on bringing the German industrialists to account for their activities before and during the war. Now the issue is biting us on the ass. They don't know your father's true identity, but they know he was an American officer, and they want to embarrass us."

I wasn't interested in the political ramifications of the issue, only the moral ones. "But what if my father really did these things? What if he was responsible for all this?" I pointed to the photographs on the table. "Aren't we hypocrites for trying to defend him?"

"Don't be so naïve," MacFarlane snapped. "Harry McCoy lived in mortal danger every day for eleven years. He did it because he loved his country. In order for him to succeed, for him even to survive, he had to pretend to be a Nazi. That meant acting like one every day, behaving in the same manner as the rest of them."

I scowled. "Did it require torturing and killing innocent human beings, too?"

"For him to be convincing in his role, I'm afraid it did."

Uncle John said, "Your father may have used evil means to accomplish a noble end. The only way I can defend him is if I prove he did so reluctantly, or that he tried to mitigate the horror."

"I hope he doesn't claim he was only following orders," I said.

Uncle John shook his head. "There's no indication of that. So far, we've only heard the Russians' side of the story. We haven't yet had an opportunity to interview your father in depth."

The British, French and American governments refused to participate in the prosecution of my father. If a trial were to proceed, the Russians would run it alone.

I said, "Isn't that a big risk? After all, their system of jurisprudence isn't exactly up to Western standards."

"We hope that won't be a problem," Uncle John said. "We won't participate in the prosecution, but we'll insist that the trial include an American judge. The Russians don't have a choice in that. If they exclude our judge from your father's trial, we could exclude their judges from trials of our choosing."

So the whole thing boiled down to politics, not justice. In the end, my father's fate wouldn't be determined by any moral imperative, but by the practical considerations of two world powers jockeying for position in the aftermath of the bloodiest war in history.

My father's own lawyer—his oldest and dearest friend—was questioning the outcome of the proceedings before they got underway. As for me, I didn't know what to think. For the past fourteen years, my father had been dead to me. For the past four months, his ghost had been a constant presence in my life, weaving a grim shroud of deception that was only now beginning to fall away.

I resolved to withhold judgment until I had the opportunity to see my father and ask him directly about his complicity in these atrocities.

CHAPTER 25

Uncle John spent the next week giving me a crash course in law. His goal wasn't to make me a lawyer; it was merely to make me familiar enough with trial procedure so I could convincingly look and act the part of law clerk in front of the Russians.

We departed for London from Idlewild Airport on Thursday, August 1, flying on the Pan American Clipper. We stayed overnight in London at Claridge's, not far from the American embassy in Grosvenor Square, and the next morning, we took a military flight directly to Berlin. Upon arriving at Tempelhof Airport, an M.P. and a JAG officer whisked us away in a staff car to AMGOT headquarters, the American Military Government command. On the way, our driver took us on a tour of the conquered Nazi capital. Berlin was a sea of devastation; hardly a single city block remained intact. Despite the spectacular August weather, postwar Berlin manifested a grim aura, as though a pall of grayness had permanently descended.

Our reception at AMGOT was businesslike—a personnel officer who barely looked up from his clipboard assigned us a master sergeant as a driver and a first lieutenant as an aide. The sergeant saw to our suitcases and our aide conveyed us to the military governor. The governor spared us little time. After a brief lecture on occupation regulations and non-fraternization, he arranged to quarter us in the suburb of Wannsee, at the Villa Marlier.

The drive to Wannsee felt like Dorothy leaving the Kansas plain and arriving in the Land of Oz. Unlike Berlin, Wannsee was virtually untouched by the war. Beautiful mansions with manicured lawns overlooking a pristine lake fronted the tree-lined boulevard leading to our destination. With its lush surrounding gardens, the Villa Marlier had a storybook quality. A wealthy industrialist built it at the turn of the century, and during the war, the *SS* used it as a vacation resort. After the fall of Berlin, Russian marines occupied it until the U.S. Army appropriated it for visiting officers.

The effects of the time difference and my heightened sense of anxiety about meeting my father were disorienting. I spent a restless night in the mansion despite the comfortable surroundings.

The next morning, our driver and aide picked us up at the villa and drove us back to Tempelhof Airport, where my father was housed in a temporary prison complex in the former Luftwaffe barracks. Upon our arrival, we were introduced to our Russian hosts, Lieutenant Colonel Vasiliy Ivanov, and Major General Andrei Timofkin. General Timofkin was a senior legal officer. They didn't say so, but Uncle John and I guessed that Colonel Ivanov was a political officer. Timofkin's English was perfect, nearly unaccented, and Ivanov's was almost as good.

We met in an institutional green conference room, furnished only with a small metal table and four folding chairs. There were no shades on the windows, and the Russians arranged the seating so that Uncle John and I faced the early morning sun, making it difficult to see their faces in the backlight. I was concerned they might see the family resemblance between my father and me, but if they did, they left it unspoken.

General Timofkin began, and he didn't mince words. "Your man is guilty. There is no doubt."

Uncle John had advised me not to speak during the meeting, so I sat back and watched them spar.

Uncle John said, "With all due respect, General, we disagree, and we strongly protest your having detained Colonel Jergens. He spent eleven years among the Nazis as an undercover agent for American military intelligence. His contribution to the Allied war effort is incalculable."

General Timofkin nodded and smiled. "I believe you, but in the course of his work for the Americans—"

Uncle John cut him off. "His work benefited *all* the Allied powers, including the Soviet Union."

"Forgive me," he said. "In the course of his work for the *Allies*, Colonel Jergens enslaved ten thousand Russians, Poles and Jews. More than half died under unspeakable circumstances."

I did my best to maintain a poker face, but it was difficult. Although he couldn't know their effect on me, each of Timofkin's words dug deep into my soul, stinging like the tines of the devil's own pitchfork.

Ivanov interjected, "There is a precedent for this, Comrades. One of our own—Major Nikolai Bartinsky—led a guerilla commando unit behind enemy lines for two years. He killed many thousands of Germans, but he also slaughtered thousands of Ukrainian civilians, women and children included." The look on his face was almost a leer. "We didn't bother with an international tribunal in his case. His crimes were committed on Soviet soil. We tried him in a Soviet court two months ago and hanged him."

Uncle John sighed. "I noted Major Bartinsky's case in the briefs you provided. But the precedent doesn't apply. Major Bartinsky was an escaped prisoner of war who organized a partisan band. He operated without the official sanction of the Soviet Government, and therefore was an independent operative. In effect, he was no more than a bandit. Colonel Jergens was, and is, an American Army officer acting under the direct orders of the President of the United States." Uncle John handed Timofkin a notarized affidavit signed by General George C. Marshall, attesting that Colonel Jergens was acting under the direct orders of President Roosevelt. "If President Roosevelt were alive, would you indict him?"

Timofkin bristled. "I doubt your president ordered Jergens to commit atrocities, and even if he did, following orders is not a defense against war crimes."

The discussions continued for another half hour, but we made no progress. In the end, the only concession they granted was that, if my father were convicted, they wouldn't hang him; rather, they'd use a firing squad in deference to his military rank.

Uncle John and I agreed it would be best if he met with my father alone at first, to prepare him for seeing me again. I waited outside, wandering around the airfield grounds while Uncle John went to see my father in his barracks cell. Like the city itself, Tempelhof Airport was divided into four zones—American, Russian, British and French. The runways and control tower were used commonly, but hangars, maintenance sheds and storage areas were apportioned among the great powers, each with clearly demarcated boundaries. It was an awkward and unmanageable situation that would ultimately change, but for the time being, one couldn't traverse the vast areas without crossing several checkpoints and showing identification at each one. My pass was good for the Russian and American zones only, so when I accidentally wandered over to the French sector, the sentries turned me away.

I returned to the Russian zone and tried striking up a conversation with an off-duty Soviet officer. He became agitated and hustled away like I was contagious. In the end, I returned to the conference room and waited alone. I must have dozed off in my chair. It was shortly after noon when the political officer, Colonel Ivanov, retrieved me. He was uncharacteristically pleasant, and he escorted me to the temporary prison complex.

On the way, Ivanov said, "Judge Barrow is a highly respected jurist in your country, Colonel McCoy. We have studied him well."

"Really? I had no idea the Red Army was interested in the careers of American judges."

"We are when a judge of his stature is sent all the way from New York City to defend someone such as your Colonel Jergens. We had no idea that Jergens was so important to your government."

"My government defends the rights of all its citizens abroad, especially its war heroes."

"Ah, yes," he said. "And I see that you, too, are a war hero." He pointed at my campaign ribbons, battle stars and my DSC ribbon. "Tell me, does the United States

Army routinely award combat decorations to members of its legal service?"

"I served in the Pacific—Fourth Ranger Battalion, Thirty-Second Combat Infantry Division, Sixth United States Army. I wasn't assigned to the Judge Advocate General's Corps until after the war."

Ivanov smiled. "Very impressive, Colonel. I am told that you graduated from Harvard University shortly before the war." He pronounced Harvard with a "w" instead of a "v". "Our information is that you never went to law school, but perhaps we are mistaken. You must be very smart indeed to have completed your legal training since your return from the Pacific."

Obviously, the Russians had a file on me, too. I wondered how much they knew, but I kept my composure. "We're prodigies in my family, Colonel Ivanov."

"Prodigies? What is prodigies?"

"It means uncommonly clever and quick to learn."

"Ah. So I see."

We reached my father's barracks, and Colonel Ivanov logged me in at a sentry station. A guard patted me down, searching for weapons, and then passed me through the main building to an interior quadrangle surrounded on all four sides by long, low, two-story barracks. The quadrangle was the size of a regulation tennis court and was paved in chalk-white asphalt. Scattered around were benches and wooden tables, some of them shaded with red umbrellas, making the area look like an outdoor restaurant. There was a flagpole in the center, atop of which flew the hammer and sickle flag. Armed sentries patrolled the perimeter, and guard boxes sat atop the roofs of each building. I was nervous, but I did my best to conceal it.

Uncle John and my father sat outside at one of the shaded tables directly in front of the far building in front of me, about fifty feet away. Uncle John spotted me first, and he and my father got up and walked toward me. As they approached, I squared my shoulders, as though I were being presented to my commanding officer instead of my father. They walked slowly, and as they got closer, I noticed my father was limping. He wore field-gray fatigues with no insignia, apparently German army surplus.

When he got close enough for me to see his face clearly, I was profoundly shocked. He looked completely different from the man I remembered, and utterly unlike the robust, smiling hero depicted in the old newsreels. His hair was steel gray and thinning on top, and his face was haggard and lined. He looked ten years older than he was, and there was no longer a family resemblance between us.

Uncle John spoke first, formally, as a show for the Russian sentries. "Lieutenant Colonel Jameson McCoy, may I present Colonel Oscar Jergens. I'll leave you two alone."

John walked back to the far building for his pre-arranged meeting with General Timofkin, leaving me with the father I hadn't seen in fourteen years. My heart swelled with emotion. For so long, I'd accepted that my father was only a distant, fading memory; a moment like this was beyond imagining. And now, despite the circumstances, despite the nagging questions in my mind, I was overwhelmed by filial love. My instinct was to reach out for him, but I restrained my impulse, knowing that suspicious and antagonistic eyes surrounded us. I didn't know what else to do, so I saluted.

"Jamie," he said warmly, and returned my salute. Tears formed in the corners of his eyes.

It was all I could do to keep from embracing him in front of the guards. Instead, I took his arm and walked him over to one of the tables close to the center of the courtyard, as far away from the sentries as I could get.

"I'm proud of you," he said. "John told me all about you, and what you did in the Pacific."

My voice cracked. "Thank you, Dad," I said. "You look different."

He laughed, though laughter hardly seemed appropriate. "So do you. Actually, a fine German doctor performed plastic surgery on me a while back—removed the cleft in my chin, narrowed my nose and padded my cheekbones. I was trying to hide a famous face, but I see you have my face now."

"I'm sorry you're here, Dad. Uncle John and I have come to get you out."

"I know. I'm sorry I'm here, too." He smiled wryly and said, "You know, before the end came, I almost made it home free. I managed to make my way to the American lines. I surrendered to a patrol of GIs and identified myself as Colonel Harry McCoy. They laughed at me. Their platoon leader said, 'Yeah, and I'm Amelia Earhart.'"

"What happened? How did the Russians get you?"

"Bad luck, really. The American patrol sent me back to the rear in a jeep, but the driver got lost, and we ended up overtaking a retreating German column. The Germans took us both into custody, and I was back to being Oskar Jürgens. They realized I was trying to turn myself in to the enemy, so they arrested me and sent me to Berlin. Unfortunately, our Russian allies made it there before the Americans did."

We talked for a long time about home and my mother. I told him about Kate and Susan, and all that had happened in Granbury. He got upset when I told him Dulcie Patch burned down our house.

"God, that woman was always crazy. I'm sorry about everything Jamie, especially about Dulcie and Eberhardt. I never meant for any of it to affect you, but I suppose I was foolish to think it wouldn't."

I said, "It's okay, Dad. Some good came out of it. I met Kate and we fell in love."

"I'm happy for you. I only wish I could go to your wedding."

"You'll be there. I want you as my best man."

He shook his head. "No, Jamie. The deck is stacked against me. Even John understands that now. The only thing I can hope for is that they won't discover my real identity and embarrass us with it."

"Does anyone else in Germany know who you are?"

"Let's see—Greta Huffmann and Karl von Sielau knew, but they're both dead. Then there was Goëbbels— he always wanted me to own up to it and broadcast propaganda, but I refused—he's dead, too. Hitler, Himmler, Bormann, Heydrich—all dead. Goering, Hess, Speer, and Sauckel—they all knew, too, but they've got problems of their own right now."

"Will they talk?" I asked.

"Not if the Russians hang me first."

"I see."

"Do you really? Although the Russians stacked the deck, my fellow Americans are dealing from the bottom.

Nobody wants me alive, Jamie. I'm a liability—the great American hero turned mass murderer."

I hung my head. "Are you guilty?"

"Look at me, son," he said. "I'm guilty of a lot of things, including giving greater devotion to my country than my family. I know now I was wrong to do that. As for the rest of it—what the Russians say I did—well, I can't give you a good answer."

"Try," I said, staring him straight in the eyes. "I need to know the truth. I've lived with lies all these years, and I think you owe me the truth now, at least. I need to know who the real Harry McCoy is—an American hero, or a war criminal."

"You're not going to make this easy, are you?"

"Why should I? You didn't make it easy on me."

"Oh, yes I did. You're a very wealthy young man. More so than you even know."

I got angry. "That's not what I mean and you know it. I'd give it all away if I could have had a father all those years. I didn't need money and I didn't need a hero. I needed a father."

He rested his hand gently on my shoulder. "I know that's not what you meant, son. I'm sorry. I'm sorry I said it, and I'm sorry I wasn't there for you."

"You still haven't answered my question. Did you do it? Were you a slave-master and a mass murderer?"

"What would you say if I told you it's all a frame-up?"

"I'd fight like hell to get you out of here," I said.

"And what if I told you it's all true?"

I didn't answer him. I just asked again, "*Is* it true?"

"Yes and no," he said quietly.

I got angry again. "Come on, Dad, give me a real answer."

"That *is* a real answer. Is it true that I used slave labor in my factories? Yes, it is. If I hadn't, I wouldn't have been able to do my job effectively—my job as an American spy, that is." He paused to let it sink in. "Did I murder thousands of innocents? No, I didn't. I did my best to stop the killing—at least the best I could without jeopardizing my position. I reached into my own pocket to feed them more than was allowed. I tried to save those I could whenever possible without arousing suspicion, but in the end, there was nothing more I could do. I didn't run the labor camps; the SS did. They just sent the workers over every day, and I did what I could to make it easier on them."

I shook my head. "I saw the photographs. The conditions in your factories were appalling."

He looked at me defiantly. "How dare you judge me? You have no idea the danger I was in. If I acted like a Jew-lover, it would have been all over for me. They would have thrown me into a concentration camp, and I wouldn't have been able to do all the good I did for the Allies."

At last, the ugliness of it all struck home. He was justifying mass murder by claiming to have served a higher goal. His involvement with Baransky and the murder of Paul Jefferson were no different. Those atrocities were just smaller in scale.

Then I asked him a question he couldn't answer. "Tell me, Dad, what would you have done if the Nazis won the war? You had a nice comfortable life here as one of the elite. Would you have continued running slave factories?"

He glared at me. The look in his eyes told me he was formulating an excuse, not an answer. Finally, he said, "When I came home from the last war, I was a big hero. It was exhilarating to be famous and admired—because of something *I* achieved, not because I was the son of a rich man. For a time, I pursued stunt flying because I liked being a celebrity, but it soon became tiresome."

My father paused. He gazed beyond me, into his own past, and then continued, determined to tell it all.

"When Kunetz and Baransky approached me, I saw a way to become more than a celebrity. I saw an opportunity to get involved in something greater than myself. You see, Jamie, I truly wanted to serve my country. I went to other people, powerful men, patriotic Americans like me, and I told them about it. It was more than just a big adventure; it made me feel like I was contributing something. But the deeper into it I got, the more dangerous it became. When at last the President of the United States, my good friend Franklin Roosevelt, called on me to make this great sacrifice for my country, I agreed, never knowing where it would lead." He paused. "Yes, son, there was a time at the beginning of the war when I thought it was possible for the Nazis to win. And yes, I contemplated what I would do if that happened. But I never gave up hope, and I never stopped trying to defeat them. I fought my quiet, secret war because it was the right thing to do, and nothing you say or think can ever change my convictions."

I tried to respond, but he cut me off.

As earnestly as he could, he said, "You know first-hand that war is a dirty business, and the dirtiest job of all is being a spy. Your entire life becomes a lie, and you have to fight every day to keep that lie from becoming real. The Russians are saying I'm a war criminal; I'm telling you I did everything I could to stop the criminals from winning."

I'd come to find a clear-cut answer, but I saw there was none to be had, at least not in this time and place. I thought about my experience in the Philippines, knowing I tried to justify my own acts of brutality in the name of a greater good. In school, I'd been taught America was a nation of laws, and it was wrong to break the law to catch a lawbreaker; but we fought enemies on both sides of the globe who didn't play by the same rules. And here was my father telling me he'd become a criminal to fight the biggest crime ever visited upon mankind.

I looked at him, trying desperately to understand what he'd done, but understanding eluded me.

"What do you want us to do for you?" I asked.

He shook his head sadly. "There's nothing you can do. Go home."

"Then why did you ask Uncle John to come?"

"I wanted to see him one last time to square things between us. I owed him that."

"What about me? Why didn't you ask for me, too? Didn't you want to square things with me?"

"Of course I did. You can't imagine how grateful I am that you came." His eyes began to tear up again. "I didn't ask for you because I was afraid the Russians would discover my true identity. They still might—that's why we have to end this now."

"I wish I could hug you, Dad."

"Me, too. But it's too dangerous. Goodbye, son. Try to remember me for the good things I did, and know that I love you."

"I love you, too."

That was all there was left to say—four words that summed up a lifetime of unanswered questions. Harry McCoy—the real Harry McCoy—stood before me as a broken man with nothing left, nowhere to go, and no one to stand up for him. From his perspective, at least, he was neither a hero nor a criminal. He was just a man who did his duty and had had the misfortune to end up on the wrong side of history.

He got up and limped to the barracks without looking back at me. Uncle John appeared at the barracks door and spoke briefly with my father; then, a moment later, Uncle John walked over and we left the courtyard together. I managed to hold back my tears until we cleared the Russian zone, and then I broke down and sobbed. Uncle John embraced me, giving me the hug my father couldn't.

CHAPTER 26

Uncle John and I walked in silence to the American sector and found our way into the officer's club, where we took a booth in a secluded corner. We ordered drinks and sat there smoking for several minutes before I mustered the courage to ask him what was going to happen to my father.

"Your father instructed me to request a writ of summary justice."

"What does that mean?" I asked.

Uncle John lowered his head solemnly. "It means your father is pleading guilty to all counts and will be summarily executed."

"I see." Despite what my father had said to me, I didn't expect him to quit so easily. My stomach knotted up and my head pounded. I wanted to scream, but I knew it wouldn't help. At that moment, I hated my country. I hated all the politicians and generals who had manipulated my father—indeed my whole family—and suckered him into a life without honor or escape. My father had briefly returned from the dead, but the living wouldn't let him stay.

Uncle John explained that my father demanded concessions as a condition of his plea. He wanted to be shot by a firing squad—something to which Timofkin had already agreed—and he wanted to be cremated and have his ashes scattered. He also demanded the Russians keep everything secret.

"Why would they agree to that?"

"General MacFarlane gave me some negotiating leverage: during the war, the Germans captured several Russian generals who turned traitor. The Russians want them back, to deal with them in their own way. They can have them in return for their pledge of secrecy about Colonel Jergens."

"I see," I said bitterly. "Politics as usual. Do you think the Russians know Colonel Jergens is really the famous Harry McCoy?"

"I doubt it, but it doesn't matter. They'll keep quiet anyway. Our side has evidence of Soviet atrocities against the Poles and the Finns."

We finished our drinks in silence. I had nothing else to say, and there was nothing more I wanted to hear. The two great world powers were about to bury my father without so much as a thank you for all he'd sacrificed. The bitterness I felt eclipsed my sense of horror and shame over the means my father employed to achieve his ends. I knew the shame would return in due course, but at that moment, contemplating my father's impending execution, I had no feelings of ambivalence.

We returned to Wannsee and spent another night at the Villa Marlier, where Uncle John wrote a report to General MacFarlane. I spent the afternoon and evening alone, drinking myself into oblivion. The following afternoon, our driver returned us to Tempelhof and we caught a flight to London, where we stayed once again at Claridge's.

By dinnertime, I recovered my composure and was fit company for Uncle John. My bitterness toward the people who used my father—General Donovan and President Roosevelt—was still intense, but I'd begun to accept my father's execution as ironic justice. Whatever his duty to his country had been, and however well he fulfilled that duty, it couldn't have included or justified the enslavement and murder of innocents.

After dinner, over coffee and cigarettes, Uncle John handed me an envelope.

"That's your father's legacy to you," he said.

Inside the envelope was a single sheet of paper on which was written a list of accounts in four Swiss banks. Each account was in my name, and each had a coded password and a balance. I mentally added the balances, and they totaled more than two hundred million dollars.

I cringed. "I don't want this. It's blood money."

Uncle John shook his head. "No it isn't, Jamie. Before your father went to Germany, he liquidated all his assets. That's the money Goddard MacFarlane tried to trace—it's the fortune your father and grandfather made in America. It's been sitting in those Swiss banks—in your name—for twelve years, increasing in value."

I was overwhelmed, but still skeptical. "What happened to the money he made from his German factories?"

Uncle John showed me another piece of paper with another list of bank accounts. "The Russians confiscated your father's German assets," he said. "The rest, about fifty million dollars, is in the Royal Bank of Sweden. Your father asked that I donate the money to the International Red Cross."

I didn't know what to say or think. Was a contribution to charity, however large, my father's way of atoning for mass murder? I doubted money could expiate his sins.

We finished our coffee and left the restaurant. As we strolled across the lobby toward the elevators, Uncle John said, "Try to remember your father kindly, Jamie. In his own way, he gave up everything for his country. I won't try to explain his actions in Germany, and you shouldn't try, either. Winston Churchill once said that if Hitler invaded hell, he—Churchill that is—would try to find something nice to say about the devil. I think your father fought the devil, and used the devil's own methods against him. We can take some satisfaction that the devil lost."

"The devil lost, Uncle John, but the cost was my father's soul."

CHAPTER 27

Like almost everyone else in the civilized world, I followed the proceedings of the War Crimes trials in Nuremberg. Justice Jackson comported himself well as prosecutor and obtained convictions of the principal Nazi leaders. General Donovan served as Jackson's key associate during preparations for the trial, gathering a mountain of damning evidence.

In the end, most of the leading Nazis were hanged; some received lengthy prison sentences. Ironically, the Nazi industrialists fared comparatively well. All charges against Gustave Krupp were dismissed; Albert Speer, Hitler's official architect, chief of Germany's war production, and employer of millions of slave laborers, got off with a twenty year sentence. Of the major war criminals implicated in Germany's slave labor program, only Fritz Sauckel, chief of labor appropriations who conscripted the slaves and oversaw their conditions of captivity, received a death sentence.

I saw Goddard MacFarlane one more time. In February 1947, he and General Donovan visited me in Boston. I was cordial to them, but not much more. Donovan had nominated my father for a second, posthumous, Medal of Honor, but President Truman rejected it without comment. Had they asked me, I would have agreed.

Freddie Crowell never completed his newspaper story. I'd like to think he abandoned the effort out of consideration for Kate and me, but the truth was I prevented him from doing a credible job. I refused to share my information, and there were no public sources to corroborate his suspicions.

Victor Eberhardt was convicted on two counts of second-degree murder in the deaths of Paul Jefferson and Henry Dietz. He received a life sentence, but he died of liver cancer after serving only eight months. His nephew was convicted in the Dietz killing and got twenty to life. He earned a parole in 1961 and returned to Granbury, but his freedom was short-lived. Three weeks after his release, he got drunk and drove his car into a utility pole on the Old Hartford Turnpike; he died instantly, not twenty yards from the spot where he shot Hank Dietz.

Dulcie's fate was tragic as well. She recovered from her burns, but was hideously scarred. Both Kate and I declined to press charges, but the decision was out of our hands; the Hartford County District Attorney indicted her for arson and assault. Dulcie retreated into her own catatonic world and refused to speak, even to her attorney. At a pre-trial hearing, the Judge found her incompetent to stand trial and committed her to a state mental institution. The hospital conditions were appalling.

As much as I loathed what Dulcie had done to Paul Jefferson and Kate, I harbored a vague sense of family guilt that my father's behavior had exacerbated her obsessions and contributed to her mental illness. I arranged to place her in a private sanatorium at my expense. Sadly, no amount of psychiatric care could pierce her delusions. She wrote love letters to my father every day—addressed to Lieutenant Jameson H. McCoy at his World War One Army Post Office number. To Dulcie, it was perpetually 1917; she was still the beautiful belle of Granbury and my father was her reluctant beau.

Presuming the letters were meant for me, the sanatorium forwarded them to my Boston address. They were pathetic. After reading the first few, I sent them back to her doctors with instructions never to send me any others. Dulcie died in 1970; Freddie Crowell made the funeral arrangements, interring her in the Patch family crypt alongside her parents and her brother.

* * *

I married Kate on April 12, 1947 at King's Chapel on Tremont Street in Boston. It was a small ceremony; Uncle John served as my best man, and five-year-old Susan was Kate's maid of honor. The other guests were Kate's parents and sister, the Glendennings, Arlen and Gwen Hardesty, Ernie Thayer and Freddie Crowell and their wives, Arthur Wiseman, and Uncle John's wife, Emily. After the ceremony, we had dinner across the street in a private dining room at the Parker House Hotel, and the next morning, Kate and I left for a weeklong honeymoon on Nantucket Island. Kate's parents stayed with Susan at the house on Van Houghton Row, spoiling her with lots of attention as grandparents are supposed to do.

Kate and I had a good life together. With all the money I inherited, we didn't need to earn a living; instead, we occupied our time with charitable work. We established the Helen and Jameson Hale McCoy, Jr. Foundation, which, in its more than fifty years of existence, has given millions to various causes, especially those supporting human rights abuse victims.

I never adopted Susan, because Kate and I wanted her to keep her father's name; but she was a better daughter than I could have hoped for. She married a veterinarian in 1968 and moved to Denver where she had two lovely daughters, both of whom are now married and have children of their own. Kate and I had two boys together, neither of whom we named Jameson. The oldest, Arlen, is an attorney in Boston; he and his wife have two boys. John is a freelance magazine writer; he and his wife have a son.

Not long after returning from Europe, I sold my property in Connecticut. Arlen and Gwen Hardesty retired to Virginia Beach in 1948, so Kate and I never had any reason to return to Granbury. It was just as well. There were too many painful memories for us there.

My sons visited Granbury once, to run in the road race and participate in a re-dedication ceremony of the McCoy Memorial Library on the occasion of its hundredth anniversary. At my request, they laid a wreath at the foot of their grandfather's monument on the town green. I suspected the town fathers wanted a contribution from the McCoy Foundation, but they never asked, and I never offered.

In 1965, Kate and I donated the house on Van Houghton Row to Northeastern University. They turned it into a fraternity house. We moved to the picturesque north shore village of Rockport that year, into a Victorian house overlooking the ocean, and remained there until Kate passed away in 1998. After Kate died, I took a small apartment in Boston overlooking the Back Bay Fens, not far from Van Houghton Row. I stroll over there every so often and, if I narrow my eyes, it's 1946 again and I can see that little girl skipping rope on the sidewalk. *Cinderella, dressed in yella, went to the ball to meet a fella.*

The details of my life since Kate died have been a little vague. But it doesn't matter. I derive most of my pleasure from visiting my sons and grandsons.

They're good kids, my grandsons. I think my father would have been proud of them. When they were little, they asked me if I'd been a hero in the war. I told them no; I was just a regular soldier who did my duty. But I regaled them with stories about their great-grandfather, Colonel Harry McCoy—and his exploits in the skies over France in the Great War, and how he was lost flying over the Atlantic one April morning in 1934.

It's funny how family legends live on when they're passed down through the generations.

—THE END—